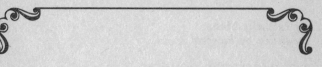

Lord Carlton assumed a most punctilious air. "My dear Miss Mathley, will you do me the very great honor to accept my hand in a fictitious engagement?"

"Oh sir, I should be honored," Melinda murmured as the dance ended and she dropped into a deep curtsy.

He smiled down at her. "Shall I execute the coup de grace to our partnership and kiss your fair hand?"

"Yes, thank you, that would be lovely."

He raised her slim, gloved fingers to his lips and gently brushed them with his warm mouth. Heat shot from her fingertips and enflamed the whole of her body.

"My goodness," she said, rising on wobbly legs from her curtsy.

"I beg your pardon?"

Melinda struggled to pull herself together. "You do that very well," she said brightly.

"Why, thank you," Lord Carlton said with a grin. "I have had years of practice. . . ."

By Michelle Martin
Published by Fawcett Books:

THE HAMPSHIRE HOYDEN
THE QUEEN OF HEARTS
THE MAD MISS MATHLEY

THE MAD MISS MATHLEY

Michelle Martin

FAWCETT CREST • NEW YORK

A Fawcett Crest Book
Published by Ballantine Books
Copyright © 1995 by Michelle Martin

Library of Congress Catalog Card Number: 95-90144

ISBN 0-449-22339-6

Manufactured in the United States of America

First Edition: August 1995

10 9 8 7 6 5 4 3 2 1

*

Chapter 1

OSWALD OMERSBY STEPPED on Melinda Mathley's battered toes once again. This—in the packed, overheated, deafening roar of the Bascombs' London ballroom—was the fourth such happenstance in the last three minutes. Apologizing profusely, he jerked Melinda back into the dance, his arms and legs flailing in all directions. Had she not suffered from similar performances these last four months, Melinda would have blushed at this graceless capering. As she had suffered through the exercise far more than any mortal should have to withstand, she retained her composure and murmured "Indeed?" and "How gratifying," as Lord Omersby continued to discuss his honorable mother's report of a recent tea she had had with Miss Mathley.

When the dance finally ended, Melinda made her curtsy with all due decorum and forestalled Lord Omersby's offer to procure her a glass of lemonade by observing that her Mama was signaling to her and she really must fly.

This was a bald-faced lie. At that moment Mrs. Catherine Mathley was engaged in a tumultuous game of whist in the adjoining salon, and so far from summoning her eldest daughter, she was wholly ignorant of her eldest daughter, her second daughter, her son, her husband; in fact, she was ignorant of everything save the hand of cards she held, the best hand she could recall holding in many a month. So glaring a lie, however, perturbed Melinda not at all. She had gained her freedom and that was everything.

Alas, the relief was short-lived. She had meant to join

1

her good friend, Miss Elizabeth Jonson, whom she had observed sitting against the far wall. But her cousin, Basil Hollis, accosted her not halfway to her goal with a malicious smile and a hand upon her arm that held her fast.

"Ah, Cousin," said Mr. Hollis, his smile revealing two rows of uneven teeth, "what a charming picture you made dancing with the devoted Omersby. You make a delightful couple. When may I wish you joy?"

"On the day you emigrate to the West Indies, Basil," Melinda sweetly replied. She tried to move away, but Mr. Hollis's grip on her arm merely tightened.

"Dear Cousin, ever the witty riposte. But you must tell me, when is to be the wedding? Omersby will have you if he can."

"He cannot."

"A bosom friend of your father's? An honorable title? Devoted to you? Come, come, Cousin," said Mr. Hollis as two fat barons and one towering countess pushed past, pressing them closer together, "you must have him. I declare you must have him."

"And I declare I must not."

"You must have some man. You have turned me down—"

"Yes, wasn't that clever of me?"

"—and how many others?" Mr. Hollis inquired, ignoring her sally. "Four? Five?"

"Five," said Melinda. "I'll make it an even dozen if I have to."

"Won't that be a lovely scandal for your family to live down," said Mr. Hollis with obvious pleasure. "I can hear the tattlemongers now: No man is good enough for Mad Melinda! Best be careful, Cousin Mel. If you turn down too many men, there won't be one left in London who will have you."

"Oh, surely my dowry will lure some worthy fellow to my side?"

"Ah yes, the *dowry*," said Mr. Hollis. "I wouldn't count

2

too heavily upon that, Cousin. You have but one brother standing between me and the Mathley fortune, and from what I have seen of Master Harry, he'll run himself into an early grave."

"Dear Cousin," said Melinda, removing Mr. Hollis's hand from her arm, "you live in a world of fantasy. Harry is strong and vigorous and young and, failing your dropping a large dollop of arsenic into his tea, he will succeed my father, and you will have to make do with the Hollis patrimony alone. But you frown! Is not the Hollis fortune large enough to keep you in the style you choose to affect? Your poverty is easily remedied. I suggest you get a rich wife, Basil. Find yourself a wife who cares naught for character, or good looks, or a loving heart. Find a rich wife eager to align herself with the great name of Hollis."

"A far easier task than you finding a husband who loves you more than your money," Mr. Hollis snapped. "The gold of your dowry, Cousin, outshines what little beauty you possess. You will be sold to a blind man, perhaps. That would be kindest . . . for your husband. He would not then have to fear the wedding night."

With a beautiful bow, Mr. Hollis decamped, leaving Melinda in seething fury and a secret fear that he might just be right. Melinda was not beautiful like her sister, Louisa. Just eighteen in her first Season, Louisa, with her golden hair, oval face, sparkling blue eyes, and expressive eyebrows, had already been proclaimed *La Belle du Ton* by the arbiters of fashion and every red-blooded young man in London. Alas, Melinda lacked any of this familial beauty and in its stead could offer only a good head of auburn hair and a decent set of teeth.

This was not hopeful. But far, far worse was the scandalous lack of inclination in Melinda's breast to flatter and cajole, simper and flirt with the men who sought her company, or rather, her dowry. Nearing the end of this, her third Season, Melinda had been accosted by every impoverished gentleman the ton could throw at her: short, fat,

3

brainless, bombastic. She believed that she had heard it all and seen it all, and none of it amused, let alone interested, her. She could not be grateful to the attentions of an inebriated viscount or the compliments of a known fortune-hunting baronet. She thought that they wasted her time, and she told them so in no uncertain terms.

Despite the increasingly desperate pleas of her parents that she marry someone, *anyone,* a bridegroom was not uppermost in her thoughts. No, she considered it her first task in life to keep her brother Harry healthy and to get him married as soon as possible and favored with sons early in life, so that Mr. Hollis's prediction of the Mathley fortune entailed away to him should never come to pass. She could then serenely live her life as an independent spinster, the only career that seemed to offer any hope of happiness.

Melinda continued to push her way through the overly perfumed throng to her friend, Miss Jonson, who was also rich and unbeautiful and unmarried. Drawing before her friend, she declared:

"Elizabeth, I have just had yet another wretched tête-à-tête with my abominable Cousin Basil. Come, will you not escort me to the balcony where I may enjoy some badly needed fresh air?"

Miss Jonson, colorless and demure, readily acceded to this plan. She rose, and the two young women, slipping their arms around each other's waists, walked out onto the balcony where the air did much to remove Mr. Hollis's prophecies from Melinda's thoughts. The ball, however, continued to oppress.

"How I hate the endless polite chatter and the same faces day after day, party after party," she said as she breathed deeply the cool evening air and looked out at the carefully manicured back garden of Lord and Lady Bascomb. "Everything is the same. There is no variety, no *life.*"

"It is wearying," Miss Jonson agreed. "But it is pleasant to dance with the young men and to have them fetch one lemonade and ask after one's relations."

4

Melinda turned and smiled at her friend. "*You* are easily pleased."

"I am three-and-twenty, Melinda," said Elizabeth. "I know the world. I know what to expect. Why ask for more that is not available to one?"

"Because you *deserve* more," said Melinda.

"Oh, la," said Miss Jonson, "if each of us received what we deserved, the world would be turned upside down."

"That might not be a bad thing," said Melinda, thinking of her odious cousin Basil.

"*I* should not like it. I prefer the world as it is. It holds no surprises for me, and I know how to get on in it fairly well."

"I wish I had your ease of getting on in the world. I try—you know, Elizabeth, how hard I try—to do what is best and right and proper. But somehow when I do it, it all seems to go wrong."

"Perhaps," said Miss Jonson with a fond smile, "it is because your views of what are best and right and proper are slightly skewed."

"No, how could they be?" said Melinda.

"I do not know how. I only know, my dear, that you treat the world as if the sun rises in the west and sets in the east. You have an excellent mind, but you trust in yourself too much, I think, and should learn instead to rely more upon others."

"That's a fool's advice," scoffed Melinda. "If I relied upon others, I should be more bored than I already am and in even worse straits. Why, I might even be married!"

Miss Jonson laughed. "There is no great harm in being married, Melinda."

"There is a good deal of harm in being married to any of the six men who have offered for me thus far!"

"Perhaps. But a little more tact and a little less independence might get you a comfortable companion."

Melinda considered this. "Do such creatures exist?"

"I believe so," said Miss Jonson. "Lord Dennis has begun to court me, and I think he is such a one."

"Lord Dennis! Pursuing *you*?"

"Yes. Do you think that so odd?"

"Not at all, only that you should like it."

"Why should I not like it, Melinda? He is still young, personable, and from a good family. I could not ask for more in a husband."

"That is just what I have been saying! You ask for a good deal less than you deserve."

Miss Jonson smiled. "Well, as to that, do we not all deserve happiness? And is there not a fair chance of my finding some happiness with Stephen Dennis?"

"With your good heart and low expectations, there is *every* chance," Melinda replied, kissing her friend's cheek. "Oh, bother! Here comes Basil. Let us hide before he sees us," she urged, grabbing her friend's wrist and pulling her behind a tall Ionic column.

Mr. Hollis stopped five feet away, his narrow back to them, a glass of champagne balanced in one hand.

"How extraordinary to have you back in town, Carlton," he said to a gentleman who was at the moment unseen. "I'd heard you'd gotten lost in the wilds of Yorkshire and hadn't been seen since."

"I had a reliable guide," came the laconic reply.

"The ladies *will* be pleased," said Mr. Hollis. "We must place an advertisement in the paper to warn every man, married and otherwise, to hide away his mistress now that the Great Lover has returned."

"You were a vulgarian and a boor in school, Hollis. I see that age has not improved you any."

"Huzzah!" whispered Melinda. A knight! A knight had entered the lists against her abominable cousin Basil!

"And you were always conceited and arrogant," Mr. Hollis snapped.

"But at least I had good cause," said Carlton, stepping at last into view.

Melinda could scarcely hold back her gasp of appreciation. This Carlton indeed had good cause for conceit and arrogance for he was the most handsome man she had ever beheld. His hair was blue-black and glistened in the chandelier light. His face was sculpted marble, the planes fascinating and beautiful. His mouth was sensual, his nose strong and lean. He was tall, broad shouldered, well muscled. And this beautiful god had entered into battle with the Vulcan Hollis!

"There's the most absurd rumor going around," said Basil, "that you're finally to come into the fortune you need to go with so grand a title. The world has run mad when Carlton has money."

"Hollis, you are an insect," said Carlton. "Go away."

Basil Hollis flushed to the roots of his pomaded brown hair. "You are insulting, Carlton."

"Ah good, you took my meaning, then."

"I should call you out for such a slap."

Amused, Carlton looked down upon Mr. Hollis, who missed his height by a good six inches. "You don't honestly think I would exert myself on *your* honor's behalf, do you?"

With a gasp Mr. Hollis turned on his heel and stalked off into the crowded ballroom.

"Oh, bravo, sir!" cried Melinda, shaking off Elizabeth's imploring grasp and stepping from behind the column. "That was magnificently done!"

Carlton turned, his dark blue gaze fixing upon her. He beheld a young woman a foot smaller than he with thick auburn hair, large brown eyes, a slender figure tricked out in pale blue silk, an engaging smile, and no beauty whatsoever.

"I beg your pardon?" he said with the lift of one dark brow.

"I mean the splendid way you routed Cousin Basil! Hollis, that is. He is the veriest viper, and you bested him so handily. I was most impressed, and most grateful. All the world runs in fear of Basil's scathing conversation and you, with just a few words, have put him to flight. I cannot thank you enough, sir!" Melinda cried, grasping his hand and shaking it firmly. "You have done me a world of good, and I am forever in your debt."

"It was . . . my pleasure. Your servant, ma'am." Lord Carlton bowed and, demonstrating tremendous good sense to go with his verbal wit and skill, turned on his heel and walked off in the opposite direction from Basil Hollis.

Her hand grasping Miss Jonson's wrist, Melinda hurried to the French windows and stared at the broad back of the departing knight.

"Who *is* he?" she murmured.

"I very much fear," said Miss Jonson with a blush, "that that was the notorious Earl of Carlton."

"Why do I know that name?"

"You should *not* know that name, Melinda. He is a rake and a scoundrel!"

Melinda turned shining brown eyes upon her friend. "He is *that* Lord Carlton?"

"Yes, I regret to say it."

"But how wonderful!" said Melinda. "I have never met a rake and a scoundrel before."

"Melinda—"

"Father is too strict and Mama too timid. How delightful to have him come to this ball and rout my cousin so easily and so well. I must introduce myself to him formally."

"Melinda, that you *must not do!*" said Miss Jonson, her hand now grasping Melinda's arm and holding her firmly in place. "He has a shocking reputation and will ruin yours merely by bowing to you."

"Oh, Elizabeth, what nonsense," said Melinda, laughing a trifle giddily. "I could have an affair with Lord Byron himself, and the Mathley name would see me through."

In this Melinda did not exaggerate. The Mathleys might not possess a title to go with their ancestral name, but they were one of the first families in the nation, friend and ally

8

to royalty, tied to nearly every noble house in the land. A mere scandal such as Lord Byron might offer could not affect them.

"But the Earl of Carlton is ten times worse—nay, *twenty* times worse than Byron!" said Miss Jonson.

"But why have I never seen him before?" Melinda demanded, her gaze following the tall earl's progress through the ballroom.

"He has most fortunately been sequestered these last three years, in Yorkshire I believe. The Carlton estates are located there. You were not yet out when he was cutting a wide swath through the town. I however, was out and did see him and did hear of his shocking escapades. The whole town talked of nothing else."

"Did he really elope with the wife of Lord Thurgood?" Melinda asked, as she turned to Miss Jonson, eyes round with excitement.

"That and much worse! Melinda, I implore you, do not think on him anymore."

"But how rude it would be of me not to formally introduce myself after conversing with him so familiarly. Elizabeth, where are your manners? I wonder who he knows that I know who could introduce us?"

"Melinda, no," said Miss Jonson firmly. "I will not have it. He knows no one of good repute. Therefore, you have no mutual acquaintance, therefore you may not and shall not be introduced!"

Melinda judged that her friend spoke true. Sadly, she knew no one of bad reputation, her father would not permit it. Very likely she and Lord Carlton did not share a mutual acquaintance. This was a great pity. Not that it deterred Melinda at all.

"Well, if there is no one to introduce me, I might as well introduce myself," she replied.

Removing Miss Jonson's hand from her arm, she sailed back into the ballroom, her friend gaping at her from the balcony.

Melinda's heart quickened with eager anticipation for she saw that Lord Carlton stood at the side of Gerald, twelfth Viscount of Fenwych, and Lord Fenwych she *did* know and he was *not* possessed of a bad reputation. The gods clearly favored her this night.

Alas, they soon deserted her for in the next moment the eldest son of the house, Nigel Bascomb, accosted her but halfway across the ballroom to remind her that she had promised him this quadrille. It was not in Melinda to fob off a polite young man, the eldest son of her host, with some paltry lie when she had given her word. So, suppressing a regretful little sigh, she placed her hand on his arm and allowed him to lead her into the dance.

Lord Carlton was indeed standing at the side of Gerald, twelfth Viscount of Fenwych, informing him in a voice filled with ennui that he was decamping.

"Now Peter, you c-c-can't leave a half hour after you have arrived!" said the viscount, a notorious stammerer. "It would be a d-d-dreadful insult to the Bascombs who were kind enough to accept my pleas on your behalf and invite you to this t-t-tedious show!"

"It was good of them—and you—indeed," Lord Carlton conceded. "But their kindness unfortunately does not extend to providing any entertainment in a room of three hundred people. Had I known that becoming a model of propriety for the next month required dodging the censorious glares of outraged matrons, avoiding the curious little flirts among the debutantes, and prattling to some old man about last year's hunts, I should have told my uncle Gilford to leave his fortune to anyone but me!"

"Now, Peter, d-d-don't be rash," the Viscount urged. "What is a month of boredom to a lifetime of financial ease?"

"Yes, you're right, of course," Lord Carlton said with a sigh. "I could build up a comfortable income for myself . . . over twenty years time, perhaps. Uncle Gilford offers me the chance to renovate and improve the Carlton estates now.

I cannot let such an opportunity pass me by, even though it means behaving like a block of wood for the next month. Blast my lordly predecessors for frittering away my fortune! I come from a line of imbeciles, Jerry."

"Hardly that, Peter. From everything I've ever heard, it took a good deal of d-d-diligent effort for them to reduce the Carlton fortune to pennies."

Lord Carlton grinned at his friend. "Yes, well we are a determined lot." His blue eyes narrowed. "I must and shall repair what they have harmed!"

Lord Fenwych removed a glass of champagne from the tray of a passing footman and sipped at it meditatively. "You needn't go through all this rigmarole you know. Your uncle g-g-gave you a month to prove you know how to behave like a gentleman. You c-c-could use that month instead to enjoy yourself and woo an heiress. You don't need a dying uncle to leave you his fortune. You need only take a rich wife."

"Thank you, no!" said Lord Carlton in some alarm. "I want no wife, only a fortune to attend to my estates as my honor demands."

"Then you are c-c-consigned to the Bascombs' ball, and the Duke of Marville's ball, and the Prince's garden party."

Lord Carlton stared bleakly at the dancers. "If this ball is any example of what I am to withstand, I don't know if I've the courage to carry on. The only spot of amusement I have had thus far was— Good God, there she is now!"

"Who?"

"Her," Lord Carlton said, pointing to Melinda dancing with Nigel Bascomb. "She accosted me in the most extraordinary manner and thanked me for routing Basil Hollis."

"D-D-Did you really put down Hollis? Good show, Peter!"

"Yes, but who *is* she?"

Peering with a slight squint, Lord Fenwych brightened. "Oh, that's Melinda Mathley."

"Who?"

"The eldest daughter of old George Mathley. Dripping with money. A sweet girl, Melinda, but she's g-g-got a rather sad reputation."

"Her?"

"Oh, no, nothing like that, Peter, on my honor!" Lord Fenwych hastily assured his friend. "It's just that she's a b-b-bit of a lunatic, you see."

"Ah. Well, that would explain it," said Lord Carlton with a sardonic smile.

"Now, now, don't go jumping to any conclusions. Melinda's good as g-g-gold, she just gets herself into the oddest scrapes. She's a dear little thing, and I'll not have a word said against her."

"Why, Jerry, have you a *tendre* for the young woman?"

"Me?" said the viscount, paling. "No, no, no! Nothing of the sort! It's j-j-just that she broke St. John Collier's nose for me some years back and I've been grateful to her ever since."

Lord Carlton had prepared to polish off the last of the champagne in his glass, but this stopped him. "She what?"

"Broke St. John Collier's nose. He was s-s-saying the most cutting things to me, you see, because of my stammering, and Melinda was there—it was at some summer house party that my m-m-mother is forever giving—and Melinda told St. John to stop being so cruel and St. John, of course, laughed at her and she hauled off and planted him a very neat facer. Broke his nose, b-b-blood all over the place. He ran crying all the way home to his dear mama. Melinda received solitary confinement in her room for ... oh dear, a good three or four days, I think. I s-s-slipped her chocolates under the door."

Lord Carlton roared with laughter. "Gad! The currents that run beneath polite society never cease to amaze me."

The gentlemen continued to converse throughout the quadrille until their hostess, Lady Bascomb, hurried up to them, got a firm grip on the viscount's arm, and carried him off to dance with one of that evening's wallflowers.

Abandoned to the mercies of three hundred boring people, Lord Carlton drank another glass of champagne and then slipped away. His uncle could not expect him to plunge wholeheartedly into decorum his first night on the town. No one could be so unreasonable. Besides, a good book awaited his lordship in his house in Curzon Street, not to mention a new shipment of brandy.

At the end of the quadrille, Melinda looked eagerly for Lord Carlton. It would not have been difficult to find so tall and handsome a gentleman, even in this crowd. She quickly realized that he was not to be found, however, and her spirits sank in a most surprising manner. She could not think that she would be fortunate enough to see him again in the se'ennight remaining to her before her family removed to the country for the summer. Whatever freak had brought him to the Bascombs' tonight would surely not take him into any of London's other noble households in the eight days remaining to her. She returned to Miss Jonson's side far more subdued than when she had left it.

*

Chapter 2

MELINDA ROSE AT nine the next morning, had a leisurely breakfast in bed, dressed at an equally leisurely pace, and then strolled downstairs to begin her day's labors. Two identical blurs wooshed past her on the polished rails of the grand staircase.

"I won!" shouted one of the blurs who had landed neatly in the grand hall.

"Did not!" cried the other blur who had landed a second behind her.

"Did too!"

"Did not!"

"Did *too!*"

"You cheated!"

"Did not!"

"Did *too!*"

"Do be quiet, girls," Melinda admonished as she reached the bottom of the staircase in a far more decorous manner. "You don't want Mama waking up and wondering why you aren't at your lessons."

Annabelle and Margaret, her twelve-year-old twin sisters, glanced up at her with identical freckled faces.

"Lessons?" Annabelle said vaguely.

"What lessons?" Margaret inquired.

"Oh, bother," said Melinda with a weary sigh. "What have you done to your poor governess now?"

"Nothing," said Annabelle.

"Nothing at all," Margaret said.

14

Abandoning their argument for now, the twins trooped down to the kitchen where they succeeded in cajoling two strawberry tarts from their butter-hearted cook.

Melinda smiled fondly after them: sliding down banisters, stealing their good friend Sally Hawthorpe's monkey, or shielding a stray and very pregnant cat in their room, her sisters knew how to enjoy themselves. More and more Melinda wished that she had the same skill. But duty called.

She conducted a thirty-minute conference with the Mathley butler and housekeeper, for her parents were giving a dinner party that evening prior to the Duke of Marville's ball, and Melinda always oversaw every detail of the Mathley parties herself. Neither of her parents were of any use in conducting household affairs, while Melinda, to their relief, had some skill in this arena. She then discussed with the butler and housekeeper her plans for the Mathley's removal to their country estate, Putnam Park, in one week's time, going over timetables, packing schedules, and the transfer of servants to Putnam.

It was just after eleven that morning when Melinda and the entire household were subjected to a piercing scream. As this was routine in the Mathley home, everyone, save Melinda and Addie, Mrs. Mathley's personal maid, resumed their duties with little comment, the footman Hawkins merely remarking to a passing parlor maid, "I wonder what's got her this time?"

Melinda, abandoning the morning post, proceeded without undue haste to discover what *had* got her this time.

Addie, reaching Mrs. Mathley's room first, found her mistress in a deep swoon upon the settee, her blond head lolling to the side, her mouth open, looking as if she were about to snore. She located the ever-present bottle of smelling salts on the sorely over-burdened dressing table just as Melinda entered the room.

"What is it this time, Addie?"

15

"I'm sure I don't know, miss," Addie replied. "I was in madame's sitting room when she collapsed."

With a sigh, Melinda took the smelling salts from Addie, strode over to her stricken mother, and held the opened bottle directly under Catherine Mathley's nostrils. She watched without expression as the bottle had its desired effect. Mrs. Mathley sneezed violently and began to strain her head away from the bottle with as much strength as she possessed. But Melinda was even more determined to keep the smelling salts under her mother's much abused nose until she was certain that she had fully regained consciousness. This took only a moment longer. Mrs. Mathley opened her blue eyes, focused them on Melinda, and immediately burst into tears.

Melinda calmly instructed Addie to fetch the cold compress and mild herb tea that habitually followed Mrs. Mathley's hysterics. She then resigned herself to being trapped at her mother's side and tried to make some sense of her hysterical ramblings.

"How could she? My own sister! Twenty thousand a year and likely more! Gone, all gone! Oh, George will be so furious. He'll die of apoplexy or gout or some such thing, and then what will become of us?" She glared up at Melinda. "I have nursed a viper in my bosom!" Heart-wrenching sobs once again wracked Mrs. Mathley's lovely form.

"Mama," Melinda said in a soothing voice bred from many years of experience, "please just take a deep breath and try to tell me—slowly—what has caused this terrible upset."

Despite the plump tears rolling down her cheeks, Mrs. Mathley began to breathe deeply and slowly and attained a modicum of calm. "There!" she cried, pointing at the newspaper lying beside her rather wide right foot. "Look there for your answer!" Her tears became more copious.

Melinda picked up the newspaper as Addie returned to the room. While Melinda scanned the pages, Addie managed to get Mrs. Mathley to lie back upon the settee with a cold compress applied to her forehead.

"Where exactly . . . ?" Melinda began.

"The announcements!" Mrs. Mathley uttered in a terrible voice, pressing the compress against her forehead.

Melinda once again scanned the paper. There were announcements of engagements, marriages, and births. As her mother never called her a viper except in reference to marriage—specifically, her lack thereof—Melinda turned to the marriage announcements. But these provided no illumination. She turned, therefore, to the engagements, an equally treacherous topic in their household, and here at last she found the cause of her mother's upset.

"Beatrice is engaged to Mr. Wentworth?" she said. "But our aunt Wells has said nothing of this!"

"Exactly!" cried her mother. "She has kept it secret while her wretched daughter has stolen away your sister's future husband! Twenty thousand pounds a year! Gone! All gone!"

"What's gone?" a voice inquired from the doorway.

Melinda turned her head and beheld the breathtaking form of her sister, Louisa. Impressed, as always, by her sister's golden beauty, Melinda was still sufficiently in command of herself to note that Louisa had had the very good sense to wait until she was quite certain that the worst of Mrs. Mathley's hysterics were over before coming to inquire after her stricken mother's health.

"What has gone?" Louisa asked again as she advanced into the room.

"It is more of a who," Melinda replied. "Brace yourself, Louisa, for some terrible news: You have lost a beau."

"Really? Which one?" Louisa inquired with perfect indifference.

"William Wentworth."

"Oh, him." Louisa sniffed. "I never cared two pins for him. He's as dull as dishwater. I never would have accepted him."

17

"Louisa!" gasped their mother. "How could you? My own daughter. My own baby turning against me!"

"Now, Mama, it is nothing of the kind," Melinda said soothingly. "Louisa is a very dutiful and obedient daughter. Mr. Wentworth is a mere nothing to us. Baronets and viscounts and marquesses pursue Louisa, and she could have any of them for a song. What is twenty thousand pounds compared to a marquess? Let Cousin Beatrice have her odious Mr. Wentworth. If she wants to be bored to death in her marriage, it is no concern of ours."

"Hildegarde has done this to spite me!" Mrs. Mathley declared with a vehemence that suggested her thoughts had not yet reached a happier plane. "Keeping the betrothal a secret from *me*. To have to read of it in the newspaper—a *common* newspaper!"

"It was very bad of Aunt Wells to be sure," Melinda agreed, "but never fear, Mama. Louisa knows her duty to the family and will selflessly trump Beatrice's Mr. Wentworth with an earl or a marquess, won't you Louisa?"

"Whichever one our mother prefers," Louisa replied with a little frown at her sister.

"Oh, dear child," said Mrs. Mathley, tears in her eyes as she clasped Louisa's hand to her heaving bosom, "you are my only consolation. Melinda enjoys teasing me into vexation by her flagrant refusal to marry, but you, dearest Louisa, *you* shall not plague me as she has done, will you?"

"Of course not, Mama," Louisa replied, kissing her mother on the cheek. "I shall be married to some glittering title by Christmas, never you fear. Now lie back and rest. You know how fatigued you are after one of your attacks."

Melinda and Louisa soon made their escape, gently closing their mother's bedroom door behind them.

"Odious Aunt Wells to play such a mean trick on Mama!" said Melinda as they walked down the hall.

"And odious Cousin Beatrice to steal Mr. Wentworth away without so much as a hint of her intentions," Louisa said.

18

"Oh, it was her mother's intentions more than hers, you may be sure. I am not fond of Beatrice, but I could wish her a less commanding mother. Aunt Wells has undoubtedly arranged the match *and* browbeaten Beatrice into accepting the greatest bore ever to put an entire ballroom to sleep."

Louisa laughed. "He is a dull fellow, but quite nice really. I hope he and Beatrice will find some happiness together."

Melinda suddenly stopped. "You know, there is a good chance that they will. They are both so meek and proper that they might have been made for each other. How clever of you, Louisa, to escape Mr. Wentworth and to no longer have the beautiful Beatrice competing with you on the marriage mart."

"As for that," Louisa said tartly, "Beatrice was never a worthy competitor. Her face is not a perfect oval, as mine is, and her hair is more withered wheat than shimmering gold."

"Where *do* you come up with such drivel?" Melinda demanded.

"From Mr. Wentworth!"

The two laughed heartily at this. Louisa returned to her room to complete her morning toilette, while Melinda went down to the dining room to check on the three maids busily polishing silver.

Just after ten o'clock that evening, the Mathleys and the twenty couples who comprised their dinner guests ventured out into the night, for all had been invited to the Marville ball. They quickly dispersed upon their arrival at the brilliantly illuminated mansion. Mr. and Mrs. Mathley started for the card salon, Louisa was captured by half the young men in the room and carried off for an evening of flattery and adoration, and Melinda was left quite alone. For the moment. She spied Oswald Omersby trotting toward her with an eager smile. Quickly she ducked behind Lady Jersey, slipped through a knot of Exquisites, and had soon placed half the room between her and her ardent pursuer.

It was then that she spied Lord Carlton. She quite failed to recall Miss Jonson's injunctions not to think on him, let alone speak to him again. She was ruled solely by the knowledge that the gods had, for whatever reason, decided to bless her once again. She knew no trepidation as she advanced upon Lord Carlton, only the keenest pleasure in discovering someone who was beyond her ken and different and perhaps exciting.

The earl was propping up a paneled wall of the ballroom, watching the dancers, his broad back to her as Melinda drew near. His tight-fitting black evening coat emphasized the breadth of his shoulders. His muscular legs were properly clad in white knee breeches and silk stockings. His black hair was carefully tousled in a romantic style that suited him admirably. She could not see the harsh expression on his face as she tapped him on the shoulder.

"I beg your pardon. You are Lord Carlton, are you not?"

He turned and stared down at her in some surprise and, it seemed, pleasure. "I am," he agreed.

"How do you do, Lord Carlton?" Melinda said, thrusting her hand at him. He took it and felt it firmly shaken once again. "I'm Melinda Mathley. I must apologize for accosting you in so strange a manner last night. It is not usually my habit to speak to a gentleman when we have not been formally introduced, but I was filled with such admiration for the way you bested Cousin Basil that I spoke without thinking. Let me introduce myself properly now. My name you know. But as for the rest, my father is George Mathley, that portly gentleman bending the ear of Lord Bascomb. We haven't any title, but we're vastly rich and well connected, even, it is said, to royalty, though not, alas, on the right side of the blanket. My mother is that gorgeous woman walking into the card salon on the Duke of Devereaux's arm. My sister is Louisa Mathley, *La Belle du Ton*. I'm the family lunatic. But then, you've probably guessed that already. I lack all the usual feminine accomplishments. I don't sing, paint, or play the pianoforte. I'm twenty years old and still on the shelf. Not that they haven't tried to marry me off. I've had six offers of marriage, probably seven if Omersby comes up to scratch, and oh I hope he doesn't! So all in all, the only thing to recommend me to your notice is an impressive family tree as long as your leg."

"Not my arm?"

"No, no! Your legs are much longer and so is my family tree."

Lord Carlton smiled. "How do you do, Miss Mathley?"

An engaging dimple burst into life. "Very well, thank you, Lord Carlton."

"Will Omersby come up to scratch?"

"I fear so. While I'm no Helen of Troy, my father is as rich as Croesus, and I have the most amazing dowry that has garnered me six proposals—"

"Possibly seven."

"Yes, and undoubtedly more. Well, what's a dowry for if it can't get you a decent amount of suitors?"

"I had wondered. And why haven't you accepted any of the past six suitors?"

Melinda cocked her head. "Well, frankly, I don't like fortune hunters. I don't like being valued for less than what I am. And I don't like being used."

Lord Carlton stared at her in some surprise. "For a young woman of only twenty years, you express the most decided opinions."

"Well, I can't see that it's wrong to tell the truth."

"No," said the earl, "but it is, in our society, a rather startling experience for others."

Melinda waved this argument away. "Oh, I know that plain language is considered inelegant and that we're supposed to talk in innuendos and around subjects and all that folderol, and I can do it with the best of them, really I can. You'd be amazed at how well I speak Oblique. It's just that I thought that with a rake and a scoundrel, why bother? It would probably bore you to tears."

21

Lord Carlton smiled again. He had a most attractive smile, particularly when it reached up to his blue eyes and banished the bitterness lurking there. "How very kind of you to be so considerate of my ennui. You must now satisfy my curiosity. Who were the six avaricious gentlemen you turned down without a care for their wounded feelings?"

"There isn't a fortune hunter alive who has feelings to be wounded. Well, perhaps Algernon Lansleif's feelings were wounded. But then, he wasn't really a fortune hunter, just not plump in the pocket."

"Who?"

"Algernon Lansleif," Melinda enunciated, "the nephew of Lord Stokely. He was quite all right as they go, I suppose. Algernon, that is. Well-breeched, polite, kind, considerate."

"Good God, he sounds a fiend!" Lord Carlton exclaimed, his blue eyes twinkling.

"Well, he was! For the thing of it was that he worshiped me."

"I beg your pardon?"

"Well, I know it seems absurd for I am the farthest thing from Helen of Troy, but the fact of the matter is that Algy worshiped me and what could be worse than that?"

"I haven't the faintest idea."

"Well, that's because you're not thinking about this thing properly. Women don't want to be worshiped."

"They don't?" said Lord Carlton faintly.

"No, of course not! Nothing could be worse, for as soon as the ring is on your hand and you settle down to wedded bliss, you're bound to come a cropper by preferring Milton to Shakespeare, or you'll take an instant dislike to a favorite pointer, or you'll make some slighting remark about a mother-in-law, and the scales will fall from your husband's eyes, and from then on every morning at the breakfast table your beloved will gaze at you with a look of deep reproach, somewhat like a haddock being pulled up out of the water to rest upon your breakfast plate, and what, I ask you, could be worse than that?"

"Having Lord Omersby for a husband?" Lord Carlton ventured.

Melinda shuddered. "You have hit it. Can you imagine having a man older than your father offer for you?"

"No, frankly I can't. But then, I'm more popular with the female set."

Melinda beamed up at the earl. "I know! Everyone's talking about it. How wonderful of you to descend upon us and bring a bit of life to this tepid ball. I'm so grateful to you. I was wondering if you would do me the very great favor of dancing with me."

"I beg your pardon?" Lord Carlton said, his head beginning to reel.

"Well, I've always wanted to dance with a rake and a scoundrel, and you seem so very attractive and entertaining that I thought, well, this is my chance, I might as well ask you."

The earl struggled to bring his abused wits into some semblance of order. "Won't the well-connected Mr. Mathley and the gorgeous Mrs. Mathley object?" he inquired.

"Oh, vehemently! But, of course, then I will have already had the dance so their outrage won't matter because I will have achieved the end. They are always shocked or appalled by whatever I do, so I'm quite used to their diatribes. Will you dance with me?"

Carlton stared at her a moment. A grin lifted his sensual mouth. "Yes, I think I will. If you don't care about the consequences, neither shall I. Will you do me the great honor, Miss Mathley," he said with a courtly bow, "of favoring me with this waltz?"

Melinda curtsied very low. "Oh, sir, the honor is all mine!"

Lord Carlton offered his arm, Melinda placed her hand upon it, and they paraded onto the ballroom floor. An electric buzz shot around the room as the ton turned as one to witness Melinda Mathley's newest lunacy.

Lord Carlton took Melinda in his arms and began to revolve her gracefully across the crowded dance floor. She experienced a sudden breathlessness out of all proportion to the rigors of the waltz.

"You . . . dance beautifully, sir."

"Thank you. It is one of the requirements of a rake. So tell me," Lord Carlton said, struggling to appear innocent in the teeth of such overwhelming evidence, "how do you come to be the family lunatic?"

"I don't honestly know," Melinda replied, a trifle pensively. "I didn't set out to be the family lunatic. I never intended to be the family lunatic. But the oddest things keep happening to me. Quite by accident, you understand. So now I'm Mad Melinda to everyone in the family and half the town. Actually, three-quarters of the town. No, probably all of the town. Now that you have returned from Yorkshire, you will undoubtedly hear the most awful rumors about me. Not as bad as the ones about *you*, of course, but still, all in all, rather scandalous. You may even hear it said that I once frequented a notorious gaming den known as the Red Lady."

"And didn't you?"

"No! It's a scandalous falsehood! I've more sense than to throw my pin money away on crooked games."

"However did such a rumor begin?" Lord Carlton inquired, enjoying himself hugely.

"It was all Harry's fault."

"*Another* suitor?"

Melinda laughed. "No, you goose. Harry is my brother. My twenty-one-year-old wastrel of a brother who hasn't the sense that God gave a flea. *He* used to frequent the Red Lady and, of course, lost every penny he had. When he couldn't find any more items to hock and when Father refused to advance him on his allowance, Harry had to tell Daniel Tarn, the reprehensible proprietor of the Red Lady,

24

that he wouldn't be able to pay his debt of honor until the next quarter."

"I would assume that Mr. Tarn took umbrage at such a declaration."

"Oh, he did! He had two of his bravos beat Harry senseless."

"Good God!" said Lord Carlton, honestly shocked. "Did Tarn not know of the Mathley family's vast connections?"

"Well, of course he did. That's why he let Harry get in so deep. But as this was the third time in less than a year that Harry had failed to come up with the blunt in a timely manner, Tarn felt that he ought to make an impression on my brother. Father was loading every gun in the house, Mama was in a perpetual swoon, and Harry could only eat gruel for a week. So, that's when I decided I had to take a hand in the matter."

Lord Carlton blinked. "But what could you do?"

"I had Mr. Tarn arrested after I got him to confess that he had had Harry beaten and that all of his games were rigged."

"No! How could you?"

"It *was* rather difficult," Melinda confessed. "But Tarn came around beautifully after I shot him."

Lord Carlton missed a step. "You *shot* a notorious gamester?"

"Only in the foot, and what, after all, is a mere foot? Of course, Tarn howled a good deal about it, which was really rather silly of him for it made a bad impression on the Bow Street Runners I had hired and they weren't at all gentle with him when they led him away. He had to hop. But, of course, word got around that I had been at the Red Lady, perhaps the Bow Street Runners let it slip, and that is how that silly gaming rumor began."

"Well, of course," said Lord Carlton, his eyes watering with suppressed laughter. "Gad, if the ton only knew the truth of the matter!"

"My point exactly! It would end that scandalous falsehood once and for all. But Father refused to allow me to explain."

"I don't wonder," Lord Carlton said with a grin as he gazed down at his dance partner. It was clear to him that Miss Mathley had no understanding that her real activities had been far more outrageous than her rumored activities.

"And how did you come to be a rake and a scoundrel?" she inquired.

Lord Carlton gaped at her a moment. "My . . . temperament and talents fitted me to the role."

She accepted this. "Is it enjoyable being a rake and a scoundrel, or is it rather a bore?"

"Oh, it was fun at the beginning," Lord Carlton replied, the bitterness returning to his blue eyes, "but a bit of a bore nowadays."

"Yes, I can quite see that," Melinda said. "It's all well and good to shock your friends and to dally with pretty, plump maidens who are not averse to throwing themselves at your feet, but after awhile I should think that all of that feminine attention and societal moral outrage would begin to pall."

"Yes, it has rather."

"Such stories I've heard of your escapades! I do hope they're all true. It would be a severe blow to discover you are not at all as black as you are painted."

Anger hardened Lord Carlton's handsome face. "Oh, I am quite as bad as the ton says."

Melinda considered him a moment. "No, sir, you are wrong. A really bad man would not repent his youthful excesses as you do."

Surprise replaced the anger. "I never said—"

"Well, you do, don't you?"

"On occasion," Lord Carlton conceded. "But how did you—"

"Speaking of repentance, whyever did you elope with Almira Thurgood? She's such a harpy!"

Lord Carlton had never felt so at sea. "Yes, well, I was

26

young and that accounts for a good deal. Young men think only of pleasure, never of consequences. Almira flattered me in a most gratifying manner, and she was, of course, quite beautiful and that, to a young man of two-and-twenty, is everything. Her beauty blinded me to her less amiable qualities."

"Men are so predictable," said Melinda with some disgust. "My friend, Miss Jonson, although quite plain, is the best woman on earth, and all she can lure to her side is the indifferent Lord Dennis. Had she been beautiful, however, she would have been crushed by a masculine stampede for she has quite a nice fortune of her own. My sister, Louisa, is proof enough of that. Why is it that when normally intelligent men behold a woman with a heart-shaped face and sparkling eyes they are rendered slobbering idiots?"

"Ah. Well, you must remember that God made Adam first, and he was something of a rough draft. God had a good deal more experience under his belt when he made Eve, and she turned out much better."

A gurgle of laughter escaped Melinda. "I knew I should like you the minute you called Cousin Basil a vulgarian."

"You honor me, Miss Mathley."

"Well, I can't see what sort of an honor it is being liked by an acknowledged lunatic."

Lord Carlton gave it up and laughed. Smiling up at him, Melinda thought that no man had ever looked so beautiful in laughter and no man had ever needed to laugh more. The knowledge came to her, unbidden, that Lord Carlton had led an unhappy life despite all of his adventures and scandals, or perhaps because of them. It had been in her power to give him the momentary pleasure of laughter. She hoped she might have an opportunity in the future to provide the same service again.

The dance ended and Melinda made an automatic curtsy to Lord Carlton's bow.

"Thank you," she murmured. "That was delightful."

Lord Carlton smiled down at her. "Miss Mathley, I cannot tell you how grateful I am that you accosted me tonight. I have enjoyed myself immensely, but I fear," he said, glancing up, "that the pleasure is to be short-lived. I detect a glowering father storming toward us."

Lord Carlton's vast experience in these matters had not led him astray. It was, indeed, Mr. George Mathley—short, dark, and grim—bearing down upon them, his face vermilion with suppressed fury.

"What the devil do you mean, sir," said Mr. Mathley as he drew before them without benefit of introduction, "by dancing and conversing with my daughter?"

"Why, sir, I meant to enjoy myself and did so," Lord Carlton replied.

"Enjoyed yourself? Yes! At the expense of *my* daughter's reputation!"

"Oh, now, Father, don't be absurd," Melinda broke in. "How could he ruin my reputation at a private ball?"

Mr. Mathley snorted. "A lot you know."

"Well, I do know," said Melinda, "that no one can accuse me of having an affair with Lord Carlton when they have seen me dancing in public with him rather than sneaking away with him to the back gardens for an illicit rendezvous."

"Melinda!" gasped Mr. Mathley. "Never utter such a disgraceful thought again!"

"Oh, Father, it would only be disgraceful if I got caught."

Lord Carlton was experiencing some difficulty in maintaining his gravity.

"You will oblige me, Melinda," said her outraged father, "by not saying another word! And you, sir," Mr. Mathley snapped at Lord Carlton, "will do me the honor of foregoing to converse or dance with my daughter again! Come, Melinda, your mother is having a spasm."

So saying, he grasped his daughter's hand and dragged

28

her as far away from Lord Carlton as the small ballroom allowed.

"Father, that was most uncivil of you," said Melinda. "Lord Carlton is a wonderful dancer, and his conversation was quite above reproach."

Mr. Mathley spent five minutes telling his eldest daughter exactly what he thought of her intelligence and understanding of propriety, and his intentions toward Lord Carlton should she ever dare to speak, let alone dance, with him again.

This perturbed Melinda a little, for she fully intended to see and speak with Lord Carlton again. Never had she known such pleasure in a gentleman's company. To reclaim that pleasure she would brave anything, even the wrath of George Mathley.

*

Chapter 3

JUST BEFORE NOON on the following day, Melinda returned
to her room following a morning call from Miss Jonson and
found two identical, freckled, eager faces smiling up at her
from her bed, which they had hopelessly rumpled.

"Margaret, Annabelle, do you know the first thing about
making beds?" Melinda inquired.

The two scurried off the bed, straightened it with a sin-
gular lack of success, and then accosted her in one voice
with the same statement.

"We know who's called on Father!"

"Has he returned from his club?" said Melinda with
praiseworthy lack of concern.

"An hour ago!" said Margaret.

"And he's got someone with him," said Annabelle.

"Someone who's important to *you*," said Margaret.

For some odd reason, Lord Carlton's name flashed into
Melinda's mind, but she hurriedly discarded it. She could
not think that even Lord Carlton would have the temerity to
call on her father.

"Really?" she said. "Who is it?"

"Oswald Omersby!" cried the twins as one.

Melinda was rooted to the spot. "Oh, no."

"He's probably making his offer for you at this very moment!" said Annabelle.

"Imagine being married to someone older than Father!"
giggled Margaret.

"I can't and I won't, so don't strain yourselves," said Melinda sharply.

"You're not going to marry him?" said Annabelle.

"No, of course not," Melinda said testily.

"But he's Father's friend," said Margaret.

"That is no reason for me to marry him," said Melinda. She suddenly stopped and stared with growing horror at the twins. "You must not say a word of this, girls! If you . . . And he . . . ! Promise me that you'll let me tell Father in my own way."

"Oh, honestly," said Margaret with disgust, "you'd think we don't know how to keep a secret the way you go on."

"I'm sorry," said Melinda, her fingers trembling slightly as she brushed a tendril of auburn hair from her forehead. "My nerves are a little on edge."

"Whose wouldn't be with Oswald Omersby in Father's study?" said Annabelle.

"Thank you for understanding," said Melinda with a fond smile.

"We don't want you to get married anyway," Margaret said.

"No?"

"No," said Annabelle. "It would be dreadfully dull with you gone, Melinda."

"And there'd be no one to keep Father's wrath from falling on our heads day in and day out," said Margaret.

Melinda gazed at her sisters with growing alarm. "Oh, bother, what have you done now?"

"Sally Hawthorpe's brother brought her a parrot when he came home on leave," Annabelle confided.

"He's awfully clever," said Margaret. "The parrot, I mean. He can swear in three languages."

The twins trooped happily out of her room.

Melinda sat down with a thump upon her bed, the air whooshing from her lungs, the blood draining from her face. The parrot was the least of her concerns. Omersby had actually done it! He had actually called on her father.

31

Still, perhaps they were only discussing hunting or fishing or Omersby's prize-winning sheep. Perhaps they weren't discussing her at all!

And perhaps she could sprout wings and fly to America to escape the coming storm. "Oh, bother," Melinda groaned aloud. "Why do all the worst men want to marry me?"

There was no doubt in her mind that she must and would refuse Omersby's offer. But what consumed all of her thoughts was how she was going to break the news to her father, who was undoubtedly handing Omersby a glass of port and a cigar at this very moment, clapping him on his back and calling him son, the two laughing together over this little joke.

Half an hour later she heard the faint sound of the front door opening and closing. Then there was a polite rap upon her door.

"Yes?"

The footman Hawkins, a pleasant young man with chestnut hair, came in without his usual smile.

"I beg your pardon, Miss Mathley. Mr. Mathley wishes to see you in his study."

"Yes, I thought he would," said Melinda, standing up. "You'd better alert Addie, Hawkins, to have Mama's strongest bottle of smelling salts at hand."

Hawkins visibly relaxed, a smile peeping out at her. "Yes, Miss Mathley! And may I say, miss, begging your pardon, miss, I'm so glad, miss!"

Melinda smiled. "Thank you, Hawkins. But I do wish it was you Father wished to see, rather than me."

"Thank you, no, miss. I'd sooner face a wounded bear."

They smiled at each other in mutual understanding. Then Melinda walked downstairs, advanced to her father's study, and entered into the bear's den.

"You wanted to see me, Father?" she said.

George Mathley sat in a red leather chair behind his large desk, regarding her soberly.

"Yes, Melinda, if you'll just have a seat for a moment."

Melinda knew that tone of voice, having heard it on six previous occasions. She longed to refuse her father's request, perhaps plead a headache, or some household disaster, and escape. But this must be got through and it ought to be now as later. She took a chair in front of his desk and watched her father pick up a pen and begin twirling it between his thick fingers. Finally, nervously clearing his throat, Mr. Mathley began.

"Melinda, I've . . . ahem . . . just had a call from Lord Omersby. You do recall Oswald Omersby, don't you?"

"Yes, Father."

"Yes, well, of course. The fact of the matter is, Melinda, that Omersby's offered for you. A fine offer, too. Yes, indeed. Not terribly well-breeched, you know, but he's got a good title and an absolutely impeccable family line. Now, I've known Omersby since our Oxford days together. He's not terribly bright, I grant you, but he's a kind man, Melinda. I can't recall ever seeing him in a temper. And he's fond of you, Melinda. Devilish fond. Has an absolute *tendre* for you, said so himself."

Taking Melinda's silence for interest, or at least acquiescence, Mr. Mathley cheerfully continued.

"You'd spend most of your year in the country, of course. Omersby isn't fond of city life. But then, you've always liked the country, haven't you? And he's still young enough, Melinda, to give you children. He's discussed the whole matter with his mother, and he assured me that she will be quite happy to receive you into her home. It's an outstanding offer, Melinda. Few girls will get the like."

Now, alas, was the time to speak.

"I cannot marry Lord Omersby, Father," Melinda said in a quiet, firm voice.

The pen slipped from Mr. Mathley's fingers. "What was that?"

"I cannot marry him, Father."

"But I've given him my consent!"

"He's fifty-one, Father, and fat and graceless and reeks of the port and cigars he is never without. His conversation consists of sheep and his mother. Nor does he have, as far as I have been able to discover, a single wit in his head!"

While Mr. Mathley considered this a fair and accurate assessment of his old school fellow, he nonetheless felt the injury his daughter meant to serve his lordship.

"He is my friend, Melinda," he said sternly.

"He is a fortune hunter, Father," Melinda countered, her hands clasped tightly in her lap, "as all the others have been. He does not care for me. He does not even know me. He would be horrified with my mad starts. He does not like me to discuss anything but the weather or his mother, he does not like me to ride or go to the theater, or read anything but *Fordyce's Sermons*. I could not live with such a man. I should be . . . suffocated!"

Mr. Mathley erupted out of his chair. "God's blood, Melinda, this is the *seventh* offer you have refused!"

"I know, Father," Melinda whispered, hanging her head.

"Seven men! Do you realize that we are becoming the laughingstock of the ton solely through your own disastrous efforts on the marriage mart?"

"I want to oblige you, Father, in everything that is right. But it is not right that I marry Lord Omersby."

Mr. Mathley began to pace furiously behind his desk. In his gruff and acerbic way, he was fond of all his children and sincerely tried to do what was best for them. But each, it seemed, was determined to exacerbate all of his tender feelings and press him into continual fury: Harry, with his drinking and gambling; the twins, with their constant attempts to keep the most motley pets in his house, from frogs to stray cats; his wife, with her rattlepated hysterics; even his beautiful daughter Louisa, who refused to encourage the Marquess of Rutherford to make her an offer when it was clear to a blind man that the marquess was madly in love with the girl. And Melinda. Melinda worst of all, for *she*, unlike every other female of every Mathley generation, had not wed by the time she was twenty and, worse, seemed determined on a course of spinsterdom. George Mathley knew his duty. He must save his daughter from herself!

"I have been patient with you, Melinda. God knows I have been patient! But this! This is the last straw!" he declared.

He placed his hands on his desk and leaned toward her. "I shall not be patient and understanding any longer. You must and shall be wed, your future secured, your wildness curbed. The next man, Melinda, the very next man that offers for you, rich or poor, young or old, handsome or ugly, you will have him."

"Father, no!" Melinda cried, the color draining from her face.

"I mean this, Melinda. You are my daughter. I have tried to give you a future of comfort and respectability. You will not cooperate. Therefore, I must take matters into my own hands. The next man, Melinda! You *will* marry him if you are fortunate enough to receive another offer, even if it means my dragging you bound and gagged to the altar! Now you may go! I've done with you for now."

"But Father—"

"Go!"

Shaking rather badly, Melinda rose on wobbly legs and left her father's study. She walked numbly back up the stairs and into her own room. She knew her father's temper. It was volatile, quick to rise, quick to pass away. He was angry with her now. She understood that. It would pass in time and with it the threat to her future happiness. But should a man offer for her before that passing, George Mathley would see her wed, if he had to drive her to Gretna Green himself.

He had set a treacherous trap. Three gentlemen had been pursuing her for nearly a year, drawing back only when they saw Oswald Omersby step to the fore, believing that as her father's friend, he would naturally have her father's ready acquiescence to any proposal. With Omersby out of the way, they would advance once again, and she couldn't abide any of them!

She had been cold with them, aloof, on occasion blunt, and still each believed he could have her. George Mathley's threat now made this probable, at least for one of them. If Freddy Lamont, for example, with his wandering hands and bad breath proposed first, Melinda would have no other recourse but to emigrate. And she was a lamentable sailor.

The Mathleys were promised to attend Lord and Lady Jersey's rout that night and never had Melinda looked forward to a party less. What did it matter that the Jerseys had invited the brightest literary stars, the fairest jewels in the upper ton, the most charming of gentlemen, and an excellent orchestra?

Her thoughts were oppressed with the aftermath of the Oswald Omersby affair. The three men whom Omersby had routed had quickly accosted her when she had entered the Jersey ballroom, each soliciting a dance. She had refused them all, pleading prior engagements and escaping into the crowd, hoping not to see them again. Whoever asked her to dance she refused, pleading a headache, pleading lameness, pleading rheumatism. After awhile she did not care what excuse she gave.

She hid behind clumps of dowagers, potted palms, packs of sporting gentlemen, and thickets of imperious matrons, avoiding everyone in her ken until she saw Lord Carlton. He had been cornered by three Vandeveres who, as she vaguely recalled, were his cousins. The Dowager Vandevere was a tall, heavily powdered woman with artificially blond hair, rouged lips and cheeks. On either side of her stood her sons, Fitzwilliam and Andrew.

Fitzwilliam was a determined dandy and had come to the ball dressed in—and Melinda shuddered to see it—a pale orange satin evening coat padded at the shoulders and across the chest to supply what nature had denied Mr. Vandevere. His shirt points were so high and stiff he could not turn his head. He stockings were puce. He was a terrible sight.

Andrew, in contrast, was not a dandy, nor did he affect the exquisite taste of a Beau. Rather, he was careless in all his habiliments. A shabrag, the normally gentle Mrs. Mathley had termed him on more than one occasion, and she, who was always in the height of fashion, ought to know. His cravat was a scarf loosely knotted at his throat, his coat was four years out of date, he wore trousers, not the knee breeches that were de rigueur for such a rout.

Lord Carlton, from his clothes to his intellect, was superior to his cousins in every way, and yet something in his expression suggested to Melinda that his cousins had him trapped and he was in some need of rescue.

Never one to stand aside when she saw a fellow creature in trouble, Melinda sailed across the ballroom, happy and eager for the first time since she had entered her father's study that morning.

"You won't last a week," Andrew Vandevere was saying.

"A week?" said Fitzwilliam Vandevere. "I don't give him any more than three days."

"Twenty guineas says you're wrong," Andrew Vandevere countered.

"Done."

"That is quite enough, boys," Mrs. Vandevere icily broke in. "Whether he fails in one week or in two, the outcome will be the same. My brother's fortune will come to us as it should."

"I believe Uncle Gilford may leave his fortune to anyone he chooses," Lord Carlton retorted, "and he told me he has no desire to leave it to you, Cousin."

"*I* am his eldest sister!" Mrs. Vandevere snapped.

"And *I* am the only child of his only male heir, a cousin, I grant you, but still a blood relation. The Gilford fortune

37

has not, as a rule, always descended upon the male line, it is true, but when Uncle Gilford considers the female line, well! The choice is clear."

"You are an abomination!" Mrs. Vandevere declared. "A blot on our family and our position. I shall make it a point to see that you fail this enterprise and fail badly!"

"I cannot tell you, Cousin, what pleasure it will give me to put you out of curl."

"There you are, Lord Carlton!" Melinda cried with a scolding voice. "You naughty fellow! How beastly of you to hide yourself away like this when you *know* you had promised me this waltz."

Lord Carlton's blue eyes, which had been shuttered but a moment earlier, now burst into life as he smiled at her.

"Miss Mathley, I beg your pardon. I was so engrossed in conversation with Mrs. Vandevere that I quite lost track of time. Allow me to give you my arm."

"Thank you, sir," said Melinda, nodding graciously at the Vandeveres. She turned with Lord Carlton and sailed onto the dance floor.

"I am most grateful to you, Miss Mathley."

"Yes, I rather thought you would be," Melinda replied with a mischievous smile.

He looked down at her as they began to dance. "What? Did you purposely rescue me?"

The breathlessness she had experienced the night before in Lord Carlton's arms had returned with a vengeance. "Why, yes," she managed. "Wasn't it neatly done?"

Lord Carlton chuckled. "Very neatly. And here I thought you were just trying to stir up some trouble for yourself."

"Oh, no," said Melinda, "I never try to stir up trouble. It just simply . . . happens to me."

"Yes, and the how remains a mystery," said the earl, blue eyes twinkling down at her.

"You are quizzing me, Lord Carlton. Do you say that I am the cause of all my own trouble?"

"The thought had crossed my mind."

"Yes, well I daresay you are right," said Melinda, thinking of Lord Omersby.

"Why so suddenly grave, Miss Mathley? Have you troubles of your own?"

Melinda offered her best nonchalant shrug. "A tempest in a teapot. I hope it will blow over before it causes real harm."

"This seems an evening for trouble," said Lord Carlton.

Melinda looked up at him in some surprise. "What? Have you troubles, too?"

"Yes, I've had to spend half an hour with my wretched cousins."

Melinda laughed. "They are not good ton," she said.

"No," said Lord Carlton dryly. "But they have the power to cause me a considerable amount of . . . trouble."

"Power over you? How can that be?"

"It is only a trifling matter, Miss Mathley."

"No, sir!" said Melinda earnestly. "Your eyes betray you. Something is weighing your spirits down. It has been my experience that troubles are often lessened to a considerable degree when you share them with someone else. Come, at least tell me what is the matter."

Lord Carlton's expression was quite odd, as if looking at and refusing to believe in something at the same time. "I don't—" he began.

"Now honestly, sir. I rattled on to you at an alarming pace yesterday. You can at least do the same by me tonight."

He smiled. "Very well. I have taken it into my head to reform—"

"Good God, sir, you can't mean it!" Melinda exclaimed, horrified.

"Only enough so that I need no longer be an outsider in my own class," Lord Carlton said with a smile as he busily sifted the true facts of the case to offer a more palatable half truth. For some reason he felt uncomfortable appearing

39

before Miss Mathley as a greedy puppet dancing to his uncle's piping. "I have grown weary of being a social outcast. I should like to associate within the ton with those who are truly superior, knowledgeable, good, and not be looked at askance whenever I set foot out my door. It is a trifle lonely standing on the outside looking in. Even with my own family. It would please me to assure my uncle Gilford of my reformation before he dies, and from what he tells me, I've precious little time to transform myself before he drops off the perch. Hence my presence at a series of damnably dull fetes. I beg your pardon, I ought to have said: Hence my presence at a series of glittering social functions. I mean to conduct myself like a proper gentleman and avoid any hint of scandal."

"Are you not asking too much of yourself?"

Lord Carlton chuckled. "It is a tremendous strain," he agreed. "But one I am more than willing to undertake. I find that age has given me a bit of wisdom, Miss Mathley, despite all my attempts to fend it off. The Vandeveres' sneers notwithstanding, I may bring myself much good if I can contrive to put at least some of my past behind me."

"But not all, I hope. You would find life too dull if you gave up all your fun."

"Yes, so I am learning."

"Well, now I have the solution to the mystery that has all of London puzzling. Why," Melinda continued in response to his quizzical look, "you have begun appearing at some of London's damnably dull fetes. I beg your pardon, I ought to have said: Why you have begun appearing at some of London's glittering social functions."

Lord Carlton grinned at her. "Yes, I thought if I surrounded myself with superior company I would not be so tempted to fall into some highly improper scrape or another. The problem is, I'm so damn bored. Oh, I beg your pardon, Miss Mathley."

"Piffle! Feel quite free to swear in front of me, particularly with such just cause. Harry does it all the time."

"Your . . . brother?"

"That's right."

"*Not* one of your six suitors."

"Seven," Melinda said morosely.

"What? Has Omersby come up to scratch so soon?"

Melinda shuddered slightly. "This morning."

"And you refused him."

"Well of course!" said Melinda indignantly. "I did not care for him."

"You seek a love match, then?"

"I seek a match of equals, sir. It will require affection, certainly, but I do not hope for the all-consuming love that is found in the more romantic novels being published today."

"Very sensible of you," Lord Carlton said quietly.

"Well, I am very sensible," said Melinda. "Why else do you think I refused Omersby?"

Lord Carlton's smile quickly faded. "Was the uproar at home so very difficult?"

Melinda blushed. "You *are* perceptive. Yes, it's been rather thick. Mama had her usual hysterics, of course, but I expected that. It was Father who caught me unawares."

"How so?"

"He has said that I must marry the very next man who offers for me."

"Good God! Can he be such a tyrant?"

Melinda managed another shrug. "Oh, it was just a threat in the heat of his fury. He will recant as soon as his anger dies down, but by then some dreadful man may have already offered for me and there I will be! Trapped! The announcement in the papers, the invitations sent out."

"Yes, I see the difficulty," said Lord Carlton. "We both seem bedeviled by obnoxious relatives."

"Father is not obnoxious, merely explosive, and my path is not so difficult as yours. I must simply hide whenever I

41

see a fortune hunter coming my way. But you . . . I wish there was something I could do to help."

Lord Carlton stared down at her in some surprise, for the wish had been quite genuine. They danced in silence for a moment. Then a tremor shook Melinda, and she stared up at Lord Carlton, her brown eyes wide, her face pale. He regarded her with some concern.

"Are you all right, Miss Mathley?"

"I believe so. My lord, I have just had the most shockingly brilliant idea I've ever had in my life."

"You alarm me, Miss Mathley."

"I alarm myself, Lord Carlton. There *is* a way that I can help you and you, perhaps, can do me a bit of good. If you are willing."

"How so?"

"By announcing to the world that you are engaged to me."

"What?" ejaculated Lord Carlton, standing stock-still in the middle of the Jersey ballroom.

"Please, sir, do not draw any more attention to us than we have already done!" Melinda said, pushing him back into the dance. "Hear me out. By entering into a false engagement with me, you will become associated with one of the first families in England. The Mathleys can open doors to you that no one else could open! Let the Vandeveres sneer if they dare. *We* can get you fairly started on your course."

"Yes. B-B-But an *engagement*?!"

"Well, you see, that's to help me," said Melinda. "My portion is *quite* large, you know, and I've already made plans for how I want to spend it in my spinsterhood. Therefore I have to keep my amazing dowry, therefore I must accept the next man who offers for me, but of course I don't want to do that, so the best thing to do is to get Father to recant his threat, and the only way to do that is to present him with something even more horrible than my spurning another suitor. And the only thing that I can think of that

42

is more horrible than spurning an eighth suitor would be for me to announce that I'm engaged to you."

Lord Carlton goggled at this.

"Father would be so outraged," Melinda blithely rushed on, "that he would quickly recant his odious threat and I should be able to emerge from under the knife unscathed. And you see, sir, during the course of our engagement, however brief it will be, you will have the acceptance of the ton! You will be invited everywhere because you are associated with the Mathleys. You would no longer be an outcast."

Lord Carlton's expression was severe. "Miss Mathley, I begin to think you as mad as you are painted. You cannot become engaged to *me*! I am a pariah in my own class. I have seduced wives, stolen away mistresses from the most important men in the land. I have wounded two men in duels. I have even espoused Jacobin sympathies! I would do you irreparable harm by agreeing to such a scheme."

"Oh, what rodomontade!" Melinda retorted, much to the earl's surprise. "You've a scandalous past, I agree, but that does not mean you have a scandalous present or will have a scandalous future. Your good conduct and association with my family will induce mass amnesia in the ton. Within a se'ennight, no one will remember your elopement with Almira Thurgood, or your duels, or any of your other . . . . indiscretions, you mark my words."

Lord Carlton was silent a moment. "To be the supposed son-in-law to George Mathley!" he said softly.

"I know it's a grim thought, but remember it is only a fantasy. You and I would know that it is not a real engagement."

"Yes, yes, yes. Let me think a moment, Miss Mathley." Suddenly Lord Carlton cocked his head. "You are a very shocking young woman."

"No, sir, I just have a very shocking mind."

43

Lord Carlton laughed. "Let me see if I understand you. We announce to the world that we are engaged."

"Yes. We would have to have the notice in the papers before we tell Father, that way he cannot deny us the engagement before we have even begun."

"Yes, I quite see that. The notice appears and before old George can even glance at the paper, you pull me into the house and say 'Surprise, Father, I'm engaged!' "

"Precisely!"

"Mr. Mathley will rant and rave, as which father would not? But you will be steadfast. . . ."

"Oh, very firm, sir."

"And he will set about trying to end the engagement."

"Oh, without a doubt, Lord Carlton."

"And in trying to end the engagement, he will be brought to take back his threat to you."

"Precisely!"

"In the meantime, I would be associating with one of the first families in England."

"Yes, sir."

"Do you think we could keep it up for a month?" Lord Carlton inquired.

"Oh, I should think Father would break down well before then, never fear."

"Yes, well even if it's just for a fortnight, that should do the trick," Lord Carlton murmured.

"Oh, undoubtedly!" said Melinda, gazing earnestly up at him. "And you see, sir, it would be *I* who would officially cry off, using Father's choler as an excuse. So the ton could not blame you for our failed engagement, and they could not really blame me either, for who, after all, would want their daughter to marry you?"

"Yes, quite," said Lord Carlton with a grin. "Miss Mathley, I am so glad you rescued me tonight."

"Oh, so am I, Lord Carlton. Are we agreed then?"

Lord Carlton assumed a most punctilious air. "My dear

44

Miss Mathley, will you do me the very great honor to accept my hand in a fictitious engagement?"

"Oh, sir, I should be honored," Melinda murmured as the dance ended and she dropped into a deep curtsy.

He smiled down at her. "Shall I execute the *coup de grâce* to our partnership and kiss your fair hand?"

"Yes, thank you, that would be lovely."

He raised her slim, gloved fingers to his lips and gently brushed them with his warm mouth. Heat shot from her fingertips and enflamed the whole of her body.

"My goodness," she said, rising on wobbly legs from her curtsy.

"I beg your pardon?"

Melinda struggled to pull herself together. "You do that very well," she said brightly.

"Why, thank you," Lord Carlton said with a grin. "I have had years of practice."

Melinda laughed. "I think this is going to be the most enjoyable adventure I've ever had. But come, we should attend to the particulars now before someone tries to separate us."

"Very wise. If you will allow me, Miss Mathley, I believe the outer balustrade will provide the fresh air you require."

"How very kind of you, Lord Carlton," said Melinda, placing her hand upon his arm.

Once on the balcony they moved away from the other couples seeking similar refreshment. Lord Carlton drew a small pad of paper and a pencil from his pocket.

"I will send the notice of our engagement to every paper in town tomorrow morning. I will need some particulars, Miss Mathley."

Melinda readily supplied her full name, her father's name and ancestry, her mother's name and ancestry, and the amount of her dowry.

Lord Carlton gaped at her. Melinda grinned at him.

"Now you know why a plain sparrow like me has received seven offers of marriage. Eight, if I may include yours."

"You are not a plain sparrow, Miss Mathley."

"Oh, don't be gallant or I shall call off our engagement here and now!"

"If you will agree not to deride yourself," Lord Carlton retorted, "I will foreswear gallantry. Sincerity, however, you will have to withstand."

He then added the particulars of his age, ancestry, and estates to the notice and read it aloud. He looked up from the paper to find Melinda chewing on her full lower lip.

"Reconsidering, Miss Mathley?"

"No, just worrying about poor Mama. I fear this will distress her very much. But still, at least it will take her mind off of Mr. Wentworth."

"One of her paramours?"

"Oh, you *are* a scoundrel," Melinda retorted. "No, sir, Mr. Wentworth, far from being my mother's lover, is a former suitor to my sister Louisa and has instead become engaged to my cousin Beatrice."

"God save me from the machinations of the marriage mart," Lord Carlton said fervently. "What think you of our announcement?"

"Oh, it reads very well. But I confess, I never thought to see my name entered willingly into such a notice."

"Nor did I, Miss Mathley. Nor did I. You know, it occurs to me that people will think it odd if we, as an engaged couple, are so formal with each other. For the sake of the charade, shall we advance to first names?"

"An excellent idea. I shall be Melinda and you shall be—"

"Peter. We will not meet again until Thursday when our announcement appears in the morning papers. What time should I present myself at your house in Grosvenor Square?"

"I shall contrive to have Father in the house by eleven in the morning."

"Very well," said Lord Carlton, pocketing both the notice and the pencil. "By eleven-fifteen we will have fully embarked upon this adventure."

"Yes, Peter. Thank you, Peter!"

"No, no, Melinda, thank *you*."

*

Chapter 4

THE CLOCK ON the morning parlor mantel had scarcely begun tolling the hour when Melinda heard the front doorbell. She rose from her chair because she could not remain seated any longer. Her nerves, it must be confessed, were not entirely steady. Shooting Daniel Tarn's foot could not compare to the temerity she would need to succeed in this newest venture. Hurriedly she smoothed her simple sea green cambric gown just as the parlor door opened.

"Lord Carlton, miss, as you requested," said the footman Hawkins with the greatest disapproval.

Lord Carlton, dressed all in white save for the ribbon of blue woven through his morning coat, followed him into the room.

"You look splendid, sir!" Melinda exclaimed as she went forward to greet him. "The neckcloth is perfection."

"A half hour of ferocious labor is thus amply rewarded," Lord Carlton said as he raised her hand to his lips. "There is rioting in the streets, Miss Mathley. Our announcement has appeared in this morning's papers. Do you still hold to your course?"

"Why certainly," said Melinda in some surprise. "I never go back on my word. Father is in his study and at the moment unencumbered."

"Have you thought how to tell him?"

"I have thought of little else," Melinda confessed with a rueful smile. "I think it best that I tell him I'm engaged to

48

you, and then bring you into the room as proof of so startling an announcement."

"No," said Lord Carlton. "I'll not let you beard that grumpy old bear alone. We shall tell him together."

"But—"

"No."

Melinda correctly divined from his stubbornly set chin that Lord Carlton would brook no argument in the matter, and she was oddly touched at his determination to play the knight errant.

"Very well," she said, "let us launch ourselves into the fray."

The earl offered her his arm and together they marched to Mr. Mathley's study. Melinda knocked firmly upon the door. A bark that might have been "Come in!" was her answer. Lord Carlton opened the door and they stepped in.

As he had two mornings earlier when he had issued his matrimonial threat, Mr. Mathley sat behind his desk, this time moodily regarding the documents spread before him.

"Yes? What is it?" he demanded without looking up.

"I've the most marvelous news, Father," Melinda said.

Mr. Mathley looked up now, his face becoming vermilion as he recognized Lord Carlton.

"What are you doing here, sir?" he demanded.

"Attending to the niceties, Mr. Mathley," Lord Carlton replied.

"Lord Carlton has been so obliging as to ask me to marry him, Father, and I have agreed," said Melinda. "We are engaged!"

Mr. Mathley wholly surprised his eldest daughter by not exploding at this announcement. Rather, he turned as white as Lord Carlton's shirt cuffs and sat back in his chair.

"What?" he gasped.

"I am going to marry Lord Carlton, Father. We were thinking of having the wedding sometime around Michaelmas."

49

"I'll see you in hell first!" roared Mr. Mathley, surging to his feet.

Melinda might have jumped back had not Lord Carlton a firm grip on her arm.

"But I thought you'd be pleased, Father," she said.

"*Pleased?*" sputtered Mr. Mathley. "To stain the honor of my family by aligning myself with this ... this *blackguard?*"

"But Father, you told me I must marry the next man who asked me, and Lord Carlton is that man! He's an earl, after all, and he's got a family tree as long as your arm—"

"Not my leg?" Lord Carlton inquired.

"No, no, it's not *that* long. Peter is perfectly suitable in every respect, Father. He asked me to marry him, and I have done my duty and agreed, just as you told me to."

Mr. Mathley launched himself into an infuriated diatribe on his daughter's character, morals, and understanding and would have gone on at some length had not Lord Carlton interrupted him.

"Though you are her father, sir, I will not stand here and allow you to insult my future wife," he said, his chin jutting in a most determined manner.

"She will never be your wife, sir!" rasped Mr. Mathley. "I'd sooner throw her in the Thames than give her to you."

"But Father, I don't understand," said Melinda, her brow crinkled in confusion. "You have been urging me to marry these last three years. Not two days ago you *ordered* me to marry the next man who offered for me. Now, when I have done all that you asked of me, you act as if I have committed some crime."

"You cannot marry this hellhound, Melinda. I won't have it!" barked her father.

"Father, I won't have you abuse Lord Carlton in such a manner," Melinda said firmly. "He may have committed some errors in his youth, but he is a good man, honest, kind, and true, and I won't have you say a word against him!"

Lord Carlton stared down at her in wonder as George Mathley sank weakly back into his chair.

"This is one of your hoaxes, isn't it, Melinda?" he said, almost pleading with her. "Another one of your reprehensible scrapes?"

"Nothing of the sort, sir," said Lord Carlton, manfully rising to the occasion. "I am exceedingly fond of your daughter and, believing her to sincerely return my regard despite our brief acquaintance, I made so bold as to offer her my heart and my hand which she very kindly accepted."

"Humbug!" said Mr. Mathley. "You're a fortune hunter like all the rest."

"While I cannot marry without some consideration of fortune, I have acted in this matter solely from the dictates of my heart," Lord Carlton proclaimed with a warmth in his blue eyes as he gazed down at Melinda that made her heart tremble within her breast. She tried to tell her heart that this was all playacting, but her heart responded by observing that Lord Carlton was playing this role particularly well and it would not be kept from reacting accordingly.

"You shall not marry her, sir, and that's final!" said Mr. Mathley.

"But Father, I must!" Melinda exclaimed. "The announcement is already in the papers."

"What?" gasped Mr. Mathley, turning rather green.

"Having won this good lady's consent," said Lord Carlton, "I could not wait to publish my success to the world. See for yourself."

He drew a newspaper from his coat pocket and handed it to his flabbergasted future father-in-law. Mr. Mathley read the circled item thrice, and then gazed up at his daughter, horror-stricken.

"This is terrible!"

"Wasn't it worded properly?" Melinda said anxiously, and it was all Lord Carlton could do to keep from laughing out loud. "Neither Peter nor I had ever written such a notice before, and we did so want to get it right."

Without a word Mr. Mathley rose and walked on stiff legs to a nearby table. There he poured a large amount of brandy from a crystal decanter into a glass and drank it down in one swallow.

"I can understand your feelings, sir," said Lord Carlton, not unkindly. "I have an appalling reputation, it's true. But my family is quite as old as your own; I have an honorable title and an unencumbered estate. My affection for your daughter is quite sincere, and I shall do everything in my power to make her happy."

Mr. Mathley regarded them bleakly. "You will make no wedding plans now."

"But Father—" Melinda began.

"You have entered into this engagement without consulting me and now, by God, Melinda, you will accede to my wishes! You scarcely know the fellow, and I insist that you agree to a long engagement before you marry him."

"How long?" Lord Carlton demanded.

"A year."

"Three months," the earl countered.

"Nine."

"Five."

"Eight."

"Six."

"Agreed," said Mr. Mathley. "This conversation is at an end. Good day to you, sir."

Blue eyes widening at such a dismissal, Lord Carlton nonetheless bowed gracefully and escorted Melinda from the room.

"Well!" said Melinda once they were safely behind the closed door of the morning parlor. "I think that went rather well, don't you?"

Lord Carlton stared at her. "You are *satisfied* with that interview?"

"Well, of course!"

"But he was very nearly volcanic in his reception of the news!"

"Yes, but I never expected anything less."

"You are *used* to such a show?"

"Why certainly! I've seen it nearly every day of my life."

"Miss Mathley," said Lord Carlton feelingly, "I think it a very good idea that you marry quickly—not me, of course—but some good fellow who will take you away from that monster!"

"But Father is not a monster, Peter," Melinda countered. "He has a sincere affection for me. It is just that it is tied to a rather explosive temper. I assure you that I don't pay his diatribes the least regard. They are just so much hot air."

The house was then rent by a piercing scream.

"Good God, what was that?" Lord Carlton gasped.

"Oh, dear," said Melinda, nibbling on her lower lip, "I told Addie to keep the morning papers away from Mama today. I'm afraid you'll have to go, Peter. I shall be trapped at my mother's side for some time."

The earl regarded her queerly. "I begin to think I *ought* to marry you, if only to get you away from this accursed house."

Melinda laughed and looped his arm through hers as she led him to the front door.

"I knew that rakish exterior hid a chivalrous nature. Please don't worry on my account, Peter, for I certainly don't. Will I see you at the Prince's garden party tomorrow?"

"Yes. Lord Fenwych was so unkind as to procure me an invitation."

Melinda laughed. "You will like it, I think. The gardens are quite beautiful this time of year, the food will be lavish, and everyone will be talking about *us*, so it should be highly diverting."

"With you there, Miss Mathley, it could not be otherwise. Adieu," said Lord Carlton, kissing her fingertips.

Melinda gazed after him as he walked down the front steps, thinking that adventure was far more enjoyable when in my Lord Carlton's company.

Despite her assurances to the earl, Melinda found the day rather hideous. It took two hours of patient work to return her mother to a whimpering calm. Then she had to soothe her sister Louisa who was exceedingly shocked by the engagement; withstand the teasing and highly impertinent questions of the twins; forestall Harry's rather risqué comments on her future as Lady Carlton; and suffer the alternately injured and infuriated glances her father directed at her whenever they were in the same room.

It grieved Melinda to wound her parents so. Had it not been a matter of self-preservation, she would have recanted then and there. Fortunately, Freddy Lamont had called on her to try to dissuade her from so ruinous a match and to persuade her instead to entrust her future to *him*, and that was all Melinda needed to make her resolute even in the face of so glaring an injury to her family.

But by midafternoon she was sorely in need of fresh air and sunshine to restore her good humor. Slipping out of the house without even a maid to attend her, she quickly walked the few blocks to Hyde Park and, to avoid the titillated stares of the newspaper-reading ton on all sides, tried to lose herself on the more secluded park paths.

The fresh air and the beauty of the park did much to revive her spirits, particularly when she remembered that she would be able to enjoy Lord Carlton's company until her father recanted his matrimonial threat. How lovely to be in London and not be bored!

She had just turned onto a small gravel walk when she saw some yards down the path a very pretty girl of no more than seventeen, her face bloodless as a multitude of tears streamed down. Embarrassed at intruding on such a private

54

scene, Melinda would have turned onto another walk had she not observed that the girl clutched a tiny babe in her arms as she pleaded with the taciturn man standing before her. The man—Melinda would not term him gentleman— was Jasper Wilmingham, a wealthy and ruthless blackguard in his mid-thirties who dipped heavily at the gaming tables and amongst the muslin set.

"But what shall I do?" wailed the girl.

"How the devil should I know or care?" Mr. Wilmingham retorted.

"But you said you loved me! You said you'd marry me!"

"Marry a little tart like you? Don't make me laugh," said Mr. Wilmingham.

The girl gasped and drew back as if she had been slapped. "How could you? How *could* you when you know it's not true. You're the only one. This is your son!"

"Bah! Strumpets like you are always claiming that men of wealth and position are the *only one*. As far as I know, that babe is the by-blow of some stable boy."

The girl began sobbing pitiably. "But my father has cast me out. I have nowhere to go. You *must* help me."

"No, I must do everything that I can to put as much distance between myself and you as possible."

"Oh, you are a wicked, wicked man," sobbed the girl. "I hate you! I hate the very sight of you!"

"Excellent. I fully return the compliment," said Mr. Wilmingham. He then turned and strode off.

The girl sank to her knees on the path, sobbing all the more, the baby pressed so close to her breast that Melinda feared it might be in some danger of smothering.

Never one to hold back when she saw anyone in trouble, Melinda hurried forward, knelt beside the young woman, and put her arms around her. "There, there, you must not cry so. It will upset the baby," she said gently. "Come, see if you can stand."

Struggling with her tears, the girl, with Melinda's help,

55

slowly rose. Led by her, she reached a bench and, with Melinda pressing her insistently, sat down beside her.

"You should not pin your hopes to the impossible, my dear," said Melinda. "You shall never receive any satisfaction from Mr. Wilmingham for he is a renowned blackguard."

"Oh, but what shall I do? What shall I do?" wailed the girl.

"Now, now, the first thing you must do is get yourself in order, for you cannot think when your head is full of salt water. I will sit here by you, and together we shall contrive some brilliant scheme."

Slowly the girl pulled herself together, using Melinda's handkerchief to good effect.

"There! That is much better," Melinda pronounced, refusing the return of the drenched handkerchief. "I am Melinda Mathley and I heard everything and would like to help you if I can, if you will allow me. But I should like to know who you are."

"Lydia," the girl whispered, blushing furiously. "Lydia Brooke."

"How do you do, Lydia Brooke? No, that's a stupid question for anyone can see that you are not doing at all well. Your son is quite young."

"Two weeks," the girl whispered.

"And your family has turned you out?"

"Yes."

"I gather Mr. Wilmingham has seduced and abandoned you?"

"He said he loved me." The girl turned pleading gray eyes up to Melinda. "I have known him since I was a child. He has a country seat near my family's estate. I have loved him for years. He said he would marry me."

"They always do, my dear," Melinda replied, carefully hiding from her face the fury she felt at a man who could abuse a lifelong friendship in such a manner. "Well, we must find some way of taking care of both you and your

56

son. There is no one in your family you can appeal to? No aunt? No cousin?"

The girl shook her head, her brown ringlets drooping sadly. "My father is ... the squire in Lower Hartnum. He fears any damage to his reputation above all else. No one in the family dares go against him. He controls the purse strings, you see, and he has a fierce temper. My brother ..."

"Yes?"

"My brother," Lydia uttered with a choked sigh, "would not help me to a living, but he would certainly like to call out Mr. Wilmingham, and I fear he may do so if he ever learns that ... Mr. Wilmingham is a noted duelist, you know."

"Yes, quite. He has killed five, that I know of. It is best that your brother avoid him at all costs."

"But Francis is one-and-twenty and will listen to nothing I say!"

"Yes, brothers are like that," said Melinda feelingly. "Here, look to your babe and let me think on the matter for a moment."

Melinda stared straight ahead of her at the green hedge on the other side of the gravel path. How paltry seemed her own troubles when compared to Lydia Brooke's difficulties! There must be a way to help her, but Melinda had no experience in such delicate matters. If only ...

"Of course!" she murmured. She grabbed Lydia's hand and pulled her to her feet. "My dear Miss Brooke, I know of just the person to unravel this Gordian knot. Come with me!"

Half dragging the dumbfounded girl, Melinda hurried out of Hyde Park and toward Curzon Street. With equal suddenness, she stopped, bumping Lydia into her. She could not, though accompanied by the daughter of Lower Hartnum's squire, go to Peter's lodgings. Even Melinda perceived the scandal in that. No, she would have to be more circumspect.

It took a minute or two before she could hail a hansom cab. Then, as they drove to Curzon Street, she hurriedly drew paper and pencil from her reticule and scribbled a few lines. When the cab stopped she had the driver deliver the note to Lord Carlton's door, and then had him drive them to Bond Street.

"We are going shopping," Melinda announced to the sorely confused Miss Brooke.

"But—but—" said Lydia.

"You need some clothes, don't you?"

"Yes, but . . . but why are you doing this for me, Miss Mathley? We are strangers."

"No one with a heart could look upon your difficulties and not do everything in her power to remedy them," Melinda pronounced.

"Yes, but what of your friend? Why would she want to help me?"

"I believe that *he* has quite a large heart and will be most eager to help."

"He?" Lydia cried, drawing back.

"Have no fear, Miss Brooke," Melinda said soothingly. "Lord Carlton is a man of the world. He would no more condemn you for Mr. Wilmingham's perfidy than I would. He is hardly a saint, but he has a good understanding, I think, of human frailty. Now do stop worrying for I know just the morning dress you should have."

Melinda spent a happy three hours buying every conceivable article of clothing for both Lydia and her son, purchasing them tea, and wondering if they really should not go back to get that lovely green hat with the pheasant feather wending its way around the crown. Then she spied Lord Carlton strolling on the opposite side of the street toward the milliner's shop where she had asked him to meet her.

"Oh, bother, we're late! Come along, Lydia," Melinda cried as she surged to her feet. "And quickly!"

Once again grasping Lydia's hand, she nearly ran from the restaurant. She had to wait for a barouche, two gigs, and a phaeton to pass before she could cross the street. The earl was nearly at the door of Madame Duarot, Milliner.

"Peter!" Melinda cried.

He turned, spied her, and evinced open surprise at being hailed thus.

"Peter, just a moment, please!" Melinda called again, and ignoring the curious stares of passersby, she tugged Lydia after her and hurried up to the earl. "I'm *so* glad I spotted you," she cried a trifle breathlessly. "We dallied over our tea. I'm so sorry."

"Your note," said Lord Carlton, eyeing Lydia and her baby warily, "mentioned a matter of some importance. Has your father recanted already?"

"Oh, no, he's got his back up now. We've got at least a se'ennight to be engaged. No, I needed to ask you about— Oh, but where are my manners? Lord Carlton, this is Lydia Brooke and her son Tristan."

Lord Carlton scarcely had time to bow before Melinda rushed on.

"Poor Lydia has been most scandalously used by Jasper Wilmingham, and so far from helping her in her hour of need, he has foresworn her entirely! So I am trying to help her. But, of course, I have no experience in these matters and did not quite know what to do when suddenly it came to me in a stroke of genius that *you* must have *vast* experience in dealing with castoffs and babies!"

Lord Carlton regarded her, dumbfounded. "I beg your pardon, Miss Mathley, but I have *no* such experience!"

"But you must!" said Melinda. "You are an acknowledged rake and scoundrel."

"I am a cautious rake and scoundrel," Lord Carlton replied. "I lack the experience, Miss Mathley, that you require. Therefore, I don't think I—"

"Well, nevertheless, you have vast experience in all other areas of life, and you must know other gentlemen who do have natural children, and therefore, the question to you, my lord, is what can be done to help poor Lydia and Tristan?"

Observing that this extraordinary tête-à-tête had not gone unnoticed by the other members of the ton promenading Bond Street, and recalling all too vividly his uncle Gilford's scrutiny, Lord Carlton searched desperately for a means of escape and found it in the appearance of Gerald, twelfth Viscount of Fenwych.

"Jerry!" called Lord Carlton with as much earnestness as Melinda had hailed him.

The viscount, recognizing his voice, obligingly pulled his team of bays to a stop, looked across the street, and spied his friend in tandem with two young women and a baby. He thought immediately of flight, but Lord Carlton was too quick. He stood at the head of his team.

"Jerry, I need a favor."

"N-N-No, dash it, Peter!" said the viscount. "Whatever it is, no!"

"Jerry," said Lord Carlton placatingly, "how can you treat one of your oldest and truest friends in this shabby manner?"

"S-S-Self-preservation, old chum. Self-preservation."

Carlton laughed and ordered his friend down from the phaeton. Grumbling and stammering and prophesying doom and gloom, the viscount descended to the street. Carlton turned to Melinda.

"Of course you already know Miss Mathley, Jerry, but I also have the honor to present you to Miss Brooke and Master Tristan. Miss Mathley, and company, this is Lord Fenwych."

The viscount executed a reluctant bow to Lydia's shy smile and schoolgirl curtsy and was about to offer his felicitations to Miss Mathley on her engagement, but he never got the chance.

"Do you drive, Melinda?" Lord Carlton inquired.

"Well, of course. But—"

"Excellent. You will be so good as to take the reins. Miss Brooke, if you will allow me?"

" 'ere now!" protested the viscount's groom from the rear of the carriage, but in a moment both young women and Master Tristan were established upon the phaeton.

"We shall rendezvous at the rose alcove near the Serpentine in Hyde Park in a quarter of an hour, Melinda," said Lord Carlton, his hand resting upon the phaeton as he looked up at her.

"You will not fail to appear?" she inquired anxiously.

"No, my sense of self-preservation is not as keen as the viscount's and is, I fear, overruled by an overweening curiosity. I must and shall hear the whole of *this* mad tale."

Melinda beamed at him, and then with a cheerful flick of the whip, set the team trotting down Bond Street, the viscount goggling after her, Lord Carlton watching approvingly. She handled the whip very neatly.

"D-D-Dash it, Peter!" the viscount exploded. "What the deuce do you mean by hijacking my carriage?"

"Propriety, my dear Jerry. Propriety in everything for the next month."

"Yes, but what has the Gilford fortune to d-d-do with Miss Mathley and a schoolgirl and some . . . Peter, you *haven't*?!"

"No," said Lord Carlton grimly, taking Lord Fenwych by the arm and moving him at a swift walk toward Hyde Park, "I haven't."

"Thank God. B-B-But why are you involving yourself with some schoolgirl and an infant, and why have you got yourself engaged not three days after t-t-telling me you wouldn't be caught dead at the altar?"

"Can you think of a better way to show myself to advantage to Uncle Gilford than by aligning myself with the noble name of Mathley?"

The viscount considered a moment, a rare frown crinkling his brow. "Seems a shabby t-t-trick to play on Miss

Mathley," he opined. "I never would have thought it of you, Peter."

"But it was Miss Mathley's idea! And I assure you, Jerry, that Mad Melinda is using me just as much as I am using her. It is an equitable arrangement on all sides. My supposed engagement to the daughter of so unassailable a family will keep me out of all scrapes and scandals for the month my uncle has decreed, and my reputation will quickly free her from the threat of a forced marriage."

Further explanation was required to reconcile the viscount to his friend's engagement and his own temporary loss of transportation. He insisted, therefore, on accompanying Lord Carlton to his rendezvous to regain his rightful property and to hear more of Mad Melinda and the abandoned petticoat.

The family lunatic she might be—indeed, all the signs pointed to her idiosyncratic position in the Mathley firmament—but Melinda had had the very good sense, Lord Carlton noted, to abandon the phaeton to the viscount's groom's care near the Marble Arch and to walk Miss Brooke and Master Tristan to their rendezvous. The gentlemen reached the small party at the allotted time to find Melinda cradling Master Tristan in her arms and cooing at his serious blue eyes. In contrast, Lord Carlton, arms akimbo, greeted her with a very severe look.

"Very well, Melinda, what is all the to-do?"

"But I told you!" Melinda replied, handing Tristan back to his mother. "Jasper Wilmingham abused a lifelong acquaintance with this estimable young woman by seducing and abandoning her to the world's censure. Miss Brooke's odious family has quite cast her off, so I mean to find some comfortable living for Lydia and her son.

"I see. You are a friend of long acquaintance?"

"Oh, no, sir!" Lydia burst out. "I have just met Miss Mathley and never have I known such goodness and kindness—"

"Just met?" Lord Carlton gasped. "Melinda, have you

62

taken leave of your senses? Do you have any idea the trouble you can bring down upon yourself by acting in this matter?"

"Fustian! Any man or woman of compassion would have rushed to Miss Brooke's aid had they witnessed how brutally Mr. Wilmingham abused her this afternoon," Melinda said stoutly. "I knew a man of your experience would feel just as I do in this matter. That is why I asked you to meet me. A situation must be found for Miss Brooke and her son."

"And some means of protecting your reputation," Lord Carlton added harshly.

"Oh, nonsense! How can I come to harm helping a poor girl in such dire straits? And how could anyone think of themselves when they look upon this innocent baby? You will help me, won't you?"

It occurred to the earl that Melinda had very expressive, and compelling, brown eyes. "Very well," he said reluctantly. "But what exactly do you expect me to do in the matter?"

"Why, come up with the situation of course!"

"I?"

"Well, at least *suggest* one!"

"I see. I fear you place a far greater value on my experience than I do, Miss Mathley, for nothing comes to mind."

"Oh, but surely with your experience of the muslin set—"

"I beg your pardon!"

"*You* know what I mean," said Melinda.

Lord Carlton very much feared that he did.

"You must have encountered similar situations before," Melinda continued. "What was the result?"

"Ah," said Lord Carlton. "Well, speaking from observation alone . . . ahem . . . I have observed little cottages in the countryside bought and paid for by the guilty fathers."

"Yes, but Lydia is a trifle young, don't you think, to have

63

her own establishment? Lydia, you would rather live with someone than alone, wouldn't you?"

"I-I-I have never lived alone," said Lydia.

"Precisely," said Melinda. "What else?" she said, looking to Lord Carlton hopefully.

He struggled against a determined grin.

"A-A-As it happens," broke in Lord Fenwych, most opportunely, "I have a suggestion."

"You?" said Lord Carlton.

The viscount flushed. "Yes, dash it! And don't you go m-m-making insinuations!"

"I never said a word," murmured Lord Carlton.

"You don't have to. You just have to l-l-look it."

"Your idea, Viscount?" Melinda tactfully inquired.

But, alas, the viscount was forestalled from stammering his reply for at that moment a young man, dressed in exceedingly dirty riding clothes, stormed up to them.

"There you are, Lydia!" he said in tones of mingled fury and disgust. "I have been looking for you through this damned swamp all afternoon."

"Francis!" faltered Lydia.

"Have you no shame?" stormed Francis. "Meeting in a public place with your paramours!"

"My *what*?" gasped Lydia.

"And who are you to make so erroneous an observation?" Melinda inquired.

"Her brother!" stormed Francis.

"Ah," said Melinda. "And, of course, uncle to young Tristan."

This served only to infuriate Francis Brooke. He spun around and glared at Lord Carlton.

"A fine piece of work you've made of things, sir! Ruining my sister and muddying our family name!" Francis thereupon planted the wholly surprised earl a rather ineffective facer. It neither stunned Lord Carlton nor knocked him to the ground, but it did successfully cut his lip.

"Here now!" said Lord Fenwych. "What the d-d-devil do you mean by attacking Carlton?"

Francis turned upon the outraged viscount. "Oh, ho! One lover is not enough for you, Lydia? You must take two and meet with both at the same time?"

He moved to wreak physical violence upon Gerald, twelfth Viscount of Fenwych, but in this he was forestalled by Lord Carlton who, taller and stronger than young Francis, grasped him from behind and swung him around to face his sister.

"If you would but let anyone get a word in edgewise, Mr. Brooke," he said scathingly, "you would hear that the viscount and I are not your sister's lovers. We are acquaintances of a half hour's standing."

"Do you expect me to believe that flimsy tale?" Francis sneered.

Murder glinted in Lord Carlton's blue eyes—he was not accustomed to being called a liar—and Lydia began to fear that she would soon be witness to further bloodshed.

"Men are a most amazing species," said Melinda conversationally. "They think nothing of exiling a sister who has been seduced and abandoned by another man. It is but the work of a moment to throw her out into the street and worry not at all how she shall live." She drew a handkerchief from her reticule and dabbed the blood from Lord Carlton's lip, talking all the while. "But when it comes to defending the family honor, they are more than willing to put themselves out and come to blows with any man who comes their way. Yes, a most fascinating study. Alas, we haven't time for it now," she said, returning the handkerchief to her reticule. "You were saying, Viscount, that you had an idea for Miss Brooke?"

Again the startled viscount began to make his reply, and again he was forestalled by Francis Brooke.

"Unhand me, sir!" he cried, struggling in Lord Carlton's grasp. "I'll call you out for this outrage!"

"You'll do no such thing, child," Lord Carlton replied,

the murderous glint quite gone now, "for I would refuse to meet you, however many aspersions you cast upon my honor. I don't fight children."

"I have attained my majority, sir, and I shall have satisfaction!"

"In that case I suggest you call on one Jasper Wilmingham, who is the true villain in the piece," Lord Carlton advised, unaware of poor Lydia's groan at this revelation. "He will very obligingly meet you on any field of honor you care to name and shoot you through your heart on whatever day and time is most convenient for you."

This stopped Mr. Brooke for a moment. He, like many a young buck, had heard much of Jasper Wilmingham's dueling skills.

"Wilmingham?" he gasped. "But if he . . . And you didn't . . . What are you doing with my sister?" he demanded, once again outraged.

"We are trying to fill the office that you and your family have forsaken," Melinda replied sweetly. "In short, we are trying to help Lydia in a time of great travail. Now, if you will be so obliging as to shut up, the viscount has an idea. Viscount, if you please."

Lord Fenwych coughed and began. "Well, I j-j-just happened to think," he said, "that my Aunt Galloway is in need of a companion, one who can amuse her, read to her, d-d-darn for her, that sort of thing."

"But would she not object to a young woman with Miss Brooke's history?" Lord Carlton inquired.

"Oh, no! She takes in strays all the t-t-time," said the viscount. "She rants and rails at the men of this world and thinks women the victims of every g-g-glance and aspersion. Oh, she would take to Miss Brooke like a fox hound to a fox."

"An unhappy allusion, perhaps," Melinda opined, "and yet to the point. Where does this Aunt Galloway reside?"

"S-S-Somersetshire."

"Excellent," said Melinda. "A pleasing and healthful

clime. Just the place to raise a young son. There should not be any difficulty dispatching Miss Brooke to Aunt Galloway, if Miss Brooke agrees to the arrangement."

Lydia, it must be confessed, was not entirely in coherent thought. Her world had been turned upside down in such very short order—Melinda coming to her rescue, the shopping, the accosting of Lord Carlton, the roping in of Lord Fenwych, the sudden appearance of her brother, the shocking violence, Lord Fenwych's very kind scheme to change her circumstances for the better—and it was all a bit too much after the many months of grief and abuse and privation she had endured.

Melinda, seeing her distress, slipped an arm about her waist. "Never mind, my dear, you needn't reply just now. I think perhaps a few more facts are in order."

In the next ten minutes she grilled the viscount mercilessly as to Aunt Galloway's age, character, residence, habits, and her opinion of children. All of these the viscount struggled to answer, though the questions came at him in a rather fast and furious fashion. Lord Carlton looked on with growing admiration for this surprisingly practical streak in Melinda's character as his hand rested upon the nape of Mr. Brooke's neck, a precaution to forestall him from executing any further outrage upon their persons. The earl was also practical.

At last Lydia confessed that she thought she could withstand the rigors of Somersetshire and the irascibility of Aunt Galloway.

"Capital," said Lord Carlton. "There is, I believe, a stagecoach leaving Charing Cross for Somersetshire in just a few hours' time. It should serve you admirably, Miss Brooke."

"No! On the contrary," Melinda broke in, "Miss Brooke has had an exhausting day. Besides, there are numerous packages that need to be collected and packed for her. She must rest tonight and have a hearty breakfast on the morrow. Nor can she simply lope off to Somersetshire and

67

thrust herself upon Aunt Galloway. She requires an escort and an introduction, both of which Lord Fenwych is more than qualified to provide."

"B-B-Beg pardon?" said the Viscount.

"I suggest we hire a post chaise in the morning," Melinda blithely continued, "along with a suitable duenna for Miss Brooke. You should reach Aunt Galloway's in only two days' time."

"And who is to provide such traveling accommodations?" Lord Carlton inquired.

"You needn't look so sardonic, sir," Melinda retorted. "I am fully aware of the wretched state of your finances. I had quite intended to use my own pin money for the occasion."

"Have you got that much pin money?" Lord Carlton demanded.

"Ye gods yes! I am far more plump in the pocket than half the tulips of fashion parading down Bond Street. Have you forgotten my dowry?"

"Any gentleman entering into an engagement with you, Melinda, would be a cad if he did *not* forget your dowry."

"How very charming of you to say so, Peter," said Melinda, twinkling up at him. "No wonder you have been so successful with the ladies of good and ill repute. "But," she continued as Lord Fenwych gaped at her, "I shall do very well with the financial arrangements for Miss Brooke's transport. As I think on it, my maid will make an excellent duenna for Lydia on the morrow. Maria has some family near Somerset, I believe. The excuse for her absence will be the work of a moment."

"No doubt," said Lord Carlton gravely. "May I suggest installing Miss Brooke in a lodging house I know in Charles Street for the night? It is reputable, clean, with a healthy and plentiful menu."

"Perfection," Melinda pronounced. "I knew you would come up with some solution to our problems."

The viscount would have taken exception to this pronouncement had he been able to get his stammer in order, but by then Melinda had persuaded Lord Carlton to release Mr. Brooke, warned Mr. Brooke not to make a further cake of himself, advised him to avoid Mr. Wilmingham and certain death if at all possible, and exhorted him to, at some future date, think upon his lack of charity and Christian kindness to a pair of blood relations.

Then, looping her arm through Lord Carlton's arm, her other arm still about Lydia's waist, she began to walk them out of the park. Lord Carlton, however, stopped her.

"However little you care for any danger to your reputation," he said, "I, if you will recall, have embarked upon the path of reformation and mean to hold you to it as well. Casting no aspersions on Miss Brooke, it would not do for me to be seen walking arm and arm with my fiancée and a young woman with a babe in her arms. It smacks of scandal, Miss Mathley, and I have adjured scandal for the present."

"Yes, I quite see the difficulty," said Melinda, to his lordship's vast relief. "It would be best if you and Lord Fenwych go on alone. I shall accompany Miss Brooke to the lodging house in Charles Street. Mr. Brooke may act as our escort. Propriety will be preserved."

Lord Carlton gazed down at her in wonder. Melinda Mathley's views of propriety were decidedly different from those of the rest of the haut ton. Was there any other woman in society who would have seen the misery and terror of an abandoned woman and done everything in her power to come to Miss Brooke's rescue?

"I have never met so good or kind a woman," Lord Carlton murmured, raising her hand to his lips. A blush stole unaccountably into her cheeks. "Ah, ah, ah, no protests. I vowed to be sincere with you, remember? I shall abandon the gentleman's role for now and go before you to Mrs. Spencer's lodging house to arrange for Miss Brooke's installation for this evening. Jerry? Coming?"

Despite the gratitude shining up at him from Lydia's gray eyes, Lord Fenwych was more than willing to decamp. This left Mr. Brooke feeling both a trifle silly and more than a little put out that he had not been able to achieve any of the satisfaction that his bloodlust required.

"Mr. Brooke," Melinda commanded, "you shall escort us to Charles Street."

Mr. Brooke might be a year older than she, but he had none of the commanding presence that Melinda could summon at a moment's notice, as she had now.

He meekly took his sister's arm and walked with them out of Hyde Park. Melinda was wholly unaware that she was the object of conversation of every member of the ton she passed. She thought not of her false engagement to Lord Carlton, nor of the uproar in her home, nor the trouble she had taken upon herself on Lydia Brooke's behalf. Rather, she thought of the warm light in Lord Carlton's blue eyes when he had kissed her hand just now. The blush stayed in her cheeks all the way to Charles Street.

*

Chapter 5

IT WAS JUST after nine the next morning when Melinda returned to her house, having successfully seen off her maid Maria, Lydia Brooke, Master Tristan, and the sleepy but resigned Gerald, twelfth Viscount of Fenwych. None of her family was aware of her early morning appointment. None of them was aware of her return, which was just as Melinda preferred it. Simply because she had done something that she felt was right and they would consider harebrained at best or horrific at worst was no reason to get into an argument with her parents on such a lovely day.

Stepping up to her as she crossed the threshold, the footman Hawkins, speaking in a low voice, urged her to accompany him into the morning parlor. Fearing further familial outcries to be his report, or an outraged demand by the Hawthorpes for the return of their parrot, she hurried after him.

"What's afoot?" she whispered when the parlor door was closed behind them.

"An adventure, miss," said Hawkins with barely suppressed excitement, "and one beyond any of your imaginings, I think, from the strained and feverish expression of Lord Wingate."

"What has Lord Wingate to do with anything?"

"He came to see you an hour ago, miss. I have, at his request, secretly installed him in the north drawing room."

"But what's the to-do?"

"I don't know, miss, excepting he's Master Harry's

71

bosom bow, and I'd swear Lord Wingate never saw his bed last night, and Master Harry hasn't returned home since last night."

This, in itself, was not startling for Harry was known to keep late hours. But the presence of his good friend Lord Wingate indicated that something indeed was afoot. Harry would not think of carousing without Lord Wingate in tow.

Thanking Hawkins for his continued presence of mind, Melinda hurried off to the north drawing room. Throwing open the doors, she beheld a pitiful sight. Lord Wingate—all of two-and-twenty, slim and fair—was sunk upon a gold chair, his shirt points quite wilted (an unheard of occurrence for Lord Wingate), his head buried in his hands.

"Good God, Eustace, what's the matter?" Melinda burst out, hurriedly closing the doors behind her. This ejaculation was not wholly indecorous. She and Lord Wingate had known each other from infancy.

Lord Wingate's head jerked up. Deep circles shadowed his hazel eyes as he hastily struggled to his feet. "Melinda, thank God you've come!" he gasped.

Becoming honestly alarmed, Melinda hurried forward. "What's the matter, Eustace? Is it Harry? Is he in some trouble? Is he . . . is he hurt?"

"No, not yet," said Lord Wingate with a desperate laugh. "But never you fear, he'll be dead this time tomorrow."

"What's this fustian?"

"No fustian. The God's honest truth. Oh, Melinda, I'm in such a quake, I don't know what to do!"

"Well, first you must sit down and tell me everything from the beginning," said Melinda calmly, pushing him back onto his chair and pulling her own chair up before him. "Very well, begin."

This Lord Wingate seemed incapable of doing. His mind was not the strongest and to assemble his thoughts in a logical order required some effort. Taking a deep breath, however, he launched himself into the tale.

"We were at the Blue Peacock last night," he began.

"Oh, bother, not that hellhole again!" Melinda groaned. Lord Wingate bristled. "All the best chaps go there."

"All the silliest chaps go there. But don't let me interrupt you, Eustace. Please continue. You went to the Blue Peacock against all the dictates of common sense and what happened?"

"We'd had a bit of luck at faro and were settling back with some champagne when we observed a fellow about our own age accosting Jasper Wilmingham—"

"Wait a minute," said Melinda, a headache beginning to form. "This young man, was he dressed in riding clothes, his hair brown, his face thin, his manner belligerent?"

"Yes! Do you know the fellow?"

Melinda cringed. "Ours is but a slight acquaintance. He accosted Mr. Wilmingham, you say?"

"And loudly, too," said Lord Wingate, shuddering at the memory. "Damned him with the most filthy names and downright dared Wilmingham to call him out. Well, Wilmingham's not the type to take that kind of abuse from anyone, particularly a stripling, so he slapped the fellow, and the fellow tried to hit him, and Wilmingham easily knocked him to the ground, and then told him to meet him this morning at dawn. Well, someone helped the fellow to his feet, and others crowded around Wilmingham telling him he couldn't call out a boy, and the next thing you know the boy hurled himself at Wilmingham and began a brawl in the middle of the Blue Peacock!"

"Shocking," said Melinda. "What a universal lot of fools young men are. Mr. Brooke has even less sense than I gave him credit for."

"Is that the fellow's name? Brooke? Well, no matter. Wilmingham made short work of him. But the thing of it is, you see, that once he had knocked Brooke down, he didn't stop! He picked Brooke up, though the poor fellow was unconscious, and hit him again and again, then he threw him to the ground and kicked him!"

"Yes, isn't that just like Jasper Wilmingham? He delights in kicking people when they are down."

"Well, Harry was outraged, as were we all, only . . . Harry . . . did something about it."

Melinda regarded Lord Wingate with growing horror. "Oh, no, Eustace, he didn't!"

"Aye, he did," said Lord Wingate, wringing his hands. "Went up to Wilmingham, told him he was no better than a dog, and planted him a very neat facer. Jackson would have been proud. Broke Wilmingham's nose by all accounts."

"I am glad to hear of any injury to Jasper Wilmingham, but I fear the incident did not end there."

"No," said Lord Wingate miserably. "Wilmingham called him out then and there. Harry answered him and named me his second and told Wilmingham that I would call upon *his* second this morning. We are to set the time and place of the duel for tomorrow morning, Melinda, and I don't mind telling you I'm scared to death. I can't be a second! I've never been a second. I don't know the first thing about it. Dueling's bad ton, everyone knows that. If my father should ever hear about it, he'd string me up by my entrails—begging your pardon—at the least whiff of such a scandal!"

"It's not your entrails I'm worried about, Eustace, it's Harry's life. Wilmingham will kill him!"

"I know!" wailed Lord Wingate, beginning to tug at his hair, a habit he had whenever he was particularly distressed. "We've got to call the thing off, but how?"

"I don't believe Mr. Wilmingham has ever backed off from a duel," said Melinda.

"Not him, particularly after so public an insult. He'll meet Harry tomorrow, make no mistake. I was thinking," said Lord Wingate, looking a trifle wild, "that we ought to escape to Canada."

"Admirable," Melinda conceded, "but Harry would never agree. Unless, of course, we drugged him."

74

This suggestion shocked Lord Wingate, and he hurriedly shook his head. "No, no, I don't want to be the one to face Harry when he wakes up and finds he's been drugged, kidnapped, shipped to Canada, and denied his moment of glory upon the field of honor."

Melinda could quite understand the sentiment. She wouldn't like to be in a similar circumstance. Harry had inherited their father's temper.

"But you're so dashed clever, Melinda! The way you got my sister Jane out of that scandal in Bath last Christmas was amazingly brilliant. Surely you can think of something to save Harry."

Melinda gazed at Lord Wingate rather pensively. She was quite used to people bringing her their problems for she was indeed very clever and always found a solution, however improper, to every difficulty. But just now, with Harry's life in real danger, she wished there was someone to share this particular burden.

Lord Wingate was ineligible for he hadn't a notion in his head save how to properly tie his neckcloth. Elizabeth Jonson, though a good friend, was too bound to decorum to come up with a creative solution to a wholly indecorous problem. Her father was too volatile, her mother too rattle-pated, her sister Louisa too caught up in the Season to think of anything beyond herself. It was up to Melinda to find a solution, but she knew very little about duels and even less about how to stop one. She needed someone with more worldly experience than she or any of her acquaintance possessed.

Lord Carlton's name came instantly to mind and she brightened a moment, then hesitated. She scarcely knew the man, and here she had already involved him in a false engagement and a fallen woman's plight. It was not right to involve him in any more of her problems. But looking at the distraught Lord Wingate, Melinda's resolution faltered. In truth, there was no one else she could turn to, and no one else who could really help.

"Carry on," she told Lord Wingate, "as if we had never spoken. Go ahead and meet with Mr. Wilmingham's second. Arrange everything for the morrow, and then tell me all your arrangements. I shall insure that Harry and Mr. Wilmingham never meet."

As she could not act until Lord Wingate had procured her the necessary details of the duel, Melinda applied herself to her household duties and tried to compose a note to Lord Carlton, but was never really satisfied with any of her drafts.

An hour after Lord Wingate had departed, the footman Hawkins reported to Melinda that Master Harry had returned home in a foul mood and had gone straight to bed. Another half hour passed, and then Lord Wingate rewarded Melinda's patience by calling on her again. It took several minutes' strenuous effort before she could wrest the details from the panicky lord, and then, however reluctant she might be, Melinda sat down and immediately wrote to Lord Carlton, requesting an audience with him as soon as he was available. She handed the note to Hawkins with orders to deliver it personally into his lordship's hand and to wait for an answer. If Lord Carlton was not at home, Hawkins was to return with Lord Carlton's itinerary for that day.

Melinda passed another anxious half hour before Hawkins returned. Lord Carlton had not been at home. Armed with Hawkins's report of her fiancé's itinerary, and glad to be doing something at last, Melinda fobbed off her mother with a tale of visiting a milliner's shop and began to hunt the unsuspecting earl through a series of less and less reputable haunts.

What little sense of propriety she could claim might have quailed at the task, but Harry's life (and her dowry) hung in the balance. Melinda was resolute, even when she ordered the driver to the last address on her list. She knew one or two qualms, to be sure, but she told herself this was nonsense. The house was in a most respectable part of town, she was coming in a hack, and she was heavily veiled. Every conceivable precaution had been taken. Still, when the hack at last stopped and the driver let down the steps, Melinda was forced to fortify herself with a deep breath before stepping out.

The footman who answered the doorbell, and the butler who succeeded him, were child's play to a young woman who had grown up with an army of servants. She was informed that *madame* had a guest with her in the red parlor and was unable to receive any visitors. It was the work of a moment for Melinda to ascertain the direction of the red parlor, fob off the servants by the soothing comment that she was expected, stride purposefully up to the parlor doors, and throw them open.

The scene that met her eyes was as bad as she had imagined. Lord Carlton and *madame* were in a private salon, which boasted two luxurious red velvet chaise longues, matching chairs, a cherry wood dining table, soft candlelight, and several oils from the new romantic school of painting that depicted, as near as Melinda could make out, plump women lolling on chaises and ottomans in various states of undress.

Lord Carlton had removed his coat and, sitting at the cherry wood table, was about to partake of a late luncheon with a buxom woman of perhaps thirty years dressed in a rose silk negligee.

"Peter! I'm *so* sorry to disturb you, but I must speak to you on a most urgent matter."

The earl jerked up from his chair, unaccountably flushing at being caught indulging his masculine prerogative. "Melinda? Melinda, what the devil do you mean by coming here? *Here* of all places!" he demanded.

"Well, it was rather difficult tracking you down," said Melinda, removing her veil. "But I had to see you on a matter of the utmost importance, and I'm so glad I came because, you see, it's been most fascinating. I've heard a good deal about Mrs. Hill, of course, but I've never met her or been to her house before."

"No, I should bloody well hope you haven't!"

"It's all quite different from what I imagined," said Melinda as she advanced into the room, Mrs. Hill calmly taking a sip of tea and regarding her over the cup. "It's in the very height of fashion. I am most impressed. Did you use a decorator?"

"I prefer to follow my own judgment and taste," Mrs. Hill replied. "I wanted the decor to reflect my personality, as it were."

"And it does!" Melinda assured her. "Passion and beauty combined into an intoxicating whole."

"Why, thank you," said Mrs. Hill with a surprised smile.

"The decorations are quite lovely," Melinda said, studying the oil of a Turkish harem on the wall to her left, "if a trifle risqué. And every furnishing in the best of taste. No wonder you've known such success. I'm *so* glad to have all my illusions shattered. It's so much better knowing the *facts* of life, don't you think?"

"There are some facts," Lord Carlton grimly replied as he jerked on his coat, "that are best left unknown."

"No! How can you say that?" Melinda cried. "Knowledge is the greatest pursuit, after spirituality and love, of course."

"Neither of which can be found here," said Lord Carlton.

"But, Peter," Mrs. Hill murmured wickedly, "you know I dote on you."

"Why, I never said they could!" Melinda replied to Lord Carlton, who was glaring at Mrs. Hill. "That isn't why gentlemen curry Mrs. Hill's favor, at least from what I understand."

"You understand a good deal too much," said Lord Carlton feelingly. Their engagement might be a charade, but his discomfort was very real. How could a slip of a girl discompose him so easily? "I begin to understand how you acquired your nickname. What the devil are you doing here, Melinda?"

"I've come to ask your advice."

Lord Carlton looked heavenward, as if appealing for divine intervention. "Could it not wait until tomorrow?"

"No, because, you see, Harry would probably be dead by then, and that's why I've come. I'd like to avoid that if at all possible."

"Harry?"

"My brother. He's gotten himself into the most dreadful fix, and I thought you could help him get out of it."

"Why me?" Lord Carlton said feelingly.

"Well, because you know much more about these matters than I do. You see, Harry is going to fight a duel with Jasper Wilmingham tomorrow."

"He *what*?"

"And I want to stop him, but I don't know the first way of going about it, and as you've fought so many duels—"

"Two," said Lord Carlton, a trifle desperately. "Only two."

"Well, even though you've fought only two duels, you still must be far more knowledgeable about the etiquette of this sort of thing than I am. How does one go about stopping a duel?"

Lord Carlton sighed and glanced across at his scantily clad companion. "I fear, Becky, that we must postpone our meal to another date."

"I'll try to withstand the blow," Mrs. Hill replied, earning a grin from the earl.

"Oh, I do beg your pardon," Melinda said contritely as she advanced on the brunette. "I've interrupted your private lunch, and I haven't even introduced myself. I'm Melinda Mathley," she said, extending her hand to the renowned courtesan.

"Becky Hill," the stunned beauty replied.

"How do you do, Mrs. Hill? I'm so glad to meet you at last for I've heard *so* much about you, and I knew it

79

couldn't all be true. And now that I've seen your home, I *know* it isn't. I've actually seen you once before. It was at the Prince's birthday ball in my debut season, and I was so thrilled. You came in on the arm of the Duke of Clarence and how the room buzzed! It was my only taste of scandal my debut year, and I was so grateful to you. I hope you'll forgive my intrusion today, but I had such pressing business. Is Lord Carlton your newest protector?"

"No," Mrs. Hill replied, quite unruffled, "merely an old friend. I'm enjoying a few months of independence just now, though I do have my eyes on a duke with a Friday-faced wife."

"The Duke of Glockson? How marvelous! He's too good a man not to have some happiness in life."

"That was my opinion," Mrs. Hill said in amusement. "You've met his wife, I take it."

"Several times," Melinda said with a grimace. "Friday-faced is too kind. —Oh, my! That is the loveliest negligee I've ever seen!"

"It is nice, isn't it," said Mrs. Hill, preening.

"I've never seen the like, and I've got the most stylish friends in London. Who is your modiste?" Melinda inquired as Lord Carlton gazed at her, bemused.

"Madame de Lombardine."

"Really? The French émigré? I've heard good things about her, but this! I really must call on her tomorrow. The design and color are perfect on you."

"I've just had a ballgown made that you'd think had been sewn by fairies," Mrs. Hill confided. "It's all gossamer and sparkles and quite, as you put it, risqué."

"Oh, how divine! Perhaps if I mention your name to Madame de Lombardine, she can set the fairies to working on my behalf."

"Ladies, if you please!" said Lord Carlton rather severely. They gazed at him inquiringly as he turned to Mrs. Hill. "*Madame*, I apologize for this unheralded interruption of our luncheon. I shall remove Miss Mathley with all haste and trouble you no further."

Mrs. Hill, vastly amused, lovingly chucked him under the chin. "Ah, now, Peter, don't you worry about that. I've enjoyed Miss Mathley's company immeasurably. I've never had such a comfortable coze before. She's a most delightful conversationalist. You know," she said, standing up and walking around Melinda, "you would show to advantage in this style."

Lord Carlton's mind—through some odd quirk he could not fathom—suddenly transposed Melinda into Becky Hill's negligee. A most startling and appealing image.

"I daresay I could do a great deal with you," Mrs. Hill announced.

"Really?" said Melinda. "What could you do with me? And how?"

"Don't answer that," Lord Carlton commanded.

"Oh, but I should like to know," Melinda pouted.

"You like to know a good deal too much that is not good for you to know," said Lord Carlton gruffly.

"On the contrary," Melinda retorted, "knowledge is the best defense against unhappiness. Indeed, I now begin to understand why it is wise not to marry young."

Lord Carlton regarded her in some puzzlement. "How so?"

"Why, if one marries young, one has no experience to draw upon to bring pleasure into the marriage. How dull the lives of two stainless youngsters must be, trapped in such a union."

Lord Carlton blinked. He was well and truly caught. "It has been my understanding that society regards it as best that a young woman, at least, have no experience prior to entering the wedded state."

"Yes, but I think that society is off by a good mile there, don't you?" said Melinda as Mrs. Hill looked on with the liveliest interest. "I don't mean that a young woman should have legions of lovers prior to her marriage, but she should

81

have had her heart broken at least once or twice and been kissed a good number of times so that she knows how to differentiate the talented from the untalented. How dreadful to be trapped with a husband who is a terrible kisser!"

"Such wives invariably turn to more talented lovers, I believe."

"Well yes, exactly! That is just my point!" said Melinda. "And their husbands turn to Mrs. Hill. The very foundation of marriage is being destroyed for lack of experience by the women entering into it. Now imagine a young woman who has had her heart broken once or twice and has kissed a good number of men. Should she receive a proposal and a kiss from a young man and discover that he was a poor kisser, she would very sensibly refuse him and would marry instead the man who both proposed and kissed well. Would not *that* marriage be a much more secure and happy estate? Would not two such people look within marriage for their happiness rather than without?"

"There's a flaw there," Lord Carlton murmured. "I am certain there is a flaw."

"No!" said Melinda. "Why should there be? It makes perfect sense."

"It does indeed," said Mrs. Hill warmly.

Lord Carlton cast her a quelling glance before turning to his faux fiancée. "And you, Melinda, has your heart been broken once or twice? And have you sampled masculine kisses?"

She could not help it. A soft blush stole into Melinda's cheeks. "As for the first, my heart has been broken innumerable times. I think I have been falling in and out of love since I was thirteen. It was all calf-love, of course, but useful in helping one distinguish between infatuation and lasting affection. As for the latter, I suppose I have been kissed four . . . no, five times. Not much, I grant you. But at least it's a start."

"A shocking statement for any fiancé to hear."

A gurgle of laughter, which Lord Carlton found wholly

entrancing, escaped Melinda. "You cannot gammon me, sir. You've seen too much of the world to be shocked by anything, even should Lady Godiva ride down Bond Street."

"Now *that* was a tasteless exhibition from first to last," sniffed Mrs. Hill.

"Oh, no!" Melinda cried. "She was wholly admirable! To risk everything a woman holds dear—her marriage, her reputation—for a lofty principle! *I* would not have such courage."

"Thank *God*," said Lord Carlton.

Melinda grinned up at him. "My hair is not long enough, you see."

Lord Carlton gave it up and laughed wholeheartedly. "Any man with *you* for a wife, Melinda, would not look at Becky Hill twice."

"Why thank you," said Melinda with a wholly charming blush.

"Well I like that!" Mrs. Hill said with a toss of her brown curls. "I can get any man in England to look at me twice, *thrice* if I choose."

"That's certainly what I've heard," Melinda agreed.

"You hear entirely too much. I hope you *do* call on Madame de Lombardine," Lord Carlton murmured as he took her hand. "It would give me the greatest pleasure in coming years to think of so delightful a young woman dressed in such scandalous habiliments." He tucked her hand into the crook of his arm. "Come, Melinda, we are leaving."

"Oh, but I don't want you to abandon your afternoon!" said Melinda, made a little breathless by Lord Carlton's gaze. "I only want to ask you one simple question and get a simple answer, and then you can go on with your luncheon and . . . whatever else you had planned."

"Thank you, no," said Lord Carlton, his lips quirking. "The mood is quite spoiled."

"Quite," Mrs. Hill agreed, struggling against her own smile.

"Oh, dear," said Melinda. "I'm so sorry, Mrs. Hill. I had

83

no intention of spoiling your luncheon. I feel dreadful about this. Simply dreadful."

"You're going to feel a good deal worse if anyone discovers that you've been here," said Lord Carlton as he drew her toward the door.

"But I wore a veil," said Melinda, "and I came in a hack. I knew to do that!"

"Wonderful," said Lord Carlton as he opened the door and led her into the hall, Mrs. Hill trailing behind. "You are the oddest—and most broad-minded—fiancée I have ever known. Produce the veil, if you please, and let us get out while we can."

"How am I broad-minded? Don't all gentlemen know courtesans? I've always heard that they did. Why should you not come here?"

"It is unfair of you to rob me of my own argument," said Lord Carlton, who forbore asking himself why he felt the need to defend himself before a fictitious fiancée, or why he was a trifle miffed that that aforementioned fiancée had not raked him over the coals for dallying in the demi-monde. "Good-bye, Becky," he said, raising her hand to his lips. "It's been . . . unique."

Mrs. Hill laughed at him. "It's the most fun I've had in years. If you come calling again, be sure you have Miss Mathley in tow."

Lord Carlton shuddered.

While he went to his own curricle to order his groom to return to Curzon Street, Melinda stood pensively on the walk. It had, of course, been a most interesting adventure. She had learned so much. Still, she was very ashamed to admit it, but in her heart of hearts she was glad she had interrupted Lord Carlton's rendezvous and she thought this very wrong. She had no hold on the man. No claim to his fidelity. Yet, seeing him in company with the voluptuous Becky Hill had been a severe blow to her accustomed sang-froid. Mrs. Hill was a perfectly amiable woman, of course, but Melinda wished Lord Carlton had not seemed so content in her company.

The earl returned and helped her into the hackney coach, sat beside her, ordered the coachman to drive on, and then regarded Melinda. "Very well, *what* the devil is all this about?"

Not at all perturbed by so forbidding an expression, for no one could match her father in a fury, Melinda concisely provided the details Lord Wingate had arranged for Harry's forthcoming demise.

"Even though Harry is a stupid clod," she continued, "I really should hate to have him murdered, particularly just now when Father is in such a foul mood on account of our engagement, and Mama is in hysterics every day because my odious Aunt Wells delights in plaguing her about our engagement, and Louisa is close to bringing the Marquess of Rutherford to his knee, despite our engagement. Besides, then there would be no direct male heir, and the estate would be entailed away to my father's loathsome nephew, Basil Hollis, and if Father should die before I marry, I would be bereft of my amazing dowry and I really wouldn't like that. It is all well and good to say that money is the root of all evil, but I've found that it provides the most wonderful comforts in living. So you see, it would be best if Harry were not murdered tomorrow."

"I do not quite understand," Carlton said weakly, "how Harry came to call out Wilmingham."

"Don't you? Well, that is all the fault of Francis Brooke."

"Brooke? That boy is beginning to give me a headache."

"Yes, he gave me one, too," Melinda replied, and then detailed the tumultuous activity at the Blue Peacock on the previous night.

Lord Carlton considered the tips of his gleaming Hessians. "Wilmingham will kill your brother, Melinda."

"I know it! And I can't have it. As much as Harry is a stupid clod—for only a stupid clod would go to the Blue

Peacock, let alone insult Wilmingham—he is the only thing standing between me and the loss of my fortune. Surely, you could not wish such a disaster upon me."

"No, I would not wish it upon you, nor would I like to see Hollis advance in the world, particularly at your expense. But why come to me, Melinda? Surely your father—"

"Do but think, Peter."

The earl stopped. "Yes, of course. How silly of me."

Melinda fixed Lord Carlton with an earnest gaze. "I did not want to involve you in this, truly I did not. But I know no one with your expertise in such matters. You've fought two duels! You must be able to think of some way to stop this one. I know nothing of the etiquette of dueling. If I attempted to interfere on my own, I would probably make a hash of everything. But with your experience, you can undoubtedly think of some brilliant scheme to save Harry's neck."

"I begin to regret more and more my reputation and the misadventures of my youth," Lord Carlton murmured. "To stop a duel is not an easy matter. Wilmingham will not cry off."

"Neither will Harry."

"Then some means must be devised of separating them for all time."

"Could we not kidnap Mr. Wilmingham and place him on a fast ship to India?"

Carlton laughed. "A colorful and not wholly unreasonable scheme. Jasper Wilmingham is a plague. I would like to rid the country of him. Let me think a moment." He studied his signet ring for two or three minutes, and then looked up at Melinda. "I believe I've thought of a scheme that will serve you."

Melinda's heart quickened. "You are a knight-errant, indeed, sir. I'm so glad I know you."

"And I would not have missed your acquaintance for the world," Lord Carlton replied with a smile. "What would you say to having your brother arrested tomorrow morning?"

Melinda seriously considered the suggestion. "Well, I should not mind him being arrested, but I would rather dislike him going to jail. Father would become choleric, you see, Mama would go into convulsions, and the house would be made quite unlivable."

"Yes, I see that," said Lord Carlton. "I can assure you, however, that Harry will not land in jail."

"Oh, well that's all right then. Have him arrested. But how will that stop the duel? Will Harry not force the issue again once he is free?"

"He will not have the opportunity, for Jasper Wilmingham will have fled the country."

"Will he?" said Melinda. "Why?"

"The Bow Street Runners will give him very little choice. They will charge him with the murder of Francis Brooke, enacted before witnesses at the Blue Peacock."

"But Brooke is not dead! At least, I don't think he is. No, he's too plaguesome to cooperate with an early demise. How can the Bow Street Runners be brought to utter such a falsehood?"

Lord Carlton failed to look innocent. "I believe their salaries are not commensurate with their duties. They would not look askance at any coin being slipped into their pockets."

"Bribery!" Melinda exclaimed. "What a marvelous idea!"

Lord Carlton gazed at her in open amusement. "Melinda, you have the oddest sense of propriety I have ever encountered."

"But bribery is quite proper. Everyone does it."

"Perhaps. But there are laws, codes, boundaries of decorum . . ."

"Fiddlesticks!" Melinda pronounced. "If the prime minister can hand out bribes left, right, and center to win a vote in Parliament, why cannot you issue a bribe to save Harry's life? Or should I provide the blunt?"

"Thank you kindly, no," Lord Carlton said firmly. "It will be a pleasure and a privilege to spend a little money to see Jasper Wilmingham ruined."

"I *knew* you would think as I do!"

"You alarm me, Melinda. Am I to become a family lunatic as well?"

"Any man who would want to seduce Almira Thurgood has long since abandoned any claim to sanity," Melinda retorted.

"That," said Lord Carlton, considering the matter, "is quite true. "I consign myself, therefore, to the rigors of lunacy. With you leading, Melinda, I know I shall quickly become an adept."

*

Chapter 6

DAWN EXTENDED ITS tendrils across the dark blue sky, tinge-
ing the occasional cloud with a soft pink, making the world
seem fresh and young.

"Oughtn't this to be a fog-shrouded morning dripping
with gloom and premonitions of disaster?" Melinda inquired.

Lord Carlton smiled down at her. "Proof positive that
you *do* read novels, Miss Mathley, your denials notwithstanding."

"Fiddlesticks!" Melinda roundly retorted. "I've heard my
friends describe them, that's all."

"Of course," Lord Carlton gravely agreed. "As for the
lack of appropriate gloom, I did warn you that there would
be nothing of interest for you in this meeting."

"You spent two hours yesterday and a full hour this
morning telling me a good deal of drivel," Melinda replied,
gazing up at him in amusement. "I wouldn't have missed
this for the world, my lord, fog-shrouded gloom or no."

"You *are* obstinate," Lord Carlton observed. "A very un-
attractive quality in a female."

"And you, sir, are parsimonious ... an equally unattrac-
tive quality in a male," Melinda retorted good-naturedly.
"Why will you not give me a larger part to play in your
melodrama?"

"As you said, I am parsimonious."

"Nonsense, sir! You have generously paraded each of
your human frailties before the whole of the ton. Therefore,

I can only conclude that you fear exposing me to some sort of danger. I will speak plainly, Peter. If your plan involves some danger, if not to Harry, then to yourself, I take umbrage at any fiancé, false or no, risking his life before the banns have even been posted."

Lord Carlton chuckled. "Nay, madam, I would not risk losing the most entertaining acquaintance of my life. There is little danger, unless Wilmingham behaves like a fool, and I have never known him to behave like a fool. A cad, certainly, but never a fool. Ah! Here they come!"

Melinda and Lord Carlton were secreted in a spinney, comfortably ensconced on his silver and blue phaeton. They were perfectly well concealed from the field of coming battle: a forty-foot-wide patch of neatly cropped grass surrounded by woods, but a few miles from the heart of town.

They watched as Eustace Wingate's sporting curricle drew to a stop at the edge of the field and Lord Wingate and Harry jumped to the ground.

"Poor Eustace," said Melinda, "he's shaking like a leaf. You will remember, Peter, to not in any way implicate Lord Wingate in the discovery of this foolish affair."

"Certainly," said Lord Carlton. "And that is your brother, eh?" The earl looked the boy up and down. "A fine-looking youth, pale, but resolute. I could admire his courage if I didn't know him to be an unholy fool."

"Oh, the Mathley men have lots of pluck, but alas very few brains."

Lord Carlton chuckled as a second carriage drew onto the ground. From this emerged a gentleman in his late thirties, dressed to perfection in silk stockings, pale yellow trousers, and a tightly fitting brown coat speckled with yellow rosettes.

"So that is the infamous Captain Perkins," Melinda murmured. "Is it true he strangled a viscount with his bare hands?"

"No, no, only a baronet."

After the captain came a gentleman with a black bag,

clearly the doctor, and at last the star of this morning's entertainment, Jasper Wilmingham himself. He was dressed as if for a morning call, as if he expected no more strenuous activity than to partake of tea with some boring dowager. He wore a frock coat of blue-green, lush cascades of white lace as a cravat, and immaculate white pantaloons. His brilliantly polished Hessians gleamed in the pale dawn light.

"Remember to wait for my signal," Lord Carlton said softly.

The four men on horseback who surrounded the earl's phaeton nodded grimly.

The players in this morning's entertainment went through the set pattern of the dance. The seconds dutifully requested their friends to abandon the quarrel and were soundly vetoed. Having expected nothing else, they checked the pistols and handed them to the combatants. Rules were stated. Mr. Wilmingham and Harry stood back to back and counted off the paces. They turned. On the order, they raised their guns.

"Hold!" shouted Lord Carlton.

Lord Wingate nearly fell to the ground as the four Bow Street Runners galloped onto the field. Lord Carlton jumped down from his phaeton and strolled after them at a more leisurely pace. Melinda had long since been ordered to remain behind.

"Throw down your guns in the King's name!" bellowed a Bow Street Runner who had not had time that morning to scrape the red stubble from his face. "You're all under arrest!"

Lord Wingate moaned and swayed on his feet. Harry obediently dropped his gun, looking both relieved and frightened at the same time, while Jasper Wilmingham neither dropped his gun nor looked relieved. Rather, he looked decidedly peeved.

"What the devil do you mean intruding on a private engagement?" he demanded.

"Why, Wilmingham, haven't you heard?" Lord Carlton

drawled as he strolled forward. "Dueling is outlawed in England."

"As if you cared for that!" sneered Wilmingham. "What the devil are you doing here, Carlton, interfering in a private matter?"

"Oh, certainly private," said Lord Carlton, "but the matter concerns me nonetheless for, you see, you were about to place a bullet in the heart of my future brother-in-law."

"So?"

"So, I thought it would behoove me to endear myself to my future in-laws by rescuing my future brother, keeping him hale and hearty so that he may continue the great name of Mathley and, not the least in this affair, protect my future bride's dowry from being entailed onto the odious Basil Hollis. Your plans for Mathley, Wilmingham, did not at all coincide with mine. Then, of course, there is the little matter of Francis Brooke."

"Who?" said Wilmingham.

"Mr. Cuthbert, if you please," Lord Carlton directed the grizzled Bow Street Runner.

"Jasper Wilmingham," pronounced Mr. Cuthbert in a voice that could undoubtedly carry to Carlton House, "I arrest you in the name of the King for the murder of Mr. Francis Brooke."

"Who the devil is Francis Brooke?" Wilmingham demanded as his second, Captain Perkins, began to back inconspicuously toward his carriage.

"Why, the boy you beat to a pulp at the Blue Peacock the other night," Carlton replied amiably.

"I didn't kill the boy, I merely gave him the whipping he deserved!" Wilmingham expostulated, the color rising in his cheeks.

"The whipping might have been deserved, but the kick was not, for the blow shattered several ribs that in turn punctured the boy's heart and lungs, thus killing him. 'Twas bad enough to kick a fellow when he's down, Wilmingham, but to do it in front of two dozen witnesses ... Tsk, tsk! Very bad ton, Wilmingham. Very bad ton."

Mr. Cuthbert began to advance on Jasper Wilmingham in the King's name until Mr. Wilmingham raised his pistol without any thought to the King's name or anyone else's save his own.

"Take one more step and I'll kill you!" he declared. "I'll not be arrested for the death of some fool calfling."

"I'm afraid," said Lord Carlton, wholly at ease, "that you've no choice in the matter."

Wilmingham, black eyes blazing with fury, turned on the earl. "*You!* You're behind all this!"

"I? I only came to stop a duel. The Bow Street Runners are here of their own accord. Better go along peacefully, Wilmingham. You're outnumbered, you know."

Lord Carlton turned to Harry. "You should be horse-whipped, boy," he informed him. "Rather than defending your honor, you have brought a good deal of trouble and embarrassment to your family."

"You should not have interfered, sir," Harry stiffly replied. " 'Twas a private matter."

"For one who's almost a member of the family? Tut, tut, boy, that excuse won't fadge."

"Peter, look out!" Melinda shouted.

Lord Carlton jerked around just as Jasper Wilmingham fired. The bullet creased my lord's coat sleeve. A thin trickle of blood appeared.

"You do have an affinity, Wilmingham, for committing murder before witnesses," Lord Carlton grimly stated. With that he planted a very neat facer that knocked Wilmingham to the ground.

But the accused murderer was made of sterner stuff. He was quickly on his feet, throwing himself at the earl, knocking *him* to the ground. The battle was closely fought for several minutes. The combatants were of similar height and weight. Both had been trained in the pugilistic arts at Jackson's Saloon.

Wilmingham landed a cutting blow to Lord Carlton's determined jaw.

"Shouldn't we put a stop to this?" one of the Bow Street Runners nervously inquired.

"Good heavens, no!" Melinda scoffed, moving up for a closer view of the entertainment. "Lord Carlton is enjoying himself hugely, I am certain of it. Do you want any interference, Peter?" she called.

"Thank you, no," Lord Carlton grimly replied as he connected with an uppercut to Mr. Wilmingham's jaw.

Fortunately, his lordship had a good deal more science than Mr. Wilmingham, who sought to make up for his lack of innate skill with a good deal of ferocity. Lord Carlton's neckcloth was hopelessly ruined. A button flew off his coat. The lip that Francis Brooke had cut but two days earlier was seen to bleed again.

Lord Carlton seemed to take umbrage at this for in three blows he quickly laid Jasper Wilmingham flat on the damp ground.

"Oh, well done, sir!" Melinda cried as she hurried forward. "Never have I seen such an exciting mill!"

"You are an habitué of prizefights as well?" Lord Carlton inquired as he collected his breath.

"Well, the gentlemen are forever talking of them," Melinda said a trifle defensively, for it came to her that young ladies of good breeding did not, as a rule, approve of the barbarities of a fistfight. "How could I not be curious? How could I not follow where curiosity led?"

"Just how many have you seen?" Lord Carlton demanded with a grin.

It was with an effort that Melinda met his blue gaze. "Five. Oh, your poor lip!" she said, dabbing at the trickle of blood with a lace handkerchief. "It will never heal at this rate. You ought to be more careful."

"I am a victim of the company I keep," Lord Carlton retorted, staring her down.

"If you will remove your coat, my lord, I will attend to your arm," said the doctor.

" 'Tis but a scratch," Carlton said, waving him away.

"Nevertheless," said the doctor, "I should like to earn my fee for this morning. Your coat, sir."

Jasper Wilmingham began to groan.

"Remember, gentlemen, he may collect one bag of clothes and however much money he can carry," Lord Carlton cautioned the Bow Street Runners, "but you are to be with him every moment, no matter what reasonable excuse he offers. You are to see that he is safely placed on the *Hyperion Queen* and that the ship sails on schedule."

"Certainly, my lord," said Mr. Cuthbert as he and his fellows bound Mr. Wilmingham's wrists behind him and hauled him to his feet.

The notorious duelist blearily opened his eyes.

"Perhaps, Wilmingham," Carlton said cheerfully, "if you offer them enough money, they will allow you to flee the country via a long sea voyage, rather than take up residence in a dark, dank, rat-infested prison."

"I'll be damned if I'll run away like a common criminal!" Wilmingham growled.

"But, my dear sir, said Carlton, "murder *is* a criminal offense. In fact, I believe it is a hanging offense, is it not, Mr. Cuthbert?"

"Aye, sir," Mr. Cuthbert replied with a broad wink. "He'll draw quite a crowd, this one. Not at all popular by all accounts, are you, sir?"

"There you have it, Wilmingham," Carlton said cheerfully. "Emigration, if these gentlemen will agree, or a hanging. I certainly know which one I'd choose for you, but I am reconciled to disappointment. The Bow Street Runners are notoriously ill paid. Perhaps you can buy an extension of your miserable life. It's certainly worth a try."

"Oh, certainly, sir," Mr. Cuthbert replied, nodding wisely. "I've six children to feed. All boys. All growing like weeds. They'll eat me out of house and home."

"Tragic," Lord Carlton murmured.

Three Bow Street Runners led Mr. Wilmingham away as the doctor and Captain Perkins stepped into their carriage and hurriedly departed. Lord Carlton turned to Harry and Lord Wingate, who had been arguing furiously for the last five minutes.

"But I tell you, Harry, I didn't say a word to anyone!"

"What is all the row about?" Lord Carlton demanded wearily.

"This so-called friend of mine betrayed me!" Harry stormed.

"Betrayed you? Nothing of the sort," Carlton retorted.

"He told you of the duel. That's why you're here, isn't it?"

"On the contrary, puppy. I heard of the duel from my own sources. I have never met this fellow in my life, have I?"

"No, sir!" Lord Wingate stammered. "I-I-I wouldn't dare!"

"Precisely," said Lord Carlton with a sardonic smile. "No, Master Harry, I have my own sources, as I said, and as I am soon to be one of the family, I thought it behooved me to interfere while I could. Your death would have postponed my wedding by a good six months, and I am not in a humor to wait."

"Nor am I," Melinda roundly added.

"*You!*" Harry seethed, rounding upon his sister. "You're behind this. It has your hand, I can see that clearly."

"Oh, piffle," Melinda retorted.

"Well said," murmured Lord Carlton.

Melinda glanced at him. "Thank you. You see nothing except the fog in your brain, Harry. This was Lord Carlton's plot from first to last. It was all I could do to discover that there *was* a plot."

"Indeed, Master Harry," said Carlton, "your sister knew naught of the duel until I informed her of it yesterday."

"You *told* her? You told a *girl* about a *duel?*" Harry gasped.

"No, sir. I told my fiancée about the forthcoming demise of her brother."

"We tell each other everything," Melinda said, gazing at Lord Carlton adoringly.

"We have no secrets from each other," Lord Carlton said with equal fervor.

"Good God!" said Lord Wingate.

"Therefore I think you owe your second an apology for abusing him in such a vile manner," Lord Carlton continued imperturbably. "He has stood your friend from first to last."

Harry glumly offered his apologies, which were far more graciously accepted.

"You needn't think I've forgotten you, Mr. Cuthbert," Lord Carlton said, turning to the grizzled Bow Street Runner who had been hanging on the fringe of their little circle. "You have some further business, I believe."

"Yes, my lord," said Mr. Cuthbert, moving toward the center of the circle. "Mr. Mathley, if you'll come with me, please."

"M-M-Me?" Harry cried, turning ashen.

"Yes, sir. Dueling is a criminal offense, you know. I've got to arrest you."

"In the King's name," Melinda murmured wickedly, catching Lord Carlton's amused glance.

"Arrest me?" Harry gulped. "But you can't! You mustn't!"

"I not only can, Mr. Mathley, I shall," Mr. Cuthbert stoutly retorted. "You've committed a criminal offense, and you shall be arrested and tried for it."

"Oh, come, Mr. Cuthbert," Lord Carlton intervened, "surely you needn't take the boy. He never fired his pistol. For all we know, he could have been out here engaging in ... oh ... target practice, or some such thing."

"Nevertheless, sir," said Mr. Cuthbert, "I've got to do my duty."

"Oh, poor Harry," said Lord Carlton, looking angelically heavenward. "Still, he must reap what he sows. I certainly have."

"Yes, sir. We've *all* heard tales about your escapades," said Mr. Cuthbert with a grin. "Come along, Mr. Mathley."

"B-B-But—" said Harry.

Believing this to be her cue, Melinda stepped into the breach.

"Oh, surely, sir, you could not be so cruel as to arrest my brother when he has just escaped the jaws of death!"

"I'm sorry, miss, but—"

Melinda summoned tears to her brown eyes and even allowed a few to trickle down each cheek. "Oh, please, Mr. Cuthbert, I beg you! My mother could not survive the agony of her only son's imprisonment. She is not at all strong. I fear the shock of his arrest may kill her!"

"But, miss, my duty—"

"Oh, Mr. Cuthbert, surely you have a heart. Surely if it was one of your six sons instead of Harry who stood upon this field, you would not want him arrested. Rather, you would plead, as I plead, for kindness, for generosity, for one last chance to redeem his life!"

"Well," said Mr. Cuthbert, scratching his grizzled chin.

"Oh, *please*, Mr. Cuthbert!" Melinda cried, throwing herself on her knees before the stunned Bow Street Runner—who was no more stunned than her supposed fiancé and older brother. Her hands were clasped in anguished prayer before her breast. "Harry will never again set foot upon the field of honor, I swear it, as does he. Don't you, Harry?" she implored, turning her tearstained face to her stupefied brother. "*Swear* that you will never again enter upon a duel! Swear that you will never again willingly or knowingly break the law of the land. Swear it, Harry!"

"Y-Y-Yes! Of course I swear it. Dash it, Melinda, get back on your feet!"

Melinda was not accustomed to obeying any of her brother's edicts. "There, you see, Mr. Cuthbert!" she cried eagerly. "He is not a threat to society. He *will* reform. Release him into our charge, I beg of you. He'll cause you no more trouble."

"Well," said Mr. Cuthbert, grateful to be returning to the script Lord Carlton had devised, "as he is a gentleman and has given his solemn oath—"

"Oh, he does! He does! Don't you, Harry?"

"Yes, my solemn oath!" said Harry, hope beginning to shine in his brown eyes.

"Very well then," said Mr. Cuthbert. "We got the murderer that we came for. I'll let the boy go. But if I ever hear, Mr. Mathley, that you have entered into another duel, or so much as pinched an apple from an apple cart, I'll have you in jail so fast it will make your head swim. Do you hear me, boy?"

"Yes, Mr. Cuthbert! Thank you, Mr. Cuthbert!" Harry gasped.

"Very well then. Good morning, miss, sir, my lord," he said with a bow before striding off to his horse.

"You are getting grass stains on your gown," Lord Carlton observed as he extended a hand to Melinda.

She placed her hand in his, and he pulled her to her feet.

"Yes, but the expression on Mr. Cuthbert's face was worth it!" she said.

"I begin to understand your devotion to helping everyone in need. You enjoy the flattering glow of the footlights."

"But didn't I do it well?"

"You were superb."

Melinda dimpled at the earl. "Thank you, my lord."

They smiled at each other for a moment, before Lord Carlton recollected the practicalities of the situation.

"Well gentlemen and Miss Mathley," he said, "I think it's time that we all return to our respective homes and pretend that none of this ever happened. And I will expect, Master Harry, that you keep your solemn vow made this day, or so help me, I will thrash you up and down the sordid length of this unpleasant town! Never again do I want to get up before dawn to save *your* worthless neck."

"Y-Y-Yes, my lord!" said Harry, all too aware of the earl's volatile character. "Thank you, my lord . . . I think."

Lord Wingate pulled Harry off to the curricle as Lord Carlton led Melinda back to his phaeton.

"I think we've got a fair chance of Harry once and for all eschewing serious mischief. Your plan was perfection, Peter, and you were wonderful! Simply marvelous!" Melinda exclaimed. "The way you milled Wilmingham down! The way you had him dancing to your tune from first to last! And to cow Harry with such ease . . . ! Simply magnificent."

Lord Carlton gazed with some amusement upon his faux fiancée. "You are the most remarkable young woman I have ever met," he stated.

"I? I am not at all remarkable. I am instead remarkably plain."

"Nonsense. Any young woman who attends a duel, cheers on fisticuffs, has her older brother dancing to *her* tune, and is not above flinging herself into melodrama at the least provocation, has got to be the most fascinating female in all of England."

Melinda stared up at Lord Carlton, a good deal astonished, a blush creeping into her cheeks as she realized the sincerity of his remarks. She could think of nothing to say as he handed her up onto the phaeton.

The earl drove her at a smart clip back to Grosvenor Square, reminding her, as he handed her down at her doorstep, that he would call on her that afternoon to escort her to the Prince's garden party, his first official outing into the sober Mathley world of society and connections. He wanted her, he fervently declared, to introduce him to *everyone*.

Melinda laughed. "I think Jasper Wilmingham hit you harder than you realize, sir."

With a grin, Lord Carlton set his matched bays off with a neat flick of his whip as Melinda walked into the house.

As it was just after six in the morning, no one was about save for a few sleepy servants who stared at her in some astonishment as she mounted the stairs. She was not at all concerned. To explain away her early morning departure and return to the house would be the work of a moment.

* Chapter 7

"Ah, there you are, Lord Neville! Allow me to introduce you to my fiancé, Lord Peter Carlton."

The two gentlemen bowed warily.

"And, of course, Lady Neville, I have the honor to present you to the Earl of Carlton."

The earl dutifully raised Lady Neville's plump hand to his lips.

"It is an honor to meet so charming and beautiful a lady," he said.

"Oh, I've heard about your wiles!" tittered Lady Neville, who was forty-five and insisted on acting as if she were eighteen. She even rapped Lord Carlton's shoulder with her fan. "Everyone is agog. Yes, simply agog at this forthcoming wedding! Whoever would have thought it?"

"We did," Melinda said. "The moment we gazed into each other's eyes."

"Indeed," said Lord Carlton, rising manfully to this cue, "one glance into the depths of Miss Mathley's dark brown eyes, and I knew that I was lost."

"How charming!" burbled Lady Neville as her husband harrumphed at her side.

"Oh, there are the Duke and Duchess of Isleton," Melinda said hastily. "I promised Peter faithfully that I would introduce him to them. Please excuse us my lord, my lady."

"You," Lord Carlton pronounced as Melinda dragged

him across the lawn, "are a fiend! You have taken me literally!"

Melinda smiled demurely up at the earl as a fluffy white cloud wafted past the sun and a gentle breeze teased her auburn hair. A string quartet offered Haydn from a tiny nearby alcove. "You must never tell me anything you don't mean, my lord. I have but a simple, literate mind."

"I begin to understand the virtues of honesty," said the earl. "I must have met fifty people in this last half hour."

"And a good sixty more to go," said Melinda. "Come along and meet one of the fiercer dragons of the ton and her adorable husband."

"I am all eagerness," muttered Lord Carlton.

"No one ever said that entering society would be easy, or even pleasurable."

"I am beginning to wonder if it is even survivable."

Melinda laughed and dragged him up to the dragon duchess and her adorable duke.

"So this is your rake, eh?" said the Duchess of Isleton when introductions had been made. "He looks as if he could keep you tolerably amused."

"Oh, I depend upon it, Your Grace," Melinda gravely replied.

The duke chuckled.

"They'll say he's marrying you for your money, my dear," the duchess continued, "but don't let that put your back up. Anyone can see he is well and truly caught."

"No man of good sense could fail to be captured by Miss Mathley's large heart," Lord Carlton murmured.

"I hear you've been settling down," said the duchess.

"Now and then," said Lord Carlton, warming to the forthright female, the second of his acquaintance.

"You'll have a rough go of it with Mad Melinda as your bride."

"I *have* heard rumors," said Lord Carlton.

"As have I," Melinda retorted, "but I don't think any the less of you, Peter."

The duke laughed outright. "Well matched, by gad. Well matched at last."

"Thank you, Your Grace," said Melinda. "I like to think so."

The Prince was announced in the next moment. He moved genially through the large, sumptuous crowd, chatting here and there, chucking a debutante under her chin, shaking a trembling youth's hand, and generally making himself pleasant to all of his guests. Then he came to Lord Carlton and Melinda.

"There you are, you dog!" said the Prince, clapping Carlton soundly upon the back. "Roped and caught at last, are you? Well, it's about time, that's all I can say, and well deserved. And this is the little lady who's won your devotion, eh? Why Miss Mathley, you've achieved a miracle. All of London is talking of it!"

"Better they talk of my engagement than the Red Lady, Your Highness."

The Prince roared with laughter, his coat threatening to burst at least two buttons. "I'm glad you've got him, Miss Mathley! You're a girl of spirit. I've always said it. You need a man of spirit to keep you happy, and by God, Carlton should do that."

"So all of the women *assure* me, and most of the men, too," Melinda blithely replied. "I own I am relieved."

The Prince laughed heartily at this as a flush rose in the earl's cheeks.

"Ah, she's a sly one, Carlton. She'll keep you on your toes."

"If this afternoon is any indication, sir, she will undoubtedly harry me into an early grave," said the earl.

"But it will be fun getting there, eh?" said the Prince, jabbing him in his ribs before moving on to Lady Jersey.

"I am black and blue all over," Lord Carlton complained.

Melinda laughed. "I should have known that you two would be cronies."

104

"We . . . dallied together over an occasional bottle of port some years back, I confess," said the earl. "But nothing really outrageous. *You* have cornered that market."

"*I?* I have never dueled nor eloped with anyone, at least not that I can recall."

"Your memory is undoubtedly deficient. It doesn't bother you, does it?" he asked, suddenly grave.

"What?"

"My reputation."

"Good God, no!" said Melinda, chuckling. "Why should it?"

"Well, most of it is deserved."

"Then good for you. I hope you enjoyed attaining it."

"Some of the time," Lord Carlton admitted with a reluctant smile.

"I think people should enjoy themselves if they can," Melinda declared. "While you may have gone into an occasional excess of pleasure, it's not what but most men in the ton have done. You were just foolish enough to be caught at it . . . time and time again."

"Yes," said Lord Carlton dryly. "I was never precisely discreet."

"I doubt that you can even *spell* subtle."

Lord Carlton chuckled. "But I am curious, why doesn't it bother you that I am a rake and a scoundrel?"

"It doesn't bother me because you *aren't* a rake and a scoundrel."

"I beg your pardon? I recall with the utmost clarity—"

"You *were* a rake and a scoundrel," Melinda interrupted. "You are not those things now. It is the present that matters to me. I can do nothing about the past. Neither can you, for that matter. But we can certainly do something about the present and the future. Why else am I introducing you to every snooty matron and lord in the place?"

"Because you delight in slow torture?"

"*No,*" Melinda retorted. "Because you want to please

your Uncle Gilford before he dies by becoming a pattern card of propriety."

"Ah yes, Uncle Gilford," Lord Carlton said mildly as he surveyed the elegant throng enjoying this mild summer afternoon. "It seems that more and more can be laid at his sickbed. Here we are, supposedly engaged, an act that has brought us to the center of attention in the polite world. Everyone is watching us, you know."

"Well, yes, of course. That is why we came, isn't it?"

"I thought we came so that you could launch me into society."

"Well, yes, but they have to look you over first, you know."

"Like a horse at Tattersall's?" the earl inquired.

"Yes," said Melinda, nodding gravely. "But as a rule they don't ask to look at your teeth."

Lord Carlton gave it up and laughed.

"Ah, there is Louisa on the Marquess of Rutherford's arm," Melinda said a trifle breathlessly. Lord Carlton had the most wonderful laugh! "That must mean Mama and Father have arrived. Oh, bother. 'Tis an end to our fun, I fear, for Father will undoubtedly scowl at you for the rest of the afternoon and Mama will weep on any shoulder near at hand."

"An unpleasant prospect," Lord Carlton agreed, "but one to which I must grow accustomed for the next month."

"No, no, Father can't hold out for more than a fortnight. He can't!"

"Make it three weeks, if he is half as stubborn as you."

"Melinda!" Louisa called as she strolled up to them on the arm of the Marquess of Rutherford, all of three-and-twenty and with a sad predilection toward dandyism.

His long neck was enveloped in yards of neckcloth that raised his head a good two inches higher than its accustomed position. He was decorated with over a dozen fobs. A quizzing glass was never far from his delicate fingers. He was, as Melinda had remarked more than once, quite a sight.

"Melinda," Louisa said again, "you must congratulate me. I am to wed the marquess."

Melinda stared. "Marry?" She stopped and then hurriedly continued. "Oh, of course I congratulate you, my dear sister. How . . . happy you must be." She kissed Louisa on both cheeks, and then turned to the marquess. "You are fortunate in your bride, sir. Louisa is the best girl in the land."

"I know it," said the marquess fervently as he raised Louisa's hand to his lips. "And I am the most fortunate man in England."

"Shall we have a double wedding, then?" Lord Carlton wickedly inquired.

Louisa paled at this. Melinda merely rapped Lord Carlton's nose with her fan.

"No indeed, sir," she retorted. "My one chance to shine in public, and you would rob me of it? No, sir! Let Louisa shine at her wedding and leave me to shine, however dimly, at my own. But tell me, Louisa," she said, turning to her far from exuberant sister, "when did all this happen? You were not engaged this morning as I recall."

"No," said Louisa with a faint smile. "Rutherford and Father met for several hours this morning to make all the arrangements. The marquess proposed to me as we drove here. It was very . . . romantic. Is not this a lovely ring?" *La Belle du Ton* hastily inquired as she held out her hand.

The emerald was a staggering chunk of green nestled in gold and sapphires.

"It must weigh a ton," said Melinda, then blushed furiously. "I mean, it is very beautiful."

Louisa laughed. "It is a little heavy," she conceded. "But I am growing accustomed to it very quickly."

"No doubt," Lord Carlton murmured. "I congratulate you, Rutherford. You are marrying into an estimable family."

"I understand that I must felicitate you as well, my lord,"

the marquess said stiffly. He was always conscious of his high position in the ton and quite aware of the low position the earl held. "You, too, are to marry into this estimable family."

"We are both fortunate, it seems," said Lord Carlton with a bow.

"I must go and tell Princess Esterhazy," said Louisa. "She will never forgive me if she is one of the last to know."

With a nod at Lord Carlton, she pulled the marquess away.

"Didn't I do that well?" said the earl with the greatest satisfaction.

"You were superb," Melinda said demurely, keeping her eyes downcast so he could not see the laughter lurking there.

But he divined its presence nevertheless. "They make a handsome couple," he said sardonically, watching the affianced pair accost Princess Esterhazy. "They look well together. That is the proper comment to make on such an occasion, is it not?"

"Mm," said Melinda, gnawing on her lip.

Lord Carlton glanced down at her. "What is wrong?"

Melinda sighed in exasperation as she looked up at the earl. "Once again I must face my own worthlessness."

"What on earth are you babbling about?"

"The Mathleys *always* marry well to serve the family. But I can make no real contribution to my own family. *I* merely attract penniless fortune hunters, while Louisa wins a *marquess*. It is very lowering."

"But you have an earl," Lord Carlton pointed out.

Melinda's smile was a little sad. "But *such* an earl. The worst of it is that Louisa doesn't even want to marry her marquess."

"Whyever not?"

"Because Louisa does not love him."

"I did not know that members of the ton married for

108

love," Lord Carlton said, withdrawing a snuffbox from his coat pocket.

"It happens more often than people realize," Melinda stated, "and it should have happened to Louisa, for she cannot be happy in marriage if she does not love her husband."

"Why, then, did she accept the marquess?" the earl inquired, taking a pinch of snuff. "With your sterling example before her, she could have refused him as she would a dish of bad oysters."

"She accepted Rutherford because the true love of her life is not worthy of her."

Lord Carlton blinked. "The man she loves is not *worthy*?"

"*Most* ineligible. You see," Melinda said kindly, "he is a plain mister, the only son of an undistinguished general. Not at all suitable for a *Mathley*. We must needs marry a glittering title or great fortune, or both, *not* a nonentity with but a thousand pounds a year. Louisa is a most dutiful daughter. It has never occurred to her that she could marry Clare. It never occurred to *him*, I suppose."

"Clare?"

"Clarence Hyde-Moore, a neighbor of ours near Putnam Park in Herefordshire. He and Louisa have known each other from the cradle, and loved each other just as long. He is a charming and intelligent young man who would suit her in every way, but alas," said Melinda with a heavy sigh, "the general—"

"The undistinguished general," Lord Carlton corrected.

"Yes. If he had been a Wellington, that might have been something. But as it is, Louisa is to marry her marquess, thus gratifying our parents and ruining at least two lives. Bother," said Melinda, gnawing on her lip again. "I wish there was something I could do. Louisa will be *so* unhappy."

"You cannot fix everyones' lives, Melinda," the earl said gently.

"No," she said with a sigh. "But I should like to try with this one." Suddenly she brightened. "But of course!"

"My experience in our brief but tumultuous acquaintance tells me to beware that look. *What* are you thinking, Melinda?" Lord Carlton demanded.

"Putnam Park!" Melinda exclaimed. "We are to remove to Putnam Park in three days. She will be in Clare's company every hour of the summer, if past experience is anything to judge by. His company *must* wear down her resolution to marry the marquess. And if we could have the marquess at Putnam . . . ! The comparison of the two men day in and day out . . . Oh! It might work. It must work! It *will* work! And you could help!"

"I?" the earl exclaimed, looking horrified.

"Certainly!" Melinda cried, brown eyes shining up at him. "The marquess is an indifferent horseman, a lackluster dancer, a pitiful player at whist. You have only to help Clare outshine the marquess in all of the usual manly endeavors. Clare is an excellent horseman, a good dancer, and a keen player at whist. A nudge here and there on your part and—"

"But I am not going to Putnam!"

Melinda was so stunned by the shock she experienced at this statement, and the understanding she gleaned that she had actually depended on Lord Carlton attending her to Putnam, that she blinked. She even paled for a moment, then rallied and turned resolutely to the earl.

"But of course you are coming to Putnam! We are engaged. It would be expected of you to come, and besides, if you are out of Father's sight, he might begin to think less harshly of you. He might even begin to reconsider forbidding our marriage. You must be with him day and night and hound him into submission. You agreed! Besides, you can't possibly want to stay in London in the *summer*. There's no company and the town stinks."

Lord Carlton, who was astute, had quickly realized that rescuing a fallen woman, thrusting himself into the midst of

110

a duel, and entering into a false engagement were not a good start toward respectability. His supposed fiancée, whom he had assumed would hold him to propriety, had him instead constantly walking on the edge of disaster. What was supposed to enroll him into decorum had instead led him into worse scrapes than he had ever gotten into on his own, and all in the name of helping others in need. It had quickly become clear that it would be impossible to attain a veneer of respectability during a month in town where Melinda's imagination and efforts on behalf of humanity could run riot.

In the country, however . . . Lord Carlton turned the matter over in his mind. In the country he would be in a respected country home, surrounded by respected members of the ton. There would be far less provocation for Melinda to enter into some mad scheme. The country began to appeal. What, after all, could happen to him in the country?

Chapter 8

"STAND ASIDE!"

"Only for a better man than I," the Earl of Carlton robustly declared.

"He stands before you, little man," Melinda retorted.

"You'll have to prove it then," Lord Carlton said, taking a gentle swipe at her auburn hair with his staff.

She easily blocked the blow and jabbed him, far from gently, in the stomach.

"Ow!"

"Little John doesn't say ow," Margaret informed him from her safe seat on the grassy bank of the river Wye.

"He thrashes Robin Hood within an inch of his life," Annabelle coached from beside her twin.

"Tell that to your sister!" Lord Carlton said as he once again entered into the reenactment of that legendary battle between two worthy foes, wondering all the while how he came to find himself standing on a log, spanning this narrow stretch of the Wye, staff in hand, doing battle with his supposed fiancée who was having at him with some vigor, the train of her skirt tucked up into the waistband of her riding habit.

He offered a silent apology to his aristocratic forebears and jabbed Melinda's toe with his staff.

"Ow!" she said, hopping gingerly on the other foot.

"Hooray!" shouted Margaret and Annabelle. "Thrash him, Little John!" cried one; he wasn't sure which. "Mash and bash him!" the other urged.

A more bloodthirsty pair of females his lordship had never met.

He obligingly set about trying to remove the staff from Melinda's hands, but she, apparently, was not au courant with the Robin Hood legends, for she seemed determined not only to retain her staff but to knock him into the river below. Females were a treacherous lot. Not only did he have to uphold literary integrity, he had his own honor to think of. To be bested by a young woman a foot smaller than he was a fate too hideous to contemplate. Even Yorkshire would not provide enough distance with which to hide his shame.

He rapped Melinda upon her head.

"Aagh!" said Melinda, or something of that ilk.

Lord Carlton was just about to execute the coup de grâce that would remove the staff from Melinda's hands and leave him the victor, when his boot heel caught on a knobby piece of tree trunk. He waved his arms wildly to try to maintain his balance. Melinda began to laugh. Seeing his chance, Lord Carlton lunged, she feinted, and they both toppled headfirst into the river Wye.

The first sound that greeted the earl as he stood up (the river here was only three feet deep) was Melinda's gasping laughter as she sat up chin deep in the Wye. The twins' shrieks of girlish laughter rent the country calm.

"Bravo!" shouted one.

"That was *stupendous*!" shouted the other as Lord Carlton pulled Melinda to her feet.

"Will you wring their necks or shall I?" he inquired.

Rather than being outraged at her sister's selfish delight in their drenching, or horrified that every effort of her maid had been ruined by the Wye, Melinda instead stood up and executed a stately bow to her sisters, who applauded wildly. With a sigh, Lord Carlton chucked his staff into the river and made his own bow to the twins.

"What's this? What's this?"

Cringing, the earl turned his head and found an elderly

gentleman in a black coat staring at them in horror from atop a rather nice bay gelding.

"Good God! Miss Mathley, is that you?" the gentleman cried.

"Hullo, Sir Cedric!" Melinda cheerfully called out, quite unperturbed to be found standing in the middle of the Wye, drenched to the skin. "Sir Cedric Creighton," she whispered to Lord Carlton, "the local magistrate."

"Of course he is," the earl groaned.

"Mr. Brewster and I were reenacting the fight between Robin Hood and Little John, and we had a slight mishap," Melinda called to Sir Cedric.

"Who?" demanded the magistrate, echoing Lord Carlton's own query.

"Mr. Adney Brewster, a friend of Harry's from town," Melinda blithely replied.

"However did you convince the gentleman to engage you in battle?" Sir Cedric inquired.

"It was all Annabelle and Margaret's doing," Melinda replied as, catching Lord Carlton's hand in hers, she began to make her way to the riverbank. "They saw the log and naturally thought of Robin Hood and pleaded so diligently to see the battle that Mr. Brewster and I had little recourse but to oblige them."

"Young scamps," said Sir Cedric, gazing at the giggling twins with some fondness. "Quite like their elder sister."

"Sir Cedric, really!" Melinda said in a scolding voice as she stood knee-deep in the river. "I am not a scamp. Trouble prone, perhaps, but not a scamp."

"Semantics," Sir Cedric retorted. "Best get back to Putnam Hall and into some dry clothes before you catch your death of cold."

"In the middle of June?"

"My cousin Archibald was carried off by a summer cold in the prime of life. Take heed, Miss Mathley."

"Yes, Sir Cedric," Melinda said demurely.

"Your servant, Mr. Brewster," said Sir Cedric Creighton, raising his riding crop in brief salute before galloping off.

Lord Carlton opened his mouth to begin a severe dressing down of his faux fiancée, but he was forestalled by the twins who ran up and pulled Melinda out of the river, assuring Lord Carlton all the while that they thought he was the most splendid man in all of England, absolutely top drawer.

"I can't wait to tell Mama," said one.

"*I'll* tell Mama, you tell Father," the second twin countered.

The first one began to leg it toward their horses, the second close on her heels, both of them arguing at full voice who was to tell whom of this most delightful adventure.

"Adney Brewster?" Lord Carlton seethed, staring grimly up at Robin Hood.

"It was all I could think of on the spur of the moment," Melinda calmly replied as she began wringing out her riding skirt.

"Engaged nearly a fortnight and yet you forget my name?"

"Don't be idiotish, Peter. Think of your poor Uncle Gilford, as I did."

The color drained from the earl's face. *"Uncle Gilford!"*

"Shocking indeed for the Earl of Carlton to be playing at children's games and falling into the river Wye. Not at all respectable, to a dying uncle's way of thinking. So you couldn't be Peter Carlton, you see. You had to be Adney Brewster."

"Adney forsooth!"

"It is an honorable old English name," Melinda said with the greatest superiority.

"Not even an Adney Brewster would be friend to that young wastrel you call brother!" Lord Carlton declared as the full injury of the charade overcame him.

"Perhaps," Melinda said, struggling without success to

115

suppress a grin. "But I thought Father would take umbrage at having you named *his* bosom bow."

"Your father," Lord Carlton stated succinctly, "would have shot me and mounted my head on his study wall by now if he hadn't been so thoughtful as to break his leg our second day here."

Melinda shuddered. "Please! Don't remind me of the hell house to which we must shortly return."

The earl considered the matter. "This is a very nice spot, pleasant, peaceful, attractive. I think I'll camp out here the rest of the summer."

"Coward."

"Self-preservation is the hallmark of a well-trained mind."

"I'll not argue semantics with a man who debauched his way through his years at Oxford. Remove yourself from the Wye, Peter, before you grow gills."

Sighing heavily, the earl sloshed his way to the riverbank. "Well?" he said, arms akimbo. "Aren't you at least going to help me out?"

It was a fatal error for it set Melinda to laughing. She managed to offer him her hand, but she laughed so hard that she lost her footing and slid onto her derriere on the grass. Lord Carlton also fell onto his posterior, in the river.

"There isn't an inch of this country that is safe when you're around!" Lord Carlton stated as he picked himself up and heaved himself out of the river, sprawling upon the grassy riverbank beside Melinda, who was laughing helplessly. He suddenly wanted to laugh as hard as she, but he had his dignity to uphold, and it was such fun crossing verbal swords with Mad Melinda. "You should offer yourself to the War Department as a secret weapon."

"You shan't rid yourself of me so easily," Melinda retorted in the midst of her giggles. "I have vowed to see you become a leader of the polite world, river dunkings or no, and not even patriotism shall swerve me from my course."

116

"I grow more terrified with each new day by your rabid determination to do good in the world."

"And what's wrong with doing a little good when I can?" Melinda demanded.

"*I* end up bashed *and* drenched!" Lord Carlton stated with a strong sense of ill-usage.

"A little river water never did anyone any harm."

"Tell that to my valet!"

"A fearsome fellow?" Melinda inquired as Lord Carlton stood up and pulled her to her feet.

"Sixty inches of ferocity when it comes to defending my wardrobe." Lord Carlton surveyed his muddied Hessians and buckskins. "I may emigrate to China."

"Be of stout heart, Peter," Melinda advised. "You can always tell him that you sacrificed his efforts on my behalf. I was drowning, you see, and you jumped in to rescue me."

Lord Carlton shook his wet head. "For a young woman with the milk of human kindness churning through her veins, you are the most adept liar I have ever met."

"I do not lie," Melinda retorted as they started walking back to the horses they had tethered nearby. "I merely invent whatever is necessary for the situation in which I find myself."

"I'll not argue semantics with a young woman who shot Daniel Tarn in the foot."

Melinda flashed him a grin. "Very wise. Come along, we have to catch the twins up before they tell everyone about Robin Hood and Little John. Remember, I slipped into the river and you helped me out and that is all."

"Will the twins agree to such a bald-faced lie?" the earl inquired as he tossed her into the saddle.

"Their greatest pleasure comes in putting one over on our parents. Come along."

Lord Carlton went along with far greater pleasure than he would ever have thought possible at the prospect of returning to a manor hall that housed a fiend in human form.

Putnam Hall, in Hereford, was an ancient and towering

edifice that had been carefully renovated over the years to retain its Gothic charm while slowly but surely driving out the harsh drafts that had sent more than one Mathley to an untimely demise. The guidebooks spoke well of it and particularly recommended the view from the eastern drawing rooms on a summer's morning. The hall was surrounded as far as the eye could see by Putnam Park, a noble and well-managed estate that bordered the river Wye for three miles. Putnam's woods were a poacher's delight. Minutely manicured rose, flower, and kitchen gardens abounded. There was even a maze in which, Lord Carlton had quickly discovered, the twins delighted in losing themselves and having half the household come search for them. Putnam was well worth a summer visit, but it had one drawback: its master.

Mr. George Mathley, who considered himself a great goer on horseback, had singularly failed to live up to this self-delusion when he, on his second day at Putnam Park, pushed his hack at a rock wall that no sensible horse would try to jump.

His horse never considered it. He dug in his front hooves three feet from the wall and sent Mr. Mathley flying over his head. Mr. Mathley, who was not accustomed to being opposed by anyone or anything, landed badly, breaking his leg in two places. Lord Carlton, when informed of the accident half an hour later, had recommended that Mr. Mathley be shot at once and put out of their certain misery. But the attending physician, while privately thinking this a very good idea, reminded Lord Carlton that there were witnesses, promised to bring a large bottle of laudanum for the invalid, or his familial nurses, whoever needed it most, and hurriedly decamped.

Lord Carlton's suggestion held more and more allure as each day passed. Mr. Mathley was not a bad patient, he was a terrible patient. Day and night he was forever ringing the little silver bell his devoted wife had placed on his bedside table or bellowing at the top of his lungs for his butler, his

118

housekeeper, a footman, a maid, and every one of his increasingly homicidal family to attend him. His pillow was not plumped, his glass of water had grown warm, the sun was too bright, the curtains were too closed, his favorite pointer wanted in, his favorite pointer wanted out.

Deserters began to thin the ranks. The twins, whose fidgets quickly brought Mr. Mathley to foam at the mouth, were a decided detriment and were barred from the ground-floor study that had been transformed into their father's sickroom. Harry spent all of his waking hours away from Putnam Park, while dark rumors of his romance with a young woman of dubious reputation wafted back to the household and were carefully kept from Mr. Mathley's ears.

Louisa, ardently being courted by her fiancé and Mr. Clarence Hyde-Moore (who had soon abandoned any pretense of an excuse for visiting Putnam Hall every day for hours on end), was worse than useless. The tenderhearted Mrs. Mathley, who could not see her husband chained to his bed of pain without going into strong hysterics, was barred from the study by the united forces of Melinda, Lord Carlton, and the entire household staff.

Mrs. Hildegarde Wells, Mrs. Mathley's widowed sister, considered it her duty to sit at her brother-in-law's bedside and read to him from a variety of published sermons, all having to do with the folly of pride which, she never ceased to inform him, was Mr. Mathley's besetting sin. Had he acknowledged the limitations of his true age and weight, she said at least once an hour, he would never have attempted so mutton-headed an exercise and his household would not now be hovering on the brink of disaster.

As Mrs. Wells's visits never failed to put Mr. Mathley out of curl, she was permitted only one (she insisted on the one) visit a day, and that lasting no more than half an hour. Mr. Mathley's nephew, Mr. Basil Hollis, obligingly presented himself in the sickroom after breakfast each morning, inquired after his uncle's progress, and then decamped within five minutes, never to think of Mr. Mathley again that day.

Miss Beatrice Wells's sensibilities were too tender to withstand a long interview with her stricken uncle. Indeed, she required the support of her fiancé, Mr. William Wentworth, an unprepossessing gentleman who felt that ten minutes in Mr. Mathley's company in one day was as much as Miss Wells, or he, could withstand.

It was left to Melinda to attend to her father's tantrums. Indeed, it had not taken Lord Carlton long to discover that *everything* was left to Melinda: the daily management of the household; the guest lists for every meal or rout; the twins' antics (how they had managed to smuggle a parrot out of London Lord Carlton did not know); Mrs. Mathley's almost daily hysterics; any and every means of distracting the Marquess of Rutherford so that Mr. Hyde-Moore could have the field of Louisa's heart to himself; which room was to be made ready for which guest; the best ways to soothe a termagant aunt and keep a milquetoast cousin and her equally ineffectual fiancé from being hammered into aspic by the aforementioned termagant aunt; and how many roses were to be transplanted to the conservatory in the south wing.

The ton might call her mad, but Melinda Mathley was the most accomplished household manager Lord Carlton had ever encountered. Why a rich young woman would take on housekeeping when she had a phalanx of servants to do it for her was a puzzle. He had enjoyed at first thinking of her as lunatic, but Melinda was far from mad, and he found he enjoyed that much more. She was the most honest woman he had ever met, honest about others, honest always about herself. There were few women, he thought, who derived so much pleasure from laughing at themselves as Melinda did.

Any right-thinking member of the ton would never have considered enacting a staff fight. Any right-thinking member of the ton would have been horrified at toppling fully clothed into a river, even the Wye. Except Melinda. Melinda had laughed because she had appreciated the absurdity of the whole adventure. She saw the absurdity in every adventure, even George Mathley's broken leg. Her absurdity was catching. Lord Carlton found himself laughing at everything and nothing. The world was absurd because Melinda's clear vision had awakened his own. The world *was* absurd, and he had never realized until now how much he enjoyed laughing at it, and himself.

But still, all was not sweetness and light.

She might be a sorceress when it came to household management, a student of truth and hilarity in all their variations, but Melinda Mathley also had a talent for trouble—all in the name of helping others—that never left Lord Carlton unscathed. A dairymaid wanted to marry a groom and somehow it had all ended with a good deal of unpleasantness among a herd of cows that left the earl's left foot badly bruised and the affianced couple running off to speak to the parish vicar. Louisa must be got to change her mind about *her* fiancé, and Lord Carlton found himself purposefully overturning his phaeton so that Mr. Hyde-Moore could win a carriage race. His groom had not forgiven him yet.

Harry's newest inamorata must be inspected to make sure he was not being caught in the coils of an avaricious social climber, and Lord Carlton ended up with a black eye, for the girl's father had heard more than was tolerable about the earl's reputation with women. Melinda's twin sisters wanted to see Robin Hood and Little John fight it out, and *he* ended up soaked to the skin.

It had all begun to make a fascinating sort of sense.

He and Melinda returned to Putnam Hall, damp but in good spirits. The lie was dutifully told to Mr. and Mrs. Mathley, the former harrumphed about his graceless eldest daughter, the latter fluttered ineffectually around them recommending hot baths and large doses of cider vinegar; no, hartshorn; no, oil of violets, for she recalled how her dear brother Benjamin had once tumbled into a river, no, it was a lake, in Essex, she thought, or was it Northumberland? And *he* had been put to bed by their nurse and dosed with oil of violets and had been perfectly all right. Or was it camphor?

Acceding to the bath—for he stank of river mud—Lord Carlton followed Melinda's example and agreed with everything Mrs. Mathley said and took none of the recommended doses. He strolled downstairs an hour later, freshly bathed, coifed, and arrayed in tan breeches and a dark brown coat, his Hessians gleaming once again. He entered the dining room to find that the usual luncheon crowd had gathered. Catherine Mathley sat at the head of the table, the chair on her right reserved for him now that George Mathley was not present to protest this mark of favor.

Deeming cordial relations to be vital to his sanity and digestion, Lord Carlton had set about wooing Mrs. Mathley to his favor from the moment he crossed the Putnam threshold. It had not taken him long to ascertain the type and amount of flattery that pleased his hostess most. He had courted her assiduously. Whenever he saw her he remarked that she grew more lovely with each passing hour. Surely she could not be the mother of his beloved Melinda. She must instead be a younger sister. The gown of silver and pink that she wore at their first dinner party was deemed to reflect all of the beauty of its wearer. Her overlong and garbled stories were termed a delight. He could listen to her for hours. Her laughter was like a fountain of music. Her nerves were precious subjects of concern.

She was his devoted slave within two days. Lord Carlton wisely forbore reminding *Mr.* Mathley of his presence at Putnam. Flattery would not work there. A blunt instrument would not work there.

The Marquess of Rutherford sat at the foot of the table, Louisa on his right. Alas for the marquess, Melinda had insured that Mr. Clarence Hyde-Moore was on *Louisa*'s right. Harry, of course, was not present; the twins took their luncheon in their schoolroom. The Wellses and Basil Hollis were only ever concerned about their own affairs. Melinda was left, therefore, to sit across from her sister, Lord Carlton at her side, and orchestrate the conversation to suit her purpose, which was to show Mr. Hyde-Moore to best advantage.

The young man in question—an attractive fellow of medium height with dark brown hair and eyes, a good figure, and a charming smile—had not been appraised of Melinda's plans on his behalf. But Lord Carlton gave the fellow full marks for seeing an opportunity and taking full advantage of it.

"Ah, there you are, Peter!" Melinda said cheerfully. "We have been discussing Milton. Are you a disciple?"

"An admirer," Lord Carlton corrected, taking the chair by her side. "I consider *Paradise Lost* to be one of England's masterpieces. But then, I also feel that way about Congreve's *The Way of the World*."

"A silly melodrama with immoral and uncivil comments on womanhood and marriage," Mrs. Wells declared opposite him.

"Drama and comedy have their merits," Mr. Hyde-Moore opined as footmen began bringing in their luncheon, "but I prefer the romance of Blake, Wordsworth, Marvell! Who can stand against those first immortal lines of Marvell's 'The Definition of Love'? 'My Love is of a birth as rare,' " he quoted, looking directly at Louisa who was a good deal thinner and paler since coming to Putnam Park, " 'As 'tis for object strange and high. It was begotten by despair upon Impossibility.' "

"Heartrending," Melinda murmured. "Have you a favorite poem, my lord Rutherford?" she inquired of the marquess who was noted among his fellows as not being in the least bookish. This was considered high praise among his fellows.

"Hm? Oh, I . . . I suppose I enjoy . . . that Shakespeare fellow. People seem to like him," the marquess replied, hurriedly taking a sip of wine.

It was all uphill for the marquess from there.

*

Chapter 9

MELINDA'S SMILE AS she strolled through the Mathley rose garden betokened a deep satisfaction. It had been a wonderful week, the best she had ever known, aside, of course, from her father's breaking his leg, that silly business with the cows, and the innkeeper's right jab. It had been a wonderful week because Peter had been there. She had known not a moment of boredom because Peter was there. She had been happy, truly happy, because Peter was there. And he didn't even seem to mind the discomforts attendant on rustication. In fact, he had laughed more and more with each new day and didn't seem to mind the occasional trouble he fell into. In fact, he rather seemed to enjoy it, which only confirmed Melinda's opinion of his amiability and sense of whimsy.

Oh, he might scowl at her and accuse her of being an unregenerate troublemaker and madcap, but his blue eyes twinkled when he said it and she thought that he was saying such things more for form's sake than anything else. After all, he *was* trying to reform and a reformed gentleman *would* think her an unregenerate madcap.

He was the most amazing man. He had bitterly adopted the ton's unflattering opinion of him, he wielded his reputation as if it were a magic shield that would vanquish all friendship, and he seemed continually astounded whenever she laughed at that very reputation, as she often did. How could she not laugh at a former rake and a scoundrel who thought nothing of entertaining two devious girls with the reenactment of a medieval staff fight? How could she not laugh when he seemed bent on wrapping every member of her family around his little finger? And succeeded?

The twins were now his adoring, if occasionally disrespectful, acolytes. Her mother, after a solid week of Peter's shameless flattery and flirtation, had melted into an adoring puddle at his feet. Everything that Lord Carlton did was the best. Everything that he said was amusing or brilliant or charming. Everything that he wore was in the first height of fashion. He had won Catherine Mathley over completely.

Even the ever-decorous Louisa had unbent so far as to smile at his jokes, dimple at his flattery, and admit to Melinda only the other night that Lord Carlton's reputation must be unjust for he was quite an amiable man.

George Mathley, of course, still loathed even the mere sound of the earl's name, but then she had not expected him to acquiesce to Lord Carlton's many worthy qualities, at least not so soon, and certainly not when plagued by a broken leg. The leg was a decided disaster, for the doctor had assured them all that he would not completely heal for a good month.

In the next moment Melinda's thoughts took a far happier turn, for she rounded a corner in the garden just in time to see Clarence Hyde-Moore and Louisa Mathley seated upon a bench, clasped in each other's arms, and locked in what seemed to be a most passionate embrace.

"Louisa!" Melinda gasped before she could think better of it. Never had she thought to see her beautiful sister in so indecorous an attitude.

Her sister and Mr. Hyde-Moore broke guiltily apart, each blushing furiously. Mr. Hyde-Moore jumped to his feet, Louisa quickly following as she stared at her sister, aghast.

Melinda, having recollected herself, assumed a stern expression. "What," she demanded, "is the meaning of all this?"

Louisa glanced anxiously at Mr. Hyde-Moore, knotting and unknotting her fingers before her. Then, raising her

126

chin in a most determined manner, she said, "Clare has asked me to marry him and I have agreed."

Melinda's mouth fell open. "You what?"

"I never wanted to marry the Marquess of Rutherford!" Louisa burst out. "I've only ever wanted to marry Clare, but he never asked me until now!"

"Louisa!" said Melinda, a good deal shocked.

"It's awful of me, I know," said Louisa, wringing her hands, "and I don't care! I love Clare!"

"No, no, you quite misunderstand me!" said Melinda hurriedly. "I am amazed! I never thought you had it in you. This is wonderful!" Then she suddenly sobered. "But, Louisa, Father will never agree. Not when he's got the marquess on his hook and safely reeled in."

"I know it," said Louisa, chin rising in the air. "That is why Clare and I are going to elope."

Melinda had never been more stunned. *"You?* Elope?"

"It seems the only way," Mr. Hyde-Moore offered tentatively.

"Well, of course, it's the only way!" Melinda retorted. "I just never thought *Louisa* would think of it, let alone agree to it. But this is marvelous! Louisa, you're turning out better than even I had hoped. Have you made any plans, discussed the details, plotted your route to Gretna?"

"No, not yet," said Mr. Hyde-Moore, for Louisa was finding speech a trifle difficult at this moment. "She had just accepted me, you see, and—"

"Yes, yes, quite," Melinda said. "I blundered in. Well, let me see if I can make it good. I've always wanted to plan and execute an elopement, and here's my chance."

"But *you're* not eloping with Clare!" Louisa burst out.

"No, no, of course not, you goose. But I *can* help you to do so. I daresay you've never given the matter any thought whatsoever, while I have fantasized about this sort of thing for years! I have dozens of schemes in my head, and I know just the person to help us carry it all off: Lord Carlton."

"Lord ... Carlton?" Louisa faltered.

"Why certainly!" Melinda said easily. "He carried off an elopement with a married woman all by himself. Not as far as Gretna, of course. He at least had enough sense not to marry the harpy. But still, it must be vastly more difficult to carry off a married woman than an unmarried one, so he's bound to know the best way to pull this one off."

"But why would he help us?" Mr. Hyde-Moore demanded.

"Oh, Peter loves a good adventure," Melinda said in all sincerity. "We'll make our plans and take them to him for refinement, and then carry the whole thing off ... tonight, I think. It's best not to delay these things, and you don't want to delay getting married, do you?"

"Oh, no!" said Louisa, clasping Mr. Hyde-Moore's hands to her breast and gazing into his equally fervent eyes.

"No," said Melinda dryly, "I thought not."

An hour later they tracked Lord Carlton down in the billiards room where he was beating himself soundly. They announced without preamble the forthcoming marriage of Mr. Hyde-Moore and Louisa at Gretna Green.

"I felicitate you both," said Lord Carlton with noted composure. After a week in the Mathley household, little could shock or surprise him. He glanced at Melinda. "I begin to think you have second sight."

Melinda smiled merrily up at him. "No, just a firm knowledge of my sister, sir. But come, you have so much experience in these matters, we've come to you for advice."

"Alas, my reputation," said Lord Carlton with a sigh. "Very well, what help do you need now?"

Melinda rattled off their plot in a wholly coherent manner and was more than a little peeved when Lord Carlton very shabbily dismissed her plans to have Louisa escape the house down a rope ladder outside her bedroom window. Knotted bedsheets were also vetoed.

"Very well then," Melinda said, a trifle testily, "what do *you* propose?"

128

Lord Carlton offered the extremely prosaic idea of having Mr. Hyde-Moore come to dinner, stay late, and rendezvous with his beloved at a side door after the household had gone to sleep.

Thus it was that he found himself creeping through Putnam Hall a little after one o'clock that night. He told himself that he was a fool to involve himself in an elopement that would damn him forever in George Mathley's eyes, if George Mathley ever discovered his involvement in this affair. And he undoubtedly would. He told himself a good many other things, all of them uncomplimentary, and yet he continued to creep through Putnam Hall, Clarence Hyde-Moore in tow, as they went to their rendezvous with Melinda and Louisa Mathley.

"What was that?" Clarence Hyde-Moore said hoarsely, dragging Lord Carlton to a stop.

"The floorboard creaking beneath our feet," the earl wearily replied. This was the fifth such stop in less than two minutes. "You must have courage, Mr. Hyde-Moore, particularly if you are about to enter the wedded state. Now come along."

"But what if we should be discovered?"

"Then we will merely say that you and I grew weary of conversing in the drawing room and decided to go for a stroll together across the grounds and discuss our life stories. Now come along, Mr. Hyde-Moore, before I cuff you."

Clare, despite his unease, grinned at the earl. "She roped you in very neatly, didn't she?"

The earl glared at him. "Very."

"Will she have you dancing to her tune when you're married, do you think?"

"I dance to no one's tune but my own, Mr. Hyde-Moore," Lord Carlton witheringly retorted. "I am participating in this mad start because I have always secretly longed to assist a runaway marriage. Now no more conversation, if you please. We are supposed to be moving *stealthily* through the hall."

129

"Yes, of course," said Mr. Hyde-Moore, hiding his grin.

They continued on and but three minutes later reached their rendezvous: a little-used side door near a seldom-used parlor on the ground floor at the north side of the hall. Lord Carlton was vastly relieved to discover that Melinda, unlike most of her sex, was punctual to a fault. She stood there, brown eyes glowing, Louisa's hand clasped firmly in her own, a valise at her feet.

"You are late!" she whispered. "Is there anything amiss?"

"No, and don't look so hopeful," Lord Carlton commanded. "We will have no adventures on this elopement if you please, Melinda."

She grinned up at him. "Oh, it is not necessary, sir! This is adventure enough. Isn't this the greatest fun?"

"I'd rather be dueling with Wilmingham," the earl said flatly. "Come along ladies, Mr. Hyde-Moore. Gretna awaits."

The side door opened out onto a broad expanse of closely cropped lawn used occasionally for picnics and croquet in the warmer months. Lord Carlton noted irritably that there was not a cloud in the sky, and the moon was three-quarters full. Still, this was a country home with country hours. Even the servants had been asleep for the last two hours. He had some hope of reaching Mr. Hyde-Moore's carriage unscathed.

Alas, he was too hopeful.

A shotgun blast rent the still night air.

"Run!" Melinda shouted.

It was the most sensible thing the earl had ever heard her say.

The quartet bolted across the lawn, a second shotgun blast pursuing them.

Outside the posting house Louisa and Melinda bid each other a tearful adieu. At last Mr. Hyde-Moore separated them and helped his bride into the chaise-and-four. With a crack of the coachman's whip, they were off on the road north.

"How sad not to see them actually take their vows," Melinda said with a sniff as she dabbed at her eyes with a handkerchief.

"I can only be grateful that we're not going to Scotland," said Lord Carlton. "You have the most amazing talent for acquiring trouble, Melinda. If we were to attend them in Gretna, the Scots would undoubtedly revolt and separate themselves from the empire forever."

"La, sir, I've never caused that much trouble."

"There is always a first time," Lord Carlton said sourly.

Melinda laughed. "I *am* glad you came. You're such fun to have on adventures. It was very noble of you, sir, to allow yourself to be shot at on my sister's behalf—"

"Nay, madam, it was entirely on your behalf. I would not risk life and limb for a mere Louisa."

"You *are* gallant," Melinda said admiringly.

"Thank you. Next time, Melinda—and God Forbid there should *be* a next time—*do* try to have a more accurate understanding of your night watchman's schedule!"

"Yes, my lord," Melinda demurely replied, but the earl was unimpressed. There was an unholy twinkle of merriment in her brown eyes.

They returned to General Hyde-Moore's barouche, as unremarkable a carriage as the general himself.

Melinda engaged the earl in conversation for the next half hour about who had the worst aunt. It was a hotly contested debate for, though Hildegarde Wells was currently in residence at Putnam Hall and Lord Carlton had felt the full impact of that termagant's tongue, he still insisted that she paled in contrast to the horrors of his Aunt Abernathy, and he would not be swayed for he was enjoying himself enormously. Never had he been so comfortable in feminine company. Never had he spent more than five minutes with a marriageable female without her flirting or flattering or

131

teasing, or God help him, simpering, doing anything to catch his eye and hold his interest.

Melinda did none of this. She was earnestly debating him on a topic of interest to her with no more thought in her head than to win the argument. Despite the late hour Lord Carlton realized that he was happy. Indeed, that he had been happier in this last fortnight than in all of his preceding thirty-one years. He was just trying to puzzle this out when the barouche lurched to a halt, flinging Lord Carlton and Melinda together. Both in the same instant heard a gruff voice cry out:

"Hold or I'll fill your worthless carcass with lead!"

"What now?" Lord Carlton groaned.

"You inside!" called the gruff voice. "Come out with your hands up and no funny business."

"A highwayman?" Melinda murmured, wholly agog. "We have been stopped by a highwayman?"

"I pray you, Melinda, do nothing to endanger your life or mine," Lord Carlton urged.

"No, no, of course not!" Melinda said hurriedly as he stepped out of the barouche, hands dutifully raised, more to help Melinda out after him than in any acquiescence to the brigand's demands.

The man in the moonlight was a ghastly looking figure: tall and cadaverous, an old felt hat pulled low over his brow, a dirty kerchief tied around his face so that only his pale eyes were visible. His clothes were an assemblage of ill-fitting trousers, shirt, and coat, though the boots were well made and of new issue.

This, Lord Carlton realized with growing concern, was no highwayman, but the lowest and most dangerous criminal of all: a footpad. His brethren were known to prefer shooting witnesses than risk a hangman's noose.

"Your money or your life!" the footpad growled.

"Oh, surely you could have thought of something more original," Lord Carlton said with a sigh as he carefully reached into his coat for his purse.

"Stop the gab and hand me your purse!"

The footpad pocketed Lord Carlton's purse, watch, and signet ring, and then turned to Melinda.

"Harm her and you'll die," Lord Carlton said pleasantly.

The footpad glanced at him. "I'll not harm her if she does as she's told. I'll have that necklace, miss, and the earrings and bracelet."

"Oh, certainly!" Melinda said as she began to remove the pearl necklace with the gold-and-diamond clasp. "I've never been fond of these anyway. Mama insists that I wear them, but really they're so very plain and I'm so very plain that they're more of a hindrance than a help in getting anyone to look at me. I need something flashier, don't you think? Something to catch people's eye, for I certainly don't. Tell me," she rattled on, "do you dress like that to frighten your victims or are you really so bad at being a highwayman that you can't keep yourself in decent clothes?"

"What?" growled the brigand.

"What I mean to say is, don't you make enough money as a highwayman to buy yourself better clothes than this? Or have the pickings been slim recently?"

"What's wrong with me clothes?"

"Well, they're very ill made and ill fitting," Melinda said, beginning to remove her earrings. "I would think that a highwayman capturing such booty as ours could afford to dress better, or at least afford to find a better tailor. Do you have a tailor? Perhaps I could direct you—"

Taking advantage of the footpad's befuddlement, Lord Carlton leapt at the brigand, knocking both him and his gun to the ground, his lordship tumbling after. The footpad was more adept with pistols than with fists. He made a few feeble efforts to defend himself, but he lacked all science or art, even any innate ability. To render him unconscious was, for Lord Carlton, the work of a moment.

"Hooray!" Melinda cried as she rushed up to the earl.

"Oh, Peter, you were marvelous! Simply marvelous! How's your lip?"

"Unscathed, thank you," said Lord Carlton, dusting himself off.

"You moved so fast I could scarcely believe it! And the way you leveled him! One, two, and out like a light! How brave of you to rush at him when he was holding a gun."

"On the contrary, my dear Melinda," Lord Carlton said, casting her an appraising glance. "He may have been holding a gun, but you held his attention, as you well know. You had the poor fellow so distracted that an elephant could have walked past him and he wouldn't have noticed. To take him unaware was child's play. You really must share in any praise for this blackguard's capture."

"Do you think there's a reward for him?"

"Do you want to supplement your pin money?"

"Now, why would anyone want to supplement what is already excessive?" Melinda demanded. "It's just that I've never received a reward before. It would be so exciting!"

Lord Carlton gave it up and laughed. Any other woman in his acquaintance would have screamed or fainted or thrown herself against him to keep him from acting as any honorable man must have done. But here was Melinda cheering him on and wondering about claiming a reward for this miscreant. She was utterly unique and wholly entrancing in the moonlight, her brown eyes shining up at him, her face aglow with excitement and admiration for the way he had tackled the footpad.

Lord Carlton understood in that moment the full danger in which he stood.

"Well done, my lord," said the coachman as he finished tying the brigand's hands behind him. "What do we do with the fellow now? Leave him here?"

"Leave him to accost others on the road?" said Lord Carlton. "No, no, no. He must be jailed. But where?"

"The militia is quartered in Derrybrook just a few miles on, my lord. Or so my daughter tells me, and girls have a way of knowing such things. Derrybrook's got a jail strong enough to hold this sorry fellow."

"Excellent. To Derrybrook then, coachman."

"Yes, my lord. Where shall I put him?"

"Oh, with us, please!" Melinda said.

"What?" demanded Lord Carlton.

"There's so much I want to ask him, and if Derrybrook really is just a few miles away, I'll have so little time to question him thoroughly, so he must ride with us. There's plenty of room."

"Oh, why don't we just adopt the fellow and have done with it?"

"Please, Peter?"

Lord Carlton had noted more than once that it was nigh on impossible to refuse Melinda anything when she looked up at him with those large brown eyes of hers.

"Oh, very well," he said gruffly. "But I draw the line at inviting him to a late supper."

Melinda laughed up at him. "No. Even *I* understand the impropriety of that."

"The world is full of wonders," Lord Carlton murmured as the footpad struggled into consciousness.

The coachman and the earl grabbed an arm apiece and lifted him, none too gently, onto the forward seat of the barouche. Lord Carlton then handed Melinda into the carriage, nodded at the coachman, and followed her in.

"Oh, my head!" moaned the footpad, slumped in the forward seat and holding his head with both hands. "What did you hit me with, an anvil?"

"No, sir," Melinda retorted. "An upper right cross. Wasn't it well done?"

"Please, Melinda," Lord Carlton remonstrated, "you'll put me to the blush."

"Oh, honestly, Peter!" Melinda said. "I've never known such a rogue. I doubt if you've blushed since you were five."

"Four," he retorted.

135

She grinned at him, and then turned back to the swarthy brigand. "What is your name, sir?"

"I'm not sayin'," he replied.

"Oh, come sir, you're going to jail, your name will come out. You might as well tell us now."

The brigand squared his grizzled jaw. "No."

"Oh, please, do tell us! There are so many things I want to ask you, and it would be so much easier if I knew your name."

Apparently Lord Carlton was not the only male incapable of withstanding Melinda's pleading brown eyes.

"Barney," the footpad growled. "Josiah Barney."

"How do you do, Mr. Barney?" Melinda said. "I can't thank you enough for trying to hold us up. It was the best adventure I've ever had! Tell me, have you always been a highwayman?"

"What kind of question is that?"

"He is a footpad, Melinda, not a highwayman," Lord Carlton corrected.

"Oh, I'm so sorry, Mr. Barney!" Melinda cried. "I didn't mean to be rude. It's just that I was wondering if you've always been a footpad or if you've had another trade before this and been thrown out of it and had to turn to thievery to support your destitute family."

"I ain't got no family."

"Oh, you poor man! Not even a brother or sister?"

"No!" growled Josiah Barney.

"Then did you become a footpad because you loved the adventure of it, the excitement, the ease?"

"You think this is easy?" Mr. Barney demanded, struggling with his bonds.

"No, I quite take your point," Melinda said gravely. "There is clearly some difficulty and danger involved in your profession. Why did you become a footpad, then?"

"I got no trade."

"Surely you could learn one?"

"Don't want to," said Josiah Barney with a challenging

tilt of his chin. "Don't want to learn no farming or smithing. Don't want to be a servant to the toffs."

"Better to steal from them, eh?" said Melinda, nodding wisely.

"Until tonight it was," said Mr. Barney.

By the time they reached Derrybrook, Melinda had elicited Josiah Barney's entire life history; examined his character, morals, and philosophical outlook; and deduced, as Lord Carlton had long since, that the fellow was an out-and-out scoundrel, with few, if any, redeeming qualities. He didn't even like dogs.

The barouche at last slowed to a stop, and a moment later the coachman opened the door. Mr. Barney was handed out.

"I'm afraid you'll have to make a statement, my lord," said the coachman.

"Of course, I'll have to make a statement," said Lord Carlton with a sigh. "The perfect end to a perfect evening."

"Come, Peter, I will support you," Melinda said, offering him her hand.

"You are too good."

"Yes, I know," Melinda retorted with a grin.

Lord Carlton helped her down, and together they followed the coachman and Josiah Barney into the jail where the sleepy young lieutenant was roused and informed that he was to arrest one Josiah Barney, footpad.

"J-J-Josiah Barney?" the boy stammered. "You've captured *Josiah Barney*?"

"Is something wrong?" Melinda inquired.

"The captain's been trying to catch him these last four months!"

"A fine cockle-brained hash he made of it, too," said Mr. Barney with satisfaction.

"Oh, dear," said Melinda, looking up at Lord Carlton, "have we imposed?"

"We could always release him and let the captain try again," the earl suggested.

"Wait right here!" the lieutenant said, hastily smoothing his hair and making sure his red coat was properly buttoned. "I'll fetch Captain Reynolds. He'll want to take this fellow in charge personally."

"Next we'll have some general inviting us to a late supper," Lord Carlton said with a sigh as he sat on the corner of the large wooden desk and swung one leg back and forth.

"I had no idea you were *notorious*, Mr. Barney," Melinda said to the footpad with obvious admiration.

"I've enjoyed a bit of renown, as they say," Mr. Barney modestly replied.

"I have more and more hopes of that reward, Peter."

The earl chuckled and shook his head at Melinda.

Two minutes later Captain Reynolds, a short, well-built man with short gray hair, stepped briskly into the room, followed by the lieutenant.

"So, you're finally going to pay for your marauding up and down our roads, are you, Barney?" said the captain. "I'm grateful to you, sir," he said to Lord Carlton.

"My pleasure entirely, Captain," said the earl, removing himself from the desk.

Josiah Barney was taken into the back of the building and placed in a cell. Then the captain returned to the front office.

"I'll need just a little information so I can have this fellow properly charged," he said as he resumed his seat behind his desk. "Your name, sir?"

"Mr. and Miss Vance," Melinda said hurriedly.

Lord Carlton and Mr. Hyde-Moore's coachman stared at her in astonishment.

"Millard and Hortense," Melinda supplied. "We're brother and sister, you see. From Shropshire. But, of course, we're only half brother and sister. My mother, you see, was his father's second wife. Well, *is* his father's second wife, for they're both still living, of course, and as hale and hearty as anyone could wish, except our father is subject to

138

rheumatism on particularly damp days and they've both got the most wretched colds just now."

"Yes, of course," said the captain, a trifle taken aback by this spew of unsolicited information.

"And this is John Coachman," Melinda blithely continued. "He's been with our family ever since I can remember. He saw Mr. Barney first."

"Um . . . yes, sir," said the coachman. "The fellow leapt up from the middle of the road, aimed his gun at my heart, and told me to stop the horses. So I stopped the horses."

"Very wise," said the captain, writing this down.

"He ordered Lor—I mean, he ordered Mr. and Miss Vance out of the carriage, took Mr. Vance's purse, ordered Miss Vance to hand over her jewels, and while she was talking to him, Mr. Vance jumped at the scoundrel, knocked the gun out of his hand, and . . . er . . . rendered him unconscious."

"Well done, sir. Well done," the captain said approvingly.

"Nothing that a few hours at Jackson's Saloon couldn't supply," said Lord Carlton. "Do you need anything further of us? We really must press on. We're dreadfully late. Our . . . cousin is getting married tomorrow, you see."

"Ah. Yes, yes, of course. Then you're not a Hereford resident?"

"Oh, no! *Shropshire*, as I said," Melinda broke in. "And our cousin resides in Gloucestershire, and we are dreadfully late. We hope to drive all night. The moon is so full and bright that it should be an easy journey. May we go now?"

"Oh, certainly, miss," said the captain, standing up to escort them to the door. "Thank you for your time and trouble."

"Oh, no trouble at all, Captain. Come along, Millard," Melinda said to Lord Carlton.

The earl gallantly offered his arm, and they sailed out to the barouche. "*Millard* and *Hortense* Vance?" Lord Carlton seethed as he handed her into the carriage.

"A sudden inspiration," said Melinda. "I thought it

139

would not do to have the Earl of Carlton involved in capturing a footpad because then, you see, you would have had to explain what you were doing out so late at night, and then, of course, it would have come out about Louisa and Clare eloping, and how would that have looked to your dying uncle?"

"You," Lord Carlton pronounced as he settled himself onto the forward seat, "are a treasure."

"Thank you, sir," Melinda said, dimpling. Her smile quickly evaporated. "Oh, bother! We forgot to ask about the reward!"

To the earl's great surprise, the rest of their journey back to Putnam Park was untinged with any further adventure.

*

Chapter 10

"WHEN DO YOU announce the elopement?" Lord Carlton asked as he and Melinda paused to rest in the shade of a beech tree grove.

"After breakfast. I thought my parents should be fortified before receiving the news."

"Very considerate."

"I have to be," Melinda said soberly, leaning against a tree trunk. "Louisa is their darling. She has never, in all her eighteen years, done the least thing to upset them. Her elopement with Clare will come as a severe blow. I only hope I can find the right words to cushion the shock."

"Do you never tire of taking care of everyone in your family?"

Melinda looked up in surprise. "But I don't!"

"That is the biggest whisker you have ever told me."

"Well, families look out for one another, don't they?" Melinda temporized.

"Not my family."

"There are exceptions to every rule."

"Yes, and you are it."

Melinda chuckled. "To what rule am I an exception?"

"To most of 'em," the earl said frankly. "It's most disconcerting."

"You haven't been disconcerted since you were ten."

"Eight. But then, I had never encountered Mad Melinda before."

"It does seem a pity. We would have had the greatest fun

together! And I daresay I could have been the one sane voice in your crowd keeping you from running off with Almira Thurgood."

"Oh, I regret the follies of my youth, but the experiences taught me much. I am a wiser man because of them."

"You are a bitter man because of them."

Lord Carlton raised one dark eyebrow. "You presume to criticize your better?"

"I prefer to think that I am your equal, sir, however inexperienced I may be in *affaires de coeur*. And I do not criticize, I merely observe."

"Be warned, Miss Mathley, I will brook no caretakers."

"But I'm not!"

"You've got that zealous look in your brown eyes, much as you did when you rescued Lydia Brooke. *I* do not require rescue!"

"Certainly not! Only happiness. Do you think you can get it on your own?"

Lord Carlton sighed heavily, folded his arms across his broad chest, and leaned one shoulder against an opposite beech. "I told you long ago that I am reforming. Reformed gentlemen, as a rule, are not happy gentlemen, at least from my observations."

"But as you said, there are exceptions to every rule."

"*You* said that."

"Did I? Well, I was quite right. You are much too skilled at having fun, Peter, and much too adept at seeing the absurdities of life and your own fallibility to do anything but laugh, frequently, at the world. Laughter is a reflection of happiness, is it not? And you have laughed a good deal in the last fortnight, have you not?"

"I am constantly impressed by the twists of logic in that mind of yours."

"My point exactly! It is perfectly logical for you to abandon the bitter cloak and take on the lighter garb of a happy man. Reformation does not necessitate boredom. Merely an occasional and welcome moment of calm."

"Then I am failing miserably, for I have not known a moment of calm since meeting you!"

"Oh, dear," Melinda said, hanging her head, "I am a bad influence."

"You," Lord Carlton said, advancing on her and tilting her chin up with his fingertips, "are a sad romp. I am supposed to be cleaving to propriety through my engagement with you, not rescuing fallen women, forestalling a duel, being pummeled by cows, tumbling into the Wye, and aiding and abetting an elopement! Uncle Gilford would be shocked. *I* am shocked. However did you entangle me in so much mischief?"

"I only asked for your help," Melinda said with a meekness wholly belied by the unholy twinkle of mirth in her brown eyes. "*You* insisted on playing the Good Samaritan."

"I have never," Lord Carlton firmly stated, brushing the tip of her nose for emphasis, "acted the Samaritan for anyone."

"Tell that to the dairymaid," Melinda retorted.

As they had not ridden, they had no need to bathe and change before breakfast and so entered the dining room at an unusually early hour.

"Melinda!" gasped Mrs. Mathley as she sat, very prettily arrayed in a gown of pink silk, at the breakfast table. "What are you doing here? Why aren't you out on your morning ride with Lord Carlton?"

"We took a walk instead," Melinda replied with a demure smile at the earl as she took her place on her mother's right.

Lord Carlton, with a warning glance, sat opposite her.

"Where is Louisa?" Mrs. Mathley inquired. "She's usually down before me."

"I haven't seen her all morning," Melinda said, hurriedly pouring herself a cup of tea.

"Idleness will be the downfall of the empire," Mrs. Wells sniffed. She was a tall woman with graying brown hair, a long thin nose, and an habitually pursed mouth. "*My* daughter is never allowed to remain in bed past nine o'clock in the morning, and I trust, Beatrice," she said, turning upon that selfsame daughter, "that you will employ the same practice with your own children."

"Yes, Mama," Miss Wells meekly replied.

"An excellent rule for every household," Mr. Wentworth agreed.

"Morning," said Harry as he strolled into the breakfast room, removing a slice of toast from a tray on the sideboard. He then took his place at the foot of the table, as was his right. Mr. Mathley and his broken leg were confined to a chaise longue in the study.

"Good heavens," said Melinda in honest amazement. "What are you doing up before noon?"

"Country hours," Harry loftily replied.

"Doesn't Miss Thornton take her morning constitutional shortly?" Lord Carlton inquired.

Harry flushed. "What's that got to do with anything?" he snapped.

"A girl of her beauty must be in need of an escort, don't you think?" said Lord Carlton. "If only to keep away the dogged pursuit of the rest of the competition."

"Ignatious Youngblood seems most determined," Melinda commented.

"And don't forget the ardent Ambrose Hunt," Lord Carlton added.

"Gossip is an ill topic for the breakfast table," Mrs. Wells frigidly opined.

"What are you all talking about?" Mrs. Mathley demanded. "The only Thornton I know is the daughter of our local innkeeper, and you can't think that any gentleman, particularly Harry, would be courting such a creature, can you? Harry is a *Mathley*. He would no more court Miss Thornton than Louisa would court a . . . a swineherd. Ugh! Dreadful smelling fellows, aren't they? Indeed, Harry, your father and I have been discussing it, and we think that you and Lady Edith Shrevely would make a marvelous match."

"Edith?" Harry exclaimed. "Freckle-faced Edith Shrevely *my* wife? Thank you, no, Mama. I'll choose my own bride, if you please."

"Oh, Harry, what nonsense! You can't choose your own wife. We're *Mathleys*. Why, your father and I were promised to each other when I was but thirteen, and even then it took two years of negotiations before we were wed."

"You married at fifteen, ma'am?" Lord Carlton inquired.

"No, no, no, I was eighteen, of course," Mrs. Mathley replied.

"But the arithmetic—"

"Engaged at thirteen," Melinda explained, "sequestered until sixteen, full arrangements debated sixteen to eighteen, debut at eighteen, marriage three months later."

"Ah."

"Edith is a very amiable girl," Miss Wells ventured in little more than a whisper.

"And sensible," added Mr. Wentworth. "She knows the value of a penny and will never be one to outstrip her household budget."

"It was a lovely wedding." Mrs. Mathley rhapsodized. "Everyone was there, even the Prince! When he wasn't so stout, you know. And the Queen was there. And the King would have been there, but he was mad at the time, poor dear. And let me see, who else? Oh, yes, of course, that dreadful Lady Ingram who meant to marry *her* daughter to George. Fortunately, my father knew how to outmaneuver *her*. She was always going on and on about how her dear Marianne was the greatest beauty London had ever seen when everyone knew that *I* was the rage of the ton."

"And still are, ma'am. And still are," Lord Carlton gallantly declared.

Mrs. Mathley blushed a very pretty pink. "Why, Lord Carlton, how kind of you to say so. But really, I'm past my first bloom. Louisa is the beauty of the ton now, and she has made a most brilliant match, don't you think? The marquess is a lovely young man and such a good family and such a large fortune! Why, catching *him* just may reconcile George to your marrying Melinda, you wait and see! I was quite fortunate to catch George's eye . . . well, really his father's eye. I was a beauty, it's true, even Hildegarde owns it! But I had only fifty thousand pounds to my dowry, and that is usually never enough to tempt a *Mathley*."

The earl's eyes widened at this.

"But you had an honorable family behind you, Mama," Melinda said stoutly.

"Yes, yes. There's nothing that can be said against the Baddingtons," Mrs. Mathley said happily.

"The Baddingtons are renowned throughout England," Mrs. Wells declaimed, "for our propriety, our standing in the polite world, and our good breeding."

"Indeed," said Mrs. Mathley, "if we hadn't taken the wrong side in that dreadful affair over Charles II, or was it Charles I? I never can remember. We might well have been earls by now. But alas, great-grandfather Herbert, or was it great-great-grandfather, or was it an uncle? I wish I could remember. Anyway, his head met the chopping block and that was that."

"Alas for England," Lord Carlton murmured.

Mrs. Wells glowered at her sister for revealing this wholly improper piece of family history and took a fortifying sip of tea.

"Ah, there you are, Rutherford!" Mrs. Mathley burbled as the marquess entered the room in all his glory. His morning coat today was lavender, as were his pantaloons, a radically new fashion that had everyone in the room staring at him. "Come sit down and have breakfast," Mrs. Mathley said faintly.

"Good morning, ma'am," said the marquess as he stepped forward and raised Mrs. Mathley's hand to within scant inches of his lips. He greeted the others in the room with a curt nod at each. The marquess was noted for his propriety on any and all social occasions. "Where is Louisa?"

"She is not yet down," said Melinda.

"How unusual," said the marquess as he took his place beside Beatrice Wells. "I thought Louisa to be an early riser. I hope she is not ill."

"Her maid would have informed us of it," Melinda said smoothly.

"I thought we would go on a drive to Putnam Hill today," the marquess said, helping himself to some ham. "Louisa informs me that the view is most pleasing."

"Oh, yes, 'tis a lovely prospect," said Melinda. "You will not find the drive too wearying?"

"No, no," said the marquess with an indulgent smile. "My curricle is well sprung, Miss Mathley, have no fear. Neither Louisa nor I shall be any worse the wear for our little jaunt."

"You must both remember to wear hats," Mrs. Wells stated, "and Louisa, of course, must also carry a parasol, for there is nothing more ruinous to one's complexion or health than the summer sun. Sunlight has never reached the top of Beatrice's head. I won't permit it. My own mother was equally strict, and that is why I enjoy so good a complexion even at my advanced stage of life. You must remember, Rutherford, to hold your team to a walk as you climb Putnam Hill for it will not do to have one of them stumble and throw you both into the road."

The marquess gravely agreed with this, and then launched into a description of the breathtaking vistas one could enjoy from his main seat in Lincolnshire. He had gone on for a good quarter hour, seemingly not pausing to take a breath, when Melinda interrupted by saying she thought she ought to go upstairs and see what was keeping Louisa.

Alas, this ploy was foiled, for suddenly a maid—cap askew, wild-eyed, and distraught—burst into the breakfast room.

"Mrs. Mathley, Mrs. Mathley! It's awful! It's terrible! It's a disaster!" the girl cried, waving a piece of paper in the air.

147

Melinda was instantly on her feet and had placed both hands on the maid's shoulders to keep her from advancing any nearer to her already perturbed mother.

"Calm down, Susan, and try to speak in a rational manner," she commanded.

"But Miss Mathley, your sister has eloped!"

Melinda looked heavenward for one moment, and then ripped the incriminating letter from Susan's hand and hurried up to her mother who was beginning to hyperventilate.

"What's this?" Mrs. Mathley cried. "What's this?'"

"Now, now, Mama, don't upset yourself," Melinda said soothingly.

"Silly girl!" Mrs. Wells bellowed at the hysterical maid. "No Mathley or anyone with Baddington blood has ever eloped!"

"Give me the letter!" Mrs. Mathley quavered.

"Really, Mama, I think I should—"

"The letter!"

Melinda reluctantly placed it in her mother's hands as Susan burst into loud sobs, declaring she should have known something was amiss when Miss Louisa ordered her not to wake her before noon this morning.

Mrs. Mathley began to read the missive as Melinda awaited the inevitable conclusion.

It was said by the Putnam servants that Catherine Mathley's scream could be heard across the whole of Hereford.

She followed this by swooning. Melinda caught her with practiced ease, Lord Carlton instantly at her side to give his support to the plump burden she now held. Together, they leaned her back in her chair. Melinda began to dab at her stricken mother's temples with a moistened napkin.

"Good God, can it be true?" cried Mrs. Wells. "Can Louisa have acted so shamefully?"

"She has indeed eloped, Aunt," Melinda said calmly. "Peter, please be so good as to ring for Addie."

"Louisa's eloped?" Harry cried with delight. "Who'd

148

have thought it of that pudding heart? Whoever did she find to run off with?"

"Clarence Hyde-Moore," Melinda stated.

"But she is to marry *me*!" the marquess protested from the opposite end of the table.

"I fear you have lost your bride, my lord," Melinda replied, beginning to fan her mother. "The letter is dated at midnight last night, so she has been gone nearly twelve hours. There is no way to recover Louisa. She will be wed to Mr. Hyde-Moore by the time any of us reach Scotland, make no mistake."

"But this is an outrage!" the marquess stated, a flush creeping into his cheeks, constrasting hideously with his morning coat. "The marriage contract has been signed! The dowry agreed upon. A wedding date set!"

"It is a terrible blow, I know, sir," Melinda said, still attempting to revive her stricken mother. "But in the end, is it not best that you should escape marriage to a woman who loves another?"

"Love Hyde-Moore? Are you insane?" the marquess exclaimed, wholly astonished. "Are you saying that Louisa loved that . . . that nonentity instead of me?"

Melinda looked up at the marquess, her eyes hard. "Precisely."

"But this is untenable!" the marquess blustered.

"Exactly," Lord Carlton stated. "Consider yourself well out of it, Rutherford."

"That any niece of mine should act in so shocking a manner—" said Mrs. Wells, horror etched on her sharp face.

"What a scandal!" Harry crowed. "Miss Thornton is nothing to this. Wait till I tell Father!"

"Harry, no!" Melinda said sharply. "You will not say a word of this to Father, or I'll have your head. *I* will break the news to him just as soon as I am sure Mama is all right. Oh, where is Addie?"

"Would it not be better if I carried your mother to her room?" Lord Carlton inquired.

"Yes, Peter, thank you," Melinda said gratefully.

"Eloped?" Beatrice Wells quavered. "Louisa actually . . . *eloped* with the man she loves?"

Mr. Wentworth was instantly at her side. "Your nerves have suffered a grievous shock. Come, let me escort you to the gardens. The fresh air will revive you."

"Take your hats!" Mrs. Wells cried.

As Mr. Wentworth led Miss Wells away, Lord Carlton lifted the limp Mrs. Mathley into his arms and carried her upstairs. Melinda opened her mother's bedroom door, and he gently placed Mrs. Mathley upon a large bed topped with a gold-satin-covered comforter.

"Should we send for a doctor?" he asked, looking down at Mrs. Mathley with some concern.

"No, no," Melinda replied as she fetched a large bottle of smelling salts from the overburdened dressing table. "The shock was great, but nothing that I can't handle. If you could keep everyone away from Father until I have a chance to break the news myself, I would be most grateful."

"Are you sure the news would not be better coming from me? He hates me already."

"No, Peter, I don't want him to kill the messenger," Melinda said with a brief smile as she began to wave the smelling salts under her mother's nose. "You've suffered enough on my account."

"You do that with remarkable composure," Lord Carlton noted.

"You have lived with us a week, Peter. Do you not know that Mama is forever fainting at something or another? We will be fine. Go attend my father and *don't* tell him anything. I shall tell him all soon enough."

Lord Carlton obligingly went off to carry out this perilous mission. He had spent no more than five minutes in Mr. Mathley's company since coming to Putman Hall. It would undoubtedly strain their already murky relationship to the greatest extent when he forced himself to outstay his welcome now.

Mrs. Mathley began to revive just as Addie entered the room, carrying a tray.

"I heard the scream, miss," she said noncommittally.

"As did half the county," Melinda said.

"Miss Louisa has eloped, miss?"

"Yes, with Mr. Hyde-Moore."

"Good for her," said Addie.

Melinda cast her a brief smile. "Very good for her. But Mama and Father will not think so for some time to come, I fear."

"Louisa, my baby!" Mrs. Mathley quavered, opening her eyes. "*Louisa!*" she shrieked, and burst into heartrending sobs.

Melinda spent two hours at her mother's side, holding her, drying her copious tears, placing new hartshorn in her trembling hands every few minutes, and eventually soothing her into a fitful sleep.

"You have your work cut out for you, Addie," Melinda said as she walked to the door, the maid taking her place at Mrs. Mathley's bedside.

"No more than I'm accustomed to, miss. Will you tell your father now?"

"Yes. Lord Carlton has been guarding the door."

"Poor man."

Poor man, indeed, thought Melinda as she left the room. She would be astonished to find both of them still alive, or at least unscathed.

She had never had the least predilection for the vapors, but entering her father's study after a timid knock, Melinda felt decidedly dizzy and more than half inclined to slip unconscious to the floor.

There were her father and Lord Carlton seated opposite each other over a chessboard.

"Ha!" said Mr. Mathley. "Check."

151

"Damnation, sir, will you cease hounding me?" Lord Carlton expostulated.

Mr. Mathley chuckled with grim satisfaction. "You've met your match, sir. Concede."

"Never!" said Lord Carlton, advancing his queen. "Do or die is the Carlton creed."

"Checkmate," Mr. Mathley retorted.

Lord Carlton stared at the board. "*Hell* and damnation," he said.

"That's fifty guineas you owe me, sir."

"And well worth it for the lesson, Mr. Mathley," Lord Carlton gallantly replied as he drew out his purse. "Ah, there you are, Melinda. Your father has just trounced me for the second time this morning."

"He is . . . renowned for his ability at the chessboard, sir," Melinda said, forcing herself to rally. "I should have warned you."

"Indeed, you should have," said Lord Carlton, smiling at her knowingly. "A paltry way to serve your fiancé."

"Very paltry, Peter. I *am* sorry."

The earl handed Mr. Mathley fifty guineas. Melinda very much suspected that Lord Carlton had deliberately, and skillfully, lost the two chess games. Her father was a fair chess player, but Lord Carlton had a cooler head and a shrewder mind. He knew when it would profit him to lose and lose well. It was a pity to end this amiable tête à tête.

"I'm afraid, Father, that I've come with some rather difficult news."

"I heard your mother shriek," Mr. Mathley said wearily as he replaced the chess pieces. "What is it this time? Your aunt hounding her again?"

"No, sir. I'm afraid this is quite serious."

Mr. Mathley looked up at her from his chaise.

"It's . . . Louisa, Father. She has eloped to Gretna Green with Clarence Hyde-Moore."

"She *what*?" George Mathley erupted, trying to rise from

152

his chaise and managing instead to twist his broken leg, sending agonizing pain throughout his stout body.

"Last night, sir," Melinda pressed on. "She left a letter. There is no way to recover her. She has too good a lead to Scotland."

"But she is betrothed to *Rutherford*! The announcement was in all the papers!"

"Yes, Father, I know. It is very bad of her. But she was so unhappy trying to do her duty, and she loved Clare so, that I think—"

"*Loved* him?" Mr. Mathley's brown eyes bulged out. "Loved a penniless nothing when she had the Marquess of Rutherford in the palm of her hand?"

"There is more to happiness, Father, than a large fortune and a good title."

"Humbug!"

Mr. Mathley spent a quarter hour venting his spleen by impugning Clarence Hyde-Moore, General Hyde-Moore, and all of the antecedent Hyde-Moores; Louisa's intelligence; the marquess's stupidity in letting such a catch get away from him; and the whole damned generation of girls raised on romantic novels.

Lord Carlton and Melinda wisely let him run his course, making no attempt to interfere.

"They shall never cross my threshold, do you hear me?" Mr. Mathley declared. "Never!"

"But, Father," Melinda said, very pale, "she is your daughter!"

"I disown her from this day forward! She'll get nothing from me but my enmity for the rest of her natural life! No notice shall I give her. No dowry. Nothing! I disown her, I disinherit her, I *disavow* her!"

Melinda's hands were clasped tightly before her. "Father, you are very angry and rightfully so. But do not say things now that you will regret later."

"Regret? *Regret?*" Mr. Mathley sputtered. "It is *she* who will regret this day's work! See how she likes living on

153

nothing. She'll come crawling back soon enough, dishonored and disgraced, and I'll have none of her!"

"I don't believe," said Lord Carlton, flicking open an enamel snuffbox with his thumb, "that a thousand pounds a year is poverty. She will not live opulently, certainly, but she will be comfortable, well clothed and fed, with a good roof over her head. There are many in this land who cannot claim the same."

Mr. Mathley went from vermilion to purple. "She is a *Mathley*, sir! A Mathley has certain standards to uphold, and Louisa has trod them under her feet! She shall suffer the consequences. Not only shall she be barred from this house, she shall be barred from ever consorting with a single member of this family. *No* Mathley shall see her or acknowledge her again!"

"But Father—" Melinda said.

"Leave me!" George Mathley thundered. "I have no more to say to either of you."

Knowing it was useless to remain, Melinda and Lord Carlton soberly left the room.

"That was bad," said the earl, once the study doors were closed behind them.

"Very," said Melinda with a little shudder. "He will eventually recant . . . I think . . . I hope. But it will take some time."

"More time than it would take to acquiesce to having me as a son-in-law?"

Melinda's smile quickly faded. "A good deal longer, sir."

"Did Louisa know?"

"She suspected. I thought it my duty to warn her of the consequences of this elopement, but she had already considered the matter. Her love for Clare was greater than her fear of Father's anger. Good for her, I say, but . . . oh, poor, Louisa! She is so tenderhearted. Father's fury will hurt her badly. Mama won't dare to cross Father by trying to see her, and Louisa and Mama are so close! I shall find a way around his edict, of course—"

"Of course," murmured Lord Carlton.

"—but it will be difficult," Melinda said with a little frown of concentration as they began to walk down the hall. "I do hope she has the sense not to have a child before Father has welcomed her back into the family. A child would just make matters worse."

"Much worse. Still, she had the sense to give up that insufferable marquess for the perfectly decent young man she loves. I think much better of her for it, despite the scandal of Gretna. I see now she had little choice in the matter."

"No, none," Melinda said softly.

"Well, she has your love and support," Lord Carlton said bracingly, "and her husband's as well. She'll do much better than you are currently faring, Melinda."

She looked up at him with a sad little smile. "You *are* sweet. I am grateful to have had your help in this time of crisis, Peter."

"Indeed," said Lord Carlton with remarkable calm. He had never before been termed 'sweet.' "I begin to wonder how you ever managed without me."

"As do I."

✳

Chapter 11

"FINALLY," SAID LORD Carlton as Melinda emerged from her mother's bedroom the next morning. He had been lounging in the hall, his broad shoulders propped against the far wall, for an extensive length of time. "How is your mother?"

"A little better, I think. I've been able to keep Aunt Wells from visiting her, and that has helped enormously."

"Your aunt," Lord Carlton stated, "is a plague. Do you have any idea of the fairy tales she's told your pretty cousin to keep her from my company?"

"Something about ravishing young mothers and eating their babies, wasn't it?"

"Something like that," said Lord Carlton, his blue eyes twinkling. "Come with me, Melinda. You've played the selfless daughter long enough. When you aren't having your mother weep on your shoulder—it's looking a bit soggy, by the by—you're letting your father use you as an audience for all of his bellicose rantings and ravings. It is time to think of yourself, of sunshine, fresh air, pleasure. You do remember what pleasure is, don't you?"

Melinda frowned in concentration. "Vaguely."

"Come with me, we haven't a moment to lose."

Lord Carlton firmly tucked Melinda's arm through his and led her out into the gardens, pointing out to her what flowers he knew and observing that life did exist beyond the walls of Hell House if she would but remember it now and then.

"You *are* chivalrous," Melinda informed him as she

tucked a tulip into his buttonhole, "however much you try to hide it from others . . . and yourself."

"On the contrary, I'm a most selfish beast. There is no one in that house capable of coherent, let alone entertaining, conversation, save you. I am going out of my mind."

Melinda laughed. "This has not been quite the peaceful summer I promised you."

"An understatement."

"But I'm so grateful to have you about. You've been of enormous help."

"You must not let yourself be constantly swept up into fantasies, Melinda," Lord Carlton said as he stared across the gardens at some distant hills, his expression harsh. "I'm a very ramshackle, worthless sort of fellow."

"I will concede that you are ramshackle on occasions. But worthless? How are you worthless?"

He glanced down at her. "A rake and a scoundrel serves no purpose in society save as a topic of conversation."

"But you are *not* a rake and a scoundrel!"

"I have been one, though. Do we ever fully shed our past selves as snakes shed their skins? I think not. Oh, I regret my youthful escapades and the spectacle I made of myself, but it does me little good."

"Oh, what . . . what *humdudgeon*," Melinda said with a stamp of her foot, her arms akimbo. "Never did I think you could be such a cabbage-head. You are a good man, Peter, with your past or without it!"

"Melinda," Lord Carlton said quietly, gazing down at her, "any man who cannot fulfill his responsibilities to his family, his tenants, or even his retainers is not good, he is worthless! A title is nothing, it is the ability to *do* that matters. I have no money to speak of. I have a good many duties and responsibilities, and I can meet none of them for I haven't the blunt to spend!"

"How can an intelligent man believe such rodomontade?" Melinda demanded. "How can a man who sees the folly of this world so clearly insist on believing the . . .

worthless opinion it holds of him? Yes, I say worthless for any uninformed, prejudiced opinion *is* worthless! Prejudice is a *convenience* that allows people like the Vandeveres to continue the fantasy that they are somehow superior to a better-educated man whose understanding, taste, and heart far exceed their own!"

"Very well then," Lord Carlton retorted, rounding upon Melinda, "let's slip this shoe on another foot: *yours*."

"Mine?" she faltered.

"Yours! You may have fooled your family and the blessed ton with your lunatic antics, but I'm on to you, Melinda, don't think that I'm not. This rabid determination of yours to do good in the world, to serve your family, to cater to everyone else's needs at the expense of your own, is merely an attempt to feel important and useful by 'helping' others. You are under the erroneous impression, my sweet, that simply because no *worthy* man has offered for you that *you* are not worthy, and you try to hide this supposed flaw by thrusting yourself into situations where you are not needed!"

"But I *am* needed!" Melinda cried. "Lydia Brooke would be starving on the streets if I had not intervened, Harry would be shot dead by Wilmingham, Louisa and Clare would probably have botched their elopement, the servants would have murdered Father in his sleep by now, and Mama would be in a perpetual swoon!"

"Melinda," Lord Carlton said gently, his hands cupping her face, "I know that you have done much good. Lydia and Harry are much better off because of you. But Louisa and Clare are clever enough to have eloped without your help, servants have their own way of surviving a tyrannical master, and your mother's maid—Addie, isn't it?—is fully capable of keeping Mrs. Mathley conscious and calm. Moreover, your butler and housekeeper are intelligent, skilled people fully capable of running this house without you looking in every half hour or so. Melinda, you are important and useful simply because of who you *are*, not because of what you *do*."

Melinda pulled quickly away, turning her back on the earl and walking a few steps toward a stone bench.

"Melinda—"

"Oh, I'm fine, Peter," she said with a little sniff as she surreptitiously dabbed at her eyes with a handkerchief. "It is just that I have never liked home truths."

"Whiskers again!"

She turned to him with a genuine smile. "Well, I have never liked home truths directed at *me*," she amended. "But I shall take them to heart . . . *after* observing that you did a magnificent job of sidestepping the few shots I sent in your direction."

"You are too quick, Melinda," Lord Carlton said with a woebegone sigh. "Nothing sneaks past you."

"You're much too tall, and I'm a very knowing sort of female."

"We both seem to have acquired negative reputations for what we have done—"

"Rather than for who we are," Melinda concluded. "I knew from the first you were not what the ton said of you."

"And I quickly discovered that you are not at all as mad as you seem." Lord Carlton stopped and cocked his head, studying Melinda intently. "Are we . . . akin to each other, do you think?" he softly inquired.

Melinda felt the heat rise in her cheeks as her heart shuddered in her breast. It was hard not to avert her gaze, but she would not appear missish, especially before Peter Carlton.

"We are . . . alike, perhaps," she said cautiously. "But I pray you, do not tell Father. He would lock me in a nunnery."

Lord Carlton threw back his head and laughed in the sunshine. Melinda's heart turned over.

"*Thank you* for accosting me at the Bascombs' ball," he said simply. "I am a far happier man—reformed or no—

because of it. But what's this I hear from my trusty valet? Something about you planning a ball for next week in the midst of so much weeping and raging?"

"Oh, yes. I always plan a ball for the end of June."

"Whatever for? And why must you do so now of all times?"

"Well, it's something of a tradition, really ... and it is also my birthday."

Lord Carlton stared. "Your birthday? You're to have a birthday next week?"

"Yes. I shall be one-and-twenty, confirming me as an official antidote in the eyes of all my relations. Each Mathley female before me, you see, has always married by the age of twenty. *I* am setting a dangerous precedent."

"Well, there's always Oswald Omersby," Lord Carlton said reassuringly.

"Not even for Father's incipient ulcer," Melinda said with a shudder.

"That's my girl!" said Lord Carlton. "It comes to me in a stroke of genius that your birthday ball is the perfect opportunity to surrender the reins of the household to your trusty butler and housekeeper."

Melinda paled. "But I *always* organize the June ball!"

"My point exactly."

Melinda, at hearing her own words turned against her, promptly stuck out her tongue at the earl, which made him laugh.

"Come," he said, "now that you have partaken of fresh air and sunshine, what would you like to do? A gallop across an open meadow, perhaps? To be trounced at chess? To hear my stirring rendition of *The Rape of the Lock*?"

Melinda laughed. "May I truly choose anything that I want? I'm allowed to on my birthday, you know."

"Anything," the earl magnanimously declared. "This shall be an early birthday present."

"Then I want to play billiards."

"Billiards?"

"Actually, I want to *learn* to play billiards. Father doesn't think it a suitable activity for a female, but I can't see what all the fuss is about. It's not as if I want to put on buckskins and sit astride a horse like a man."

"A most charming picture indeed," Lord Carlton said, gazing down at her with an odd smile. He took her hand in his. "Very well, billiards it is."

In making the request to learn the game, Melinda had in no way anticipated the method of instruction Lord Carlton would employ. It entailed him standing close behind her, his arms around her, as he showed her the proper way to hold and maneuver a cue stick. She had not been in his arms since they had last danced at the Jersey ball in May, and she found it now almost impossible to hear, let alone understand, his instructions, for her heart was pounding painfully in her breast. She was also encountering some difficulty in breathing. She could feel the heat of his body against her. She shivered a little as his lips pressed close to her ear as he murmured further instructions.

She desperately clutched the cue stick as his hands covered hers to guide them to the proper position. Escape suddenly seemed of paramount importance. She turned suddenly in his arms, her excuse dying in her throat as she gazed up at Lord Carlton, her hands pressed against his chest and registering his own erratic heartbeat.

"Your hair is the softest silk," he murmured, his long fingers caressing one auburn ringlet, "and smells of roses and sunshine."

The wild idea that he was going to kiss her flashed into Melinda's mind. Whether it was fantasy or reality she would never know, for there was a discreet cough from the doorway.

"I beg your pardon, Lord Carlton," said Hawkins, the footman, "but there is a gentleman here to see you."

The earl abruptly released Melinda and took a step away from her.

"What gentleman?" he demanded, a trifle harshly.

"He gave his card, sir. Lord Fenwych."

"Jerry? What the devil is he doing here?"

"I've come to garner your c-c-congratulations, of course," said Lord Fenwych as he strolled into the room. "I'm married."

"Married?" said Lord Carlton and Melinda as one.

"To Lydia," said Lord Fenwych with the greatest satisfaction.

"Lydia?" said Lord Carlton and Melinda as one, as Hawkins discreetly left the room.

"Are you foxed?" Lord Carlton demanded, striding up to his friend, grasping him firmly by the shoulders and shaking him vigorously.

"Drunk on l-l-love, perhaps, but nothing more," Lord Fenwych returned with a grin.

"Married?" said Lord Carlton, staring at him. *"You,* married?"

"It happens to the best of us, my dear fellow," Lord Fenwych replied, breaking free to stride up to Melinda. "I m-m-must thank you, Miss Mathley," he said, raising her hand to his lips, "for introducing me to so estimable a young woman."

"This is not some hoax?" she demanded. "You are really married to Lydia Brooke?"

"Why is it so hard for you to believe me?" Lord Fenwych demanded, a trifle put out. "Is not L-L-Lydia beautiful, charming, intelligent, sweet, kind?"

"Yes, all of those things, I'm sure. But you've known her only a fortnight!"

"I married her after only a se'ennight," Lord Fenwych airily informed Melinda. He raised a quizzing glass to one eye as he turned in place. "A charming room, this. In very g-g-good taste."

"I need a drink," Lord Carlton stated as he went to the sideboard.

"Champagne seems appropriate," Melinda said dazedly.

162

He cast her a stern glance. "We will have to settle for port."

"Brandy, at least," Melinda countered.

He glanced at her once again, and then poured out the brandy. He handed the glasses around and raised his own in toast.

"To the most insane summer of my life," Lord Carlton said. He then drained the contents of his glass with a single swallow. The others followed suit. "Very well, Jerry, out with it. *What* has happened?"

"It's all your doing, so d-d-don't go glowering at me!" Lord Fenwych replied, refilling his glass. "There I was, trapped in Lydia's company for two days in a post chaise, and then for five days after that at Aunt Galloway's. How could I not come to love and admire Lydia when her many w-w-worthy qualities were before me day and night?"

"Your aunt—" Melinda began.

"Was the witness," Lord Fenwych supplied.

Lord Carlton's shoulders began to tremble.

"And where is Lydia?" Melinda demanded. "Where is your bride?"

"Oh, I wanted to tell you first, cushion the shock so to speak, b-b-before you see her. She's waiting in the front hall."

"Good God, sir, you are an absolute barbarian to leave Lydia all alone in a strange house!" Melinda cried before she hurried from the room.

"Thought that would give us a moment alone together," Lord Fenwych said with the deepest satisfaction.

"It is clear I must begin to look at you with new eyes," said Lord Carlton, greatly impressed.

"I've learned a lot about women in the last fortnight."

"As have I," Lord Carlton murmured. "Have you told your doting parents the good news?"

Lord Fenwych regarded his shoes for a moment. "T-T-Truth to tell, I'm going to Arrington now. I thought it best

163

to tell them in person, you see. But the thing of it is, P-P-Peter . . . I haven't the least idea how to do it!"

"Ah ha! An ulterior motive for this surprise visit. You've come to me for advice, no doubt, because of my reputation as a—"

"Rake and a scoundrel," Lord Fenwych finished, nodding vigorously. "Exactly. As I recall you had to break all sorts of news to *your* parents when they were alive. What do you advise with mine? H-H-How shall I go about it?"

"Truthfully?"

"Please."

Lord Carlton assumed the stance of one of the more famous orators of the time. He looked most impressive. "I only had recourse to this ploy once in my life, but it proved very effective. I recommend that you write a brief letter, stating the simple facts of the case—I suggest that you claim Master Tristan as your natural son, might as well start the story now as later—post the missive—I'll even frank you—and then embark on a long sea voyage with your wife and son."

Lord Fenwych sat down rather suddenly in a nearby Elizabethan chair. "You think they'll take it b-b-badly, then?"

"I think they'll disembowel you. Get out while you can, Jerry. It's the only way."

"I'm quite fond of the sea, actually," Lord Fenwych mused. "And I've always wanted t-t-to see Rome."

"That's the ticket," Lord Carlton said heartily, clapping him on his back.

"Here is Lady Fenwych," Melinda announced, escorting the blushing bride and slumbering stepson into the room.

Lydia Fenwych née Brooke looked far different from when Lord Carlton had last seen her. She wore a charming pelisse trimmed in ermine, and the ribbons on the hem of her blue gown were copious. Her brown hair had been cropped and modishly styled, with entrancing ringlets teasing her ears. Her face was no longer wan and thin, but pink

164

and pretty, highlighted by a pair of shining gray eyes that gazed at Lord Fenwych with obvious adoration.

The viscount didn't precisely throw himself at her feet, but he came close. He hurried up to her, slipped a protective arm around her waist, and murmured something in her ear that made her blush.

Feminine adoration, Lord Carlton mused to himself, seemed the long hoped for cure-all Gerald, twelfth Viscount of Fenwych, had always needed to remove him from the influence of his domineering father and tyrannical mother. He silently saluted Lady Fenwych.

"What a large house this is," Lydia said shyly.

"My dear Lady Fenwych, I felicitate you," Lord Carlton said, striding up to her and kissing her on both cheeks, which instantly flamed with color. "You have made Jerry a happy man at last and must, therefore, be forever in my debt."

"That is very kind of you, Lord Carlton," Lydia said, nearly inarticulate with shyness at this point.

"Come, come, come. The wife of my best friend must needs be my dear friend as well! I am Peter, and don't you forget that," Lord Carlton said, tapping Lydia on the tip of her nose.

She smiled shyly up at him. "And I . . . Lydia . . . if you would like, sir."

"I like very much," Lord Carlton said, smiling gently down at her.

Lydia began to perceive that the earl was not so fearsome as she had supposed at their first meeting. He was, in fact, rather sweet. She began to understand why her dear Gerald held him in such esteem. Never had she expected such kindness from so lofty a member of the quality!

"And do you like being married, Lydia?" Lord Carlton inquired.

"Oh, sir, I cannot believe that anyone could be this happy! It is like a fairy tale. Gerald has been a knight

165

charging to my rescue, and the amazing thing is that he loves me!"

"Nothing amazing about it," Lord Fenwych said stoutly as he pulled his bride and stepson back into his arms. "Most reasonable thing in the world," he said, kissing her forehead.

"Gerald has brought in his old nurse to help with Tristan," Lydia confided to the others. "She's quite . . . imposing at first, but really she's the dearest thing and I love her already."

"She rules the roost as she's always done," said Lord Fenwych fondly. "She's taken both Lydia and Tristan to her ample bosom and woe betide any man or woman who dares to cross her!"

Melinda laughed. "A comfy household, it seems. But this is astonishing and wonderful! Come, you must tell me all about it. When did you first know you were in love? How did he propose? What was the wedding like?"

For the next hour Lord and Lady Fenwych happily answered all of these and many more questions that Melinda advanced, Lord Carlton looking on with what might have been a sardonic smile had it not been for the affection lurking in his blue eyes as he gazed on this scene. It did not escape his notice that when in company with his wife, the viscount completely forgot to stammer. Lydia Brooke, it seemed, had been a godsend.

Master Tristan at last interrupted the conversation by waking up and announcing that he was hungry. Melinda insisted that not only would the Fenwychs stay to lunch, they would stay to dinner, and stay the week so they might attend her birthday ball before continuing their journey. Lord and Lady Fenwych protested this decree, but Melinda would brook no argument and as neither was eager to break the news of their marriage to Lord Fenwych's parents, they agreed. Lord Carlton was grateful. In love they might be, but Jerry and Lydia were two of the only three sane people

166

in this house, aside from himself, and he wasn't willing to let them go so soon.

As George Mathley was still confined to his study, Catherine Mathley still confined to her sickbed, and the Marquess of Rutherford departed in a huff long since, it was a somewhat diminished party that met at dinner that night. Mrs. Wells, upon ascertaining that the Fenwych marriage had occurred after the entry of Master Tristan into the world, refused to sit down with such shocking adulterers and forbade her daughter and future son-in-law from polluting themselves with such an acquaintance. Basil Hollis, alone, represented the rest of the family. The twins took their dinner in their schoolroom, and Harry was off courting Miss Thornton, so there were only five at the table.

"A bit of a patched up affair," Mr. Hollis commented, cutting into a beefsteak, "but with your fortune behind you, Fenwych, I'm sure you'll carry it off."

"If you can't say anything civil, Hollis, say nothing at all," Lord Carlton said in a low, commanding voice Melinda had not heard before.

"I believe that I may say what I choose in my uncle's home, Carlton," Mr. Hollis retorted.

"Certainly, as long as it is not within *my* hearing."

"*You've* no right to adopt so superior an air! At least Fenwych had the decency to marry *his* indiscretion."

Melinda raised her wineglass at this juncture and calmly poured its contents onto her cousin's lap.

"Oh, my," she murmured, "How clumsy of me."

Mr. Hollis shot up from his chair. "You did that on purpose!"

"Nonsense!" Melinda said with a bland smile. "You know how graceless and clumsy I am, Cousin. You are forever remarking on it."

Mr. Hollis glared at her a moment, and then stormed from the room.

"I always say it's so much nicer having four to dinner,

167

don't you?" Melinda said as Lord Carlton refilled her wine-glass.

The meal continued far more pleasantly, the four talking together long after the cover had been removed. At last Melinda, her arm around Lydia's waist, and Lord Carlton, with Gerald's arm tucked in his, escorted the newlyweds to their room for the night.

"Will Rome be far enough away, do you think?" Melinda inquired as Lord Carlton at last escorted her to her room.

"Just barely," he replied.

"I've always wanted to see Rome. So much history there, so many wonderful pieces of art, so much good food."

Lord Carlton chuckled. "And the wine is superb."

"I begin to envy Lydia and Jerry."

Lord Carlton turned and gazed at the Fenwychs' bed-room door. "As do I," he murmured.

"Everyone's getting married," Melinda said with a little sigh as they reached her bedroom door, "and I haven't got-ten to see a single wedding."

"They're usually a crashing bore," Lord Carlton replied.

"Yes, when they're arranged marriages, to be sure. But when it's a love match . . . I don't know. Somehow they're different, sweeter, more exciting. I can't explain it."

"You don't have to. I understand you perfectly. Good night, Melinda," Lord Carlton murmured, raising her fingers to his lips, holding her hand there a moment longer than was strictly necessary before releasing her and striding down the hall to his own room.

The next three days, in Lord Carlton's experience of the Mathleys, approached the idyllic, primarily because they were spent with none of the Mathleys save Melinda. She and the earl walked the grounds with the Fenwychs, went picnicking and punting and riding with the Fenwychs, and in short, spent a most pleasant three days.

It was the most convivial company—once Lydia over-came her shyness—the earl had ever known. Somehow they all found much to laugh at. They were in perfect agreement on the poets and the playwrights, while Lydia took in good part the teasing she received for stoutly declaring that she *liked* Radcliffe's *The Mysteries of Udolpho.* She made up for this deficiency in her literary taste by having a lovely voice that—cajoled by her doting husband—she used to sing them up and down the Wye. Lord Fenwych became the quartet's clown, Melinda their riveting storyteller, and Lord Carlton the best audience any of them could wish.

On the fourth day of the Fenwychs' visit, Catherine Mathley rose from her bed and, wan and a trifle thinner, appeared once again in the family dining room for lunch. She was warmly greeted by Lord Carlton and Melinda. A hushed inquiry after her health by Beatrice Wells went unheard and Mrs. Hildegarde Wells launched into what had become her habitual tirade against undutiful children and scheming neighbors, which included the emphatic assertion that *her* children would never behave in such an atrocious manner as Louisa had done.

A few tears slipped down Mrs. Mathley's wan cheeks, but with Melinda and Lord Carlton on either side holding her hands, she was able to pull herself together sufficiently to embark on a lengthy, albeit jumbled, monologue sparked by her recollection that Mr. Mathley had warned in Louisa's girlhood that she might be snared by an ineligible bridegroom if they were not on their guard.

"And he was quite right of course," she said with a sniff, "but then George is always right about everything."

"Oh, not everything, madam, surely?" Lord Carlton said with a suspicious twinkle in his blue eyes.

"Yes," Mrs. Mathley replied, nodding like a wise little owl, "everything. Do you know, he even knew that Harry would be a boy, before he was born, I mean. Harry, that is. The minute I told George that I was with child, he declared that the baby would be a boy and refused to discuss it again. I kept asking him what he would do if the baby

169

should be a girl, but George would only say 'It will be a boy' in that dreadfully determined way of his, and then go back to reading his paper. I used to get quite faint at times just considering what might happen if the baby should be a girl—George was so adamant, you see. I kept thinking, what if George makes me raise it as a boy, or perhaps he'd say we had to drown it or expose it like Oedipus and kittens and silkworms, and I didn't know what to do! But Harry was a boy, just like George had said he would be, and so everything was all right."

"I must remember never to question one of Mr. Mathley's decrees," Lord Carlton murmured, buttering a slice of bread. "Heaven knows I would not like to be exposed on a hilltop. Only think of the scandal!"

A shout of laughter escaped Melinda. She quickly clapped a hand over her mouth, glaring at Lord Carlton as he raised an inquiring brow at her. Mrs. Wells directed a piercing glance at Melinda to indicate her displeasure at such a breach of propriety, the Fenwychs hurriedly hid their smiles, while Mrs. Mathley sat at the head of the table at a complete loss to account for this newest example of Melinda's lamentable behavior. She thoroughly agreed with Lord Carlton: being exposed on a hilltop *would* cause a dreadful scandal.

She hurriedly stepped into the gap in the conversation made by Melinda's newest social solecism, and so the meal continued in a generally convivial mood.

They at last disbanded, Mrs. Wells shepherding her daughter and Mr. Wentworth on a constitutional through the Putnam gardens and Mrs. Mathley going upstairs to inquire after the twins. For his part, Lord Carlton began to make his way toward Mr. Mathley's study, as had become his habit, to take yet another drumming in chess.

"I don't know why you insist on thrusting yourself into the lion's den day after day," Melinda said as she escorted him down the hall.

"Don't you?" Lord Carlton said, smiling down at her. "Because I am currying his favor, of course."

Melinda pulled the earl to a stop. "You're not serious!"

"Entirely."

"But whyever would you want *Father*'s favor? He can't abide you!"

"Precisely why I curry his favor. I yearn for the rabid devotion of all of your family, Melinda, saving your aunt and Basil Hollis, of course."

"Good God, why?"

Lord Carlton's smile grew. "Call it a matter of pride. Toddle off now," he said, rapping on the study door. "You needn't thrust yourself into the lion's den unless it's absolutely necessary. You're reforming, remember?"

Melinda wrinkled her nose at the earl and decamped.

Later that afternoon Mr. and Mrs. Hyde-Moore, still in traveling dress, appeared at the front door of Putnam Hall and were denied entrance by the Mathley butler.

"But Reeves," said Louisa, turning ashen, "you must let us in!"

"I'm sorry, Miss Louisa," said the butler, not unkindly. "But Mr. Mathley has left express orders that you are not to enter the hall. That, in fact, you are to be escorted out of Putnam Park, at gunpoint if necessary."

"But Louisa is his daughter!" Mr. Hyde-Moore cried.

"I regret to inform you, sir, that Mr. Mathley has frequently in the last se'ennight stated that he disowns Miss Louisa and any connection she may form."

"At least let me see Mama," pleaded Louisa. "Let her see me and know that I'm all right."

"I'm sorry, miss," Reeves began, but was interrupted as Melinda ran down the stairs.

"Louisa?" she cried out. "Louisa, it *is* you!" she said, throwing herself into her sister's arms. "I saw the carriage from a window and hoped it was you! And Clare!" she cried, hugging her brother-in-law. "Oh, it is so good to see

171

you both! How well you both look. Marriage agrees with you. I knew that it would."

"Melinda," Louisa said, hurriedly brushing away a tear, "Reeves says that we may not enter!"

Melinda glanced at the family retainer, and he, understanding that look, bowed and went back into the hall, shutting the door behind him.

"It is quite true," said Melinda. "Father is in a fury, of course, as I warned you he would be."

"As I knew he would be," Louisa said, shuddering. "But I had no choice—"

"No, no, of course you didn't! It goes without saying."

"But it's been over a se'ennight since we left," Mr. Hyde-Moore protested. "Surely he would have calmed down by now."

"No," Melinda said. "He had such hopes of Rutherford, you see. He's forbade us all to see either of you. Not that *that* matters, of course," she said hurriedly as Louisa sagged against her husband, "for I shall slip away every day to call on you. And I'm sure Annabelle and Margaret will contrive several visits a week. Harry will come, if only to disoblige Father."

"But Mama—" Louisa faltered.

Melinda took her sister's chin in her hand and made her look the truth squarely in the eye. "She dares not oppose Father, at least not now."

"But Louisa is his *daughter*!" said Mr. Hyde-Moore in disbelief. "I've known him all my life, and never have I thought he could be so cold, so hard, so unjust! How can he behave this way to a daughter who has acted honorably by marrying the man she loves?"

"I make no excuses for our father, Clare," Melinda said quietly. "You are perfectly right: he *is* most unjust in this, and unkind. But even this shall pass. We must be patient until he comes around, and he will come around! Louisa is his favorite, you see. That is why he is in such a rage, and that is why he cannot stay mad at her forever. He loves her,

172

he wants what is best for her. If you want to gain entrance into this house, all you have to do is prove to him how happy you can make Louisa. That *you* are, in fact, what is best for her."

"Never fear, I'll do that," said Mr. Hyde-Moore, hugging his wife to him.

"We must be brave," Louisa quavered.

Melinda kissed her on both cheeks. "Peter and I will come visit you tomorrow during our usual morning ride. And the Fenwychs will be with us. Oh, I've so much to tell you! You'll see. You'll have so much company, you'll soon grow heartily sick of us all."

Louisa produced a watery smile. "My dear sister."

Mr. Hyde-Moore led her down the front steps, helped her into the carriage, and then turned back to Melinda.

"He *will* come around?"

"I give you my word, Clare."

"Then we can be happy, in spite of him."

Mr. Hyde-Moore stepped into his carriage. With a flick of the whip, the coachman bowled down the gravel drive.

Melinda had not the heart to enter Putnam Hall just yet, so she walked down the front steps and struck out toward the woods to the east, a favorite walk of hers whenever her thoughts oppressed her, as they did now. She had not gone more than a dozen yards into the woods when she found herself stumbling a good deal, for it was difficult to see through the haze of tears. She sat down on an ancient stump, drew out her handkerchief, and wept wholeheartedly.

"What's this?" a gentle voice murmured. Warm fingers brushed the tears from her cheeks. "Mad Melinda crying? It is not to be thought of!"

Melinda gave Lord Carlton a watery smile as he knelt before her. "I'm being very silly," she said.

"Sorrow is never silly. But refusing to share it is. Come, what's the matter?"

"Louisa and Clare were here."

"Yes, so Reeves informed me."

"It's just not fair!" Melinda burst out. "They love each other. They're happy together. And yet, they can't fully enjoy their happiness because of *Father* and his . . . *willfulness* and pride! When two people love each other, they have the right to be happy, don't you think?"

"Yes. Yes, I do," said Lord Carlton.

"When I think of poor Louisa, in what should be the happiest days of her life, crying herself to sleep because of Father's odious edict—"

Lord Carlton uttered a cough. "You'll forgive me, Melinda, but I think you're off by a good mile there."

She looked up inquiringly to find one of the earl's more mischievous, not to say wicked, grins twinkling at her. "How so?" she demanded suspiciously.

"She has a husband to . . . distract her from any unhappy thoughts at night."

A blush flamed in Melinda's cheeks. "Oh, you are a scoundrel!"

Lord Carlton laughed. "Besides, if Louisa and Clare love each other as much as I believe they do, *these* are not the happiest days of their lives. The coming years will provide those as they grow into their union and bring children into that union. As I understand it, the first weeks of wedded life are often pure, unmitigated hell for a bride and groom. The Hyde-Moores are no exception. It takes a bit of getting used to, to become the mistress of a new home, the husband of a new bride. Old George's edict is probably a blessing in disguise. It gives them the chance to grow accustomed to their change in circumstances, to grow into their new roles, if you will, unencumbered by parental snooping and unsolicited advice. Why, it's probably the best thing that could have happened to them!"

"Doing it *much* too brown, Peter," Melinda stated, trying to hide her smile.

"On the contrary! I have just waxed lyrical on a subject

174

of which I know nothing. Uncommonly daring of me, don't you think?"

"You *are* an idiot," Melinda said fondly.

"That is not an original accusation," Lord Carlton said, offering her his hand. "Come, walk with me through this sylvan glade. Let us pretend for a few brief, glorious moments that George Mathley does not exist, that your mother is not a complete rattlepate, and that the twins are not hoarding a secret snake collection in their room."

"Oh, bother," Melinda said with a laugh as she placed her hand in Lord Carlton's and stood up, "is that what they're secreting?"

"I was admitted into their confidence when I was able to inform them with some certainty that garden snakes are not poisonous."

"And what do you know about snakes?" Melinda demanded as he tucked her arm through his and led her farther into the woods.

"I, my dear Melinda, had the best snake collection in all of Yorkshire when I was a lad," Lord Carlton loftily replied. "My mother fainted dead away when she discovered them one day in my book chest. It was the most fun I had that entire summer."

*

Chapter 12

"I won!"

"Did not!"

"Did *too*!"

"You cheated!"

"Did not!"

"Did too!"

"Haven't you two caused enough mischief without starting a public brawl?" Melinda demanded as she advanced upon the twins, who were locked in heated verbal combat at the foot of Putnam's grand staircase. "I still have nightmares about that parrot."

"We were having a championship banister race," Margaret said righteously, "and I won."

"Did *not*!" Annabelle exploded.

"Did too!"

"You cheated!"

"Did not!"

"Did—"

"I believe," Melinda remarked with some asperity, "that this is where I came in. I should like to know, Annabelle, just how you think Margaret cheated."

"False start," Annabelle declared.

"Did *not*!" Margaret shouted.

"Did too!"

"Did not! I'm the champion and that's that!"

"Now wait just a minute," Melinda said. "You are no

176

more the banister racing champion than Annabelle because *I* am already the champion."

"What a fudge," Margaret retorted with no hint of respect toward her elder sibling.

"I, my dear child, won the title nine years in a row against both Harry and Louisa," Melinda stated.

"But that was years ago," Annabelle countered. "It don't mean a thing now."

"Unless," Margaret said with sudden inspiration, "you race *us* today!"

Melinda regarded her sisters with growing alarm because she was pretty well convinced that a banister race would be great fun, even at her advanced age. *Mad Melinda* began pounding on her brain.

"Don't be absurd," she said hastily. "Why, I haven't . . . I am twenty and I can't possibly . . ." She ground to a halt. "Champions don't have to accept a challenge."

"You're just scared," Margaret said.

"I am not," Melinda said with some heat.

"Are too!" Annabelle and Margaret chorused.

"It is just that my racing days are over."

"Then you can't be champion," Annabelle stated.

"Well, I'll not stand by and allow either of you two upstarts to claim the title!"

"It can't be helped," Margaret said. "If you won't race us, you have to forfeit the title."

The nine victories she had claimed in the ancient and noble art of banister racing were dear to Melinda's heart. She could no more forfeit them than she could let Harry die at Wilmingham's hand.

"I'll judge the first race," she said, squaring her shoulders, "and the loser can judge the second."

Ecstatic shrieks greeted this proposal as Annabelle and Margaret dashed upstairs to the starting line. After nervously checking to the left and the right (her parents disapproved most vehemently of such activities and Mrs. Wells was rabid on the subject), Melinda looked up the long curved staircase and watched as the twins positioned themselves at opposite banisters.

Just as she was about to give the signal to start, the footman Hawkins cleared his throat and said, "I beg your pardon, miss—"

Melinda hurriedly shooed him away.

"Ready?" she called up to the twins.

They answered in the affirmative. Hearts pounding, they heard at last that treasured cry: "Go!" Adrenaline surging through every capillary, Annabelle and Margaret threw themselves up and astride their respective banisters with a speed connoting great skill. Dresses hiked up to midthigh, they began the long and arduous slide downward. Every nuance of the fine art of banister racing was brought into play: the most effective positioning of the body for speed and balance; the light touch of the fingers on the rail for guidance; the eyes constantly alert to determine which new curve or bump was approaching.

They swung neck and neck into the last long sweeping curve. But Annabelle's balance faltered for a fraction of a second, and Margaret swept into the lead. The race was over in the next moment. Margaret sailed backward off the end of her banister to land, in excellent form, upon her feet a good yard from the staircase. Annabelle, desperately trying to at least tie her odious sister, threw caution to the wind as she opted for speed over balance and consequently flew in a haphazard fashion off her banister to land most painfully upon her derriere on the tiled floor.

Margaret, at first overcome by a fit of very ungracious laughter, began to crow: "I win! I win! That's twice now, Annabelle, and that proves I'm champion."

"You have yet to race me," Melinda reminded the upstart in icy tones. "I would not place the laurels upon your head just yet."

"Now or one minute from now, what's the difference," Margaret retorted as she sauntered back up the stairs. "Coming?"

"With pleasure," Melinda muttered.

She picked up the despondent Annabelle, and after ascertaining that nothing was damaged save her pride, she followed Margaret up the staircase, grimly determined to prove the superiority of age and experience over youth and exuberance. She took up her position opposite Margaret, one hand clasping her skirt, the other placed firmly upon the banister, as her heart began to pound beneath her bodice.

"Ready?" Annabelle glumly called up to them.

"Ready," Melinda and Margaret said as one.

Both heard in the same instant Annabelle's starting cry. They threw themselves into position to begin their slippery trek downward . . . to the vast amusement of Lord Carlton who had been standing well back with Hawkins (who had, in good faith, tried to announce that his lordship had returned from his trip to the village and wished a word with Melinda) from the beginning of the competition.

Despite the restrictions of her adult female attire, and blissfully ignorant of the earl's presence, Melinda had been able to claim a good position upon her banister. Margaret, however, to whom modesty meant nothing, had slung herself into position, revealing two strong adolescent legs as she swept to an early lead over the first quarter.

By the halfway post, however, Melinda had pulled even with Margaret. Excitement coursing through her veins, every fiber of her being focused on the perils of the race, Melinda saw from the corner of her eye that she had actually begun to take the lead at the three-quarter post, having negotiated the long sweeping curve in excellent form. With one last adrenaline-fed effort, she slid into the homestretch.

"I win!" she cried out just as she flew backward into the air and landed solidly against a tall male form that collapsed beneath her with a startled "Oomph!"—two strong arms reflexively wrapping themselves around her.

Giving her head a shake to collect her scattered wits, Melinda found herself sprawled upon Lord Carlton, who was convulsed with laughter, as were the twins, and Hawkins who had remained on the sidelines. An image of herself, legs and arms flying as she sailed into the earl, flashed into Melinda's mind, and she succumbed to an overpowering fit of giggles, her head sinking down upon Lord Carlton's broad chest.

"I must say," Lord Carlton said, gasping for air, "that that was the most enthusiastic welcome I have ever received."

This shattered the last shred of decorum to which Melinda had clung. Peal after peal of laughter tumbled out of her as she and Lord Carlton lay sprawled on the floor, too weak from hilarity to move.

"Not the most elegant finish I've ever observed," said his lordship, when Melinda at last dragged herself off of him and he was able to sit up.

"But I won," Melinda said triumphantly as she sat beside him on the floor. "I am now the undisputed banister racing champion of the Mathley household."

"Let the world tremble at your feet!" Lord Carlton pronounced, which sent Melinda into another fit of giggles. Grinning, he stood up and then, bending down, got a firm grasp on her arms and, with very little effort, pulled her to her feet. Still holding her, he said, "You will have to race me sometime if you ever fancy stiffer competition."

Melinda found herself staring up into Lord Carlton's dark blue eyes, suddenly aware of their hidden highlights and depths, and overwhelmingly conscious of the closeness of his sensual mouth, his strong arms, his muscular body. Her heart pounding out of all proportion to the exertion of the race or the succeeding laughter, Melinda could think of nothing to say for the first time in their acquaintance.

As Lord Carlton made some comment upon his own superior form and many years of training and expertise in the ancient and honorable sport of banister racing, Melinda realized how much she relished the sound of his voice, the touch of his hands upon her flesh, and the close proximity of his tall, masculine form. It came to her rather suddenly, with great force, and with no effort whatsoever that she loved Peter Carlton. This revelation so stunned Melinda that she could only stand, dumbstruck, staring up into the earl's handsome face. A quizzical smile tugged at his lips.

"Are you all right, Madam Champion?"

This commonplace civility succeeded in returning Melinda to a more coherent frame of mind.

"Oh . . . oh, yes!" she said hastily as she backed away from him.

"You seem a bit dazed."

"The thrill of victory and all that," Melinda said as she ran a trembling hand through her tousled auburn locks, and gazed at everyone and everything in the entry hall save Lord Carlton. "What in the world are you doing back so early from town? I thought you had gone seeking asylum."

"I found it in a pint of beer and have returned to turn the reins of my chestnuts over into your capable hands for the afternoon drive I promised you."

"I beg your pardon! I had quite forgotten. The race distracted me. It will take me just a moment to change. Girls," Melinda said rather desperately to her sisters, "you really must return to your schoolroom. Come along now."

"You were wonderful, Melinda, simply wonderful!" Annabelle rhapsodized. "And you *aren't* the champion, Margaret, so there!" she said, sticking her tongue out at her twin.

Melinda refereed the ensuing argument all the way up the stairs.

"A *most* remarkable young woman," Lord Carlton murmured.

"Yes, my lord," said Hawkins, studying him closely.

Melinda, meanwhile, ushered the twins into their schoolroom, freed their governess from the closet in which they had locked her, locked the schoolroom door behind her, went into her own room, and locked the door after her. Glancing into a mirror, she saw not Melinda Mathley, daughter of an ancient and respected family, but a madwoman, hair flying in all directions, cheeks bright pink, brown eyes shining, breast palpitating.

In love with Peter Carlton! How could she have been so stupid?

But how could she not have fallen in love with him? Melinda groaned and sat wearily upon her bed. His ability to cut to the heart of a matter, his quick mind, sense of humor, and large heart seemed to have been designed expressly to appeal to her. He was real and fallible and wonderfully honest, and she loved him. Loved him wholeheartedly. Loved him with every breath she took. Would love him until her dying day.

For weeks she had thought she was using Peter for her own ends, when in fact she had been *pursuing* him from the very start!

Groaning, Melinda fell back onto her bed. *This* was why she had wanted the false engagement. *This* was why she had involved him in every adventure that came her way. She loved him, she wanted to be with him, however uncomfortable the circumstances. They *were* akin to each other, for Melinda, at least, had truly found herself in Peter. Both had accepted the ton's judgement of themselves, both had been hurt, both had been wrong. It was a revelation to see herself as Peter saw her, not as the ton saw her. She had begun to reclaim her true self from the moment she had first gazed up into Peter Carlton's blue eyes.

Had she in any way been able to do the same for him? Oh, she hoped she had! She hoped he had begun to see himself, not as the rake and scoundrel the ton considered him, but as the good, kind man he truly was. How she hoped he had learned this truth, for she loved him and wanted no pain to touch him, no unease to disturb his mind.

She loved him. And loving him, what could she expect?

A future without Peter Carlton at her side not only held no allure, it was impossible to consider. So she did not consider it. She would turn her fictitious fiancé into a real husband because there was no other option. There were obstacles in her path, certainly. More like the Swiss Alps standing in her way. She had nothing to recommend her to him save a good head of auburn hair and a decent set of teeth.

This was not hopeful. Peter Carlton was used to dangling the most beauteous damsels in his train. Still, she seemed to have the knack of making him laugh, and that skill was far more valuable than beauty. Really it was. Perhaps if she could keep in his company long enough, he would find other things to like in her. If she could only stay at his side, he might grow to appreciate her, to become fond of her.

"Well, it's a plan," Melinda said, getting off her bed and tugging the bell rope for her maid, "and it will do until something better comes along."

Guests began arriving for Melinda's birthday ball three days before the event. One of the first was her good friend, Miss Elizabeth Jonson, who brought the glad tidings that she was engaged to marry Lord Dennis. She also brought Lord Dennis. It took but a day for Melinda to acknowledge that Lord Dennis was a worthy man, sensible, and sincerely fond of her best friend. By nightfall she was perfectly reconciled to the engagement. Dramatic exhibitions of romance—as Clare and Louisa had provided—were not, after all, for everyone.

Putnam Hall was large, but so was Melinda's acquaintance, and soon the house was full to overflowing with, as the irritable George Mathley put it, the greatest convocation of jabberers in the British Isles.

Lord Carlton was tempted at first to agree with his host, until he found much to amuse him in the jabberers. They certainly talked a good deal, but with Melinda as their friend the earl thought this merely followed from a keen sense of self-preservation. Even he was talking more than he ever had in his life. Her friends were all well-educated, opinionated, witty (even the most demure), and after an initial cautious survey, broad-minded enough to admit him into their circle and think no more of his past. Even the punctilious Miss Elizabeth Jonson had sat beside him throughout an entire tea and calmly conversed with him on the history of Putnam Park. The earl felt very much as if the world had been turned upside down.

He also grew more and more concerned as the day of the ball advanced, for Melinda had gone an entire se'ennight without an adventure, let alone any form of disaster, and he was convinced that such an unnatural state of affairs could only be ended by an eruption of volcanic proportions. He awaited the event with both trepidation and keen anticipation for he had discovered that he had never had half so much fun as when he was caught in the midst of one of Melinda's schemes.

"Happy birthday!" shrieked the twins as they jumped on their sister.

Melinda, who had been asleep in her bed until this moment, neither screamed nor boxed the twins' ears, for this was their habitual greeting on her birthday since that first treacherous day they had learned to walk. She was long inured to the ritual. She wrestled them both onto the bed, gleefully tickling them without respite until, screeching for mercy, Annabelle and Margaret tumbled off the bed and demanded to know how it felt to officially be the first Mathley old maid.

"Get out or die," Melinda said sweetly.

Giggling, the twins ran from the room. Melinda composed herself, settling the covers about her as she awaited her habitual morning tray of hot chocolate and buttered bread.

One-and-twenty and unwed. Ah, well. There were worse fates. Oswald Omersby came to mind. Nor had she learned to despair of Lord Carlton. While she could not credit that he had formed a *tendre* for her, he seemed to genuinely enjoy her company, which she had inflicted upon him at the least opportunity. With George Mathley's leg broken and Louisa eloped, she doubted if her father's temper would cool enough in the next month to acquiesce to her faux engagement. So she had time on her side in the siege for Peter Carlton's heart. But how was she to carry the day?

Unable to seek advice from any knowing female as to how to capture a man's heart, for all of the knowing females in her acquaintance would whisk her off to Ireland rather than see her carry off Lord Carlton, Melinda had no one to turn to for the advice she sought. Elizabeth Jonson was a case in point. At every private meeting or tête à tête, she admitted Lord Carlton's amiability and still tried to impress upon Melinda the impropriety of wedding such a one as he. Melinda could answer each argument with aplomb, but it was wearying and depressing as well. How could she convince her father to like Lord Carlton, when she could not even convince her best friend to acquiesce to the earl's better qualities? It was sweet of Elizabeth to be concerned for her, but why could no one see Peter's large heart and generous nature, devilish whimsy, and gentle kindness, as she did? It seemed that for the whole of her life she had seen everyone and everything in the world differently from everyone else, and now she was being made to suffer for it.

She put away these thoughts as Maria, her maid, entered the room with a cheery "Happy birthday, miss" and a tray bearing a cup of hot chocolate and a slice of bread and butter. Thus fortified, Melinda dressed in a new riding habit and went downstairs for her habitual birthday morning gallop. Not a step did she direct toward the dining room. No one had ever been able to convince Catherine Mathley that breakfast must and should be taken before eleven in the morning. As there were a good three hours before breakfast could be hoped for, Melinda could look forward to a long ride.

She found Lord Carlton waiting for her at the bottom of the stairs.

"Happy birthday, my dear. Why, you look no older than twenty," he greeted her, looking her up and down.

"You are too kind," Melinda dryly replied.

Anything else she might have said was interrupted by a *whoosh!* on either side of her as the twins came sailing down the handrails of the grand staircase.

"Ha! That's twice I've beaten you now!" said Annabelle. "That proves I'm better."

"You must have gained weight," Margaret said suspiciously.

"Not a bit of it. I've just more skill, and it's time you acknowledged it."

"Never!"

And so the battle might have been joined had not Melinda stepped in at this juncture. "How are your snakes?" she inquired.

"Splendid!" said Margaret, instantly distracted.

"One of them shed his skin yesterday," said Annabelle.

"We're saving all their skins," Margaret said.

"For what purpose?" Melinda demanded uneasily.

The twins grinned at her. "We don't know yet," said Margaret.

"But something splendid," said Annabelle.

"Something to frighten Aunt Wells," Margaret suggested.

Annabelle's eyes glowed. "That's brilliant!"

"Do not discuss the details in front of me, I beg you," Melinda stated. "Let me reap the pleasures of the aftermath and know nothing of the plot. Are you ready to go romping?"

"Yes!" the twins chorused.

"Do you mean to tell me," said Lord Carlton, arms akimbo as he feigned outrage, "that these grubby infants are to accompany us?"

"We always have a morning gallop with Melinda on her birthday," said Annabelle.

"It's tradition," Margaret said.

"Ever since they could sit a horse," Melinda said, gazing

wryly up at Lord Carlton. "I hope you won't mind the escort."

"But can they keep up with us?" Lord Carlton demanded.

"We'll outpace you," said Annabelle.

"Just you wait and see," Margaret said.

"That is a challenge no red-blooded Englishman could withstand. Come along, ladies. The morning awaits."

They returned two hours later, gloriously windblown and dusty, out of breath, cheeks bright with exercise and sunshine and laughter.

"Good God!" drawled Basil Hollis in the entry hall as, raising a quizzing glass to one disapproving eye, he surveyed Lord Carlton from head to toe. "I trust you do not mean to breakfast in that horrific state. I shall quite lose my appetite if you do."

"Have no fear, Hollis," Lord Carlton replied as he watched Melinda race the twins upstairs, beating them only by a step. "I intend to change into proper raiment."

"I take it you've been cavorting with the Mathley hellions," Mr. Hollis said, studying the earl's dusty riding boots through his quizzing glass with a look of utter disgust. "I own it has been an amazing fortnight watching you play the devoted fiancé, playmate to those two monsters, consoler to my ninnyhammer of an aunt, adviser to my wastrel cousin Harry, and boon companion to my vermilion-hued uncle. It has been a most entertaining performance, Carlton. How long do you think you can keep it up?"

The earl eyed Mr. Hollis with distaste. "And what role would you have me essay?" he inquired in a silky voice that unfortunately did not alarm Mr. Hollis.

"Why, the wooer of women, of course. Come, come, Carlton! There are a bevy of beauties currently housed in the hall. Surely you would find your time more profitably spent pursuing their charms rather than trying to find some topic of conversation with my Friday-faced cousin. Why on

187

earth are you marrying her? Oh, yes, yes, yes, I know. Her fortune is wonderful. But, good God, Carlton, there are literally dozens of beautiful, rich women in the kingdom. Perhaps hundreds. With your face and figure and title, you could have them flinging themselves at you with just the slightest nod of your head. Why settle for Cousin Mel?"

There was a dangerous glint in Lord Carlton's blue eyes that belied the casual attitude he affected. "You have succeeded once again, Hollis, in revealing yourself as a rag-mannered, nearsighted swine. Melinda Mathley is superior to every other young woman in the kingdom, rich or no. And if you had any heart or a mind that could comprehend real goodness rather than the netherworld of sycophants, jealousy, and bitterness that you inhabit, you would know it. One who tries to impress the world with his superiority by sneering at others, merely impresses the world as an ill-bred, distempered boor who delights in pulling wings off of butterflies."

Lord Carlton strolled upstairs, leaving Mr. Hollis behind to seethe with impotent and inarticulate fury.

In his heyday, Lord Carlton had been a man known to dally a good three-quarters of an hour before his mirror getting his neckcloth just right. It had come to him in Yorkshire that this was a silly waste of his valuable time, and he had become, to his valet's great distress, a quick dresser. He had already bathed and changed into proper morning attire when he knocked on Melinda's door to find his faux fiancée just finished with her own bath and clad in nothing but a black velvet dressing gown embroidered with emerald green vines, her auburn hair a charming tumble about her shoulders.

"You should wear your hair down more often," Lord Carlton observed as he sauntered into her room, "it suits you."

"Peter, what are you doing? Get out! Get out before someone sees you!" Melinda demanded, a blush burnishing her cheeks.

"Who is to see me but you and your maid, and I am certain that your maid—Maria, is it not?—will keep silent. As for you, well of course silence is too much to hope for, but nevertheless . . . I've brought you your birthday present."

Pink crept higher into Melinda's cheeks as surprise lit her brown eyes. "Peter! You shouldn't have. I never expected—"

"No, that is your one fault, Melinda. You never expect what is your due."

She held the flat, gaily wrapped box in her hands, staring at it almost with disbelief. "May I open it now?"

"Please do."

Rampant curiosity drove her to be less than tender with the wrapping paper. It was soon removed, the box opened. The only sound in the room was Melinda's sharp intake of breath.

"*Peter!* It's . . . incredible!"

"Quite beautiful, I agree. And just a trifle flashy, as you requested."

Lord Carlton removed the necklace from the box. Melinda seemed rooted to the spot. He slipped the necklace around her slim throat, securing it in the back, and then, hands on her shoulders, pushed her in front of her mirror.

"There," he murmured, "it looks as well as I thought it would."

It was a ruby necklace. A dozen small red jewels caught in gold netting. Melinda stared at herself. She looked . . . different somehow.

"But . . . But Peter, you can't give me such an incredible gift! It's . . . It's . . . It's *improper!*"

Lord Carlton gave a shout of laughter. "Your version of propriety has differed so often from the world's that that argument won't fadge, my girl. It looks very well on you, Melinda, and I'll not take it back. It was my mother's, and her mother's before her. I've wanted you to have it for some time. Your birthday was as good an excuse as any."

Melinda spun around, face pale, eyes wide. "Your moth-

189

er's? Oh, well that's that, then. I cannot accept it, Peter," she said, beginning to work at the clasp at the back of her neck. "You will want to give it to your wife when you marry someday."

Lord Carlton took her hands and firmly held them in his own. "Nonsense! You would condemn this necklace to gather dust in a bank vault somewhere, for what sensible woman would have me?"

Melinda stared up at him, dizzy and hot and uncaring of anything but truth. "I—" she began and was instantly thwarted by an eager rap on her door, followed instantaneously by the entrance of Annabelle and Margaret, bathed and dressed, their brown locks in a far from decorous jumble on top of their heads.

"Come on!" Annabelle said. "I'm starving!"

"And we want to see your presents," Margaret added.

"I shall be down presently," Melinda said as she tried to get her heart to start beating again and remove the blush from her cheeks. Never had she thought she would be grateful for the twins' rudeness!

"Well at least you can come along, Lord Carlton," said Annabelle, grabbing one of his hands.

"Yes," said Margaret, taking his other hand. "We want to hear the rest of the story you started about climbing on the window ledge outside your aunt's bedroom to release two dozen spiders onto her bed. However did you catch so many spiders?"

Lord Carlton was borne relentlessly away on this adolescent tide of enthusiasm. They were gone. Melinda turned to stare at herself once again in the mirror, the dark rubies glittering just a little in the light.

Breakfast was held in the formal dining room, for it had the only table large enough to accommodate all of the Mathleys, the Wellses, Mr. Hollis, Mr. Wentworth, and twenty other houseguests. Melinda, in a new morning gown of beige with gold piping, entered the room to a thunderous applause and hearty cries of "Happy birthday!" She

190

dropped them all a low curtsy before walking with stately grace to her place of honor beside her mother at the head of the table.

Breakfast, despite the stiffly formal presence of Hildegarde Wells and the mocking sneer of Basil Hollis, was a merry affair as Melinda opened her many birthday presents, exclaiming equally over a Norwich silk shawl from her mother, a Greek figurine from Elizabeth Jonson, and a volume containing the legends of Robin Hood from the twins. George Mathley, who had advanced to crutches, benevolently presided over this festive meal from the foot of the table, his broken leg propped up on a chair.

"The birthday wish! The birthday wish!" the twins cried when all of the presents had at last been opened and most of the breakfast consumed.

"Yes, yes," said Mr. Mathley, calming his daughters. "It is time once again, Melinda, for your birthday wish. Ask for whatever you want, and you shall have it."

"Oh, that is simplicity itself," Melinda replied.

Mr. Mathley leaned back in his chair with a genial smile. "Ah! I knew it. Once again you want to wear the Mathley sapphires at your birthday ball."

"On the contrary, Father. Lord Carlton has given me a necklace that I wish to wear tonight. You will hold to your promise, won't you, that I may have whatever I want today?"

"Oh, certainly. I can probably return it to the store tomorrow," Mr. Mathley replied, which made several of his guests laugh at his returning wit. "What is your wish, Melinda?"

"I want to have Louisa, Clarence, and General Hyde-Moore attend my birthday ball tonight."

There was a stunned silence at the table. Even the twins paled. This was followed by an uneasy shifting en masse in the gold brocade dining chairs as Mr. Mathley's face turned vermilion.

"Have I, or have I not, said that they shall never cross

191

the threshold of my home again?" he demanded in an awful voice.

"But this is my home as well, Father, is it not?" Melinda riposted with admirable calm.

Lord Carlton found that he was holding his breath.

"And you did avow before everyone present that I might have anything I desired for my birthday wish," Melinda relentlessly continued. "I want the Hyde-Moores. I don't say that they should move in with us. I don't say that you should ever let them in the house again. You need not even acknowledge their presence tonight. But for this one night, for my birthday ball, I want them here with me and for you to restrain yourself from throwing them out or causing a scene."

"Reeves!" Mr. Mathley thundered as he struggled to rise from his chair. *"Reeves!"*

The butler was instantly behind him, helping him up, getting his crutches situated properly, and helping Mr. Mathley stump from the room.

"Oh . . . my," said Mrs. Mathley faintly.

"Well," Melinda said brightly, "that went much better than I expected."

Lord Carlton rose from his chair, walked up to Melinda, and raised her hand to his lips.

"You have the heart of a lion, my dear, the wits of a fox, and the survival instincts of a lemming."

Melinda burst out laughing. "It's his broken leg, you see. He can't throttle me if he can't catch me."

This set everyone else (except, of course, for Mrs. Wells and Mr. Hollis) to laughing and broke the tension that Mr. Mathley's outburst had generated.

Melinda, with the help of two footmen and her maid, carried her booty up to her room, distributing and arranging the gifts in her bedroom and sitting room to her satisfaction. She had just started downstairs as Lord Carlton started up, when Annabelle and Margaret grabbed her arms and held her back.

"Melinda!" Annabelle whispered hoarsely. "We need your help!"

"Oh, bother, what now?" Melinda moaned.

"It's not a crisis," said Margaret. "Only a . . . difficulty."

"I can't tell you how relieved I am," Melinda replied, forcing back a grin. "What is it now?"

"Archie and Fanny have escaped!" Annabelle said.

"Who?" Melinda inquired faintly.

"Two of our snakes," said Margaret.

Melinda's life flashed before her eyes. "How many do you have?" she quavered.

"Five, only there's three now," Annabelle said.

"Could not they have been . . . eaten?"

"Oh, don't be silly," Margaret said with disgust. "Snakes aren't cannibals."

"Pity," said Melinda as Lord Carlton reached her side.

"Why the look of comic dismay, my sweet?" he inquired of her. "What new mischief is afoot?"

"Not mischief," Melinda said with a shudder, "disaster in the making."

"I expected nothing less. What is it this time?"

"Archie and Fanny have escaped," said Annabelle.

"Good God. We must begin searching for them at once," said Lord Carlton.

Melinda stared at him. "You know who Archie and Fanny are?"

"Well of course. After my initiation into the Secret Snake Society, I was consulted about reptilian name preferences. I instantly thought of my plethora of greedy cousins and named the snakes accordingly. Come along, we haven't a moment to lose. We don't want some hapless maid discovering them in a linen cupboard."

"Maybe they've been kidnapped!" Margaret said.

"Who would want them?" Melinda demanded.

"Harry might have taken them," Annabelle retorted.

"Did Harry know about them, too?"

193

"No. But you never know what Harry's going to get up to," said Margaret.

"But Miss Thornton does," said Lord Carlton, casting a grin at Melinda before following the twins into their room. "Very well, where do you keep them?"

The twins lifted a large dollhouse off its stand, which, as it turned out, was hollow and housed three snakes entangled in their early afternoon nap.

"Looks like five to me," Melinda said.

"Don't be a wet goose," Annabelle commanded. "Anyone can see it's three snakes."

"Indeed," said Lord Carlton severely. "I am amazed, Melinda, that you can be so unobservant."

"You should be currying *my* favor, not theirs," Melinda warned. "After all, I am the one arranging the place cards for dinner tonight."

"I hang upon your lips, my dear," Lord Carlton avowed. "What shall we do first?"

"Well, the first thing is to search this room," said Melinda, looking about her.

"But we've done that!" said Annabelle.

"Thoroughly!" Margaret appended.

"We will do it again," Melinda said. "And then we will check your schoolroom. Hurry, girls! We must find those wretched snakes before anyone else does!"

Melinda and Lord Carlton thoroughly searched the twins' bedroom. They looked in toy chests, on tea tables, through wardrobes and commodes. Lord Carlton found himself examining a variety of dolls, searching through a baby carriage, and even encountering some very bad needlepoint the twins were working on for two of their father's footstools.

"Ow!" the earl ejaculated as a needle pricked his finger. "Damn your sisters!"

Melinda couldn't help but laugh. "This is not at all how I planned to spend my birthday. It is the most absurd situation. Whoever would have thought to find the notorious

194

Lord Carlton ransacking an adolescent female's stitchery in search of two adventurous snakes?"

"I have a strong inclination to entomb those twins of yours in the Putnam dungeon!" Lord Carlton snapped. "*Is* there a Putnam dungeon?"

"Heavens, yes! Our ancestors were a bloodthirsty crew in their day. But we're more civilized now. The dungeon has become the wine cellar."

"Not even I," said Lord Carlton with a shudder, "could withstand the horrors enacted if your sisters ever became drunkards. Keep looking. I'll think of a less dangerous punishment."

But Archie and Fanny were nowhere to be found.

"Very well," said Lord Carlton when the twins rejoined them, "that's two rooms out of what? A hundred?"

"Eighty-six," Melinda said. "Oh, *where* are they hiding? No, I must not panic. We must simply be more logical. Where is the absolutely worst place those two wretched snakes could be?"

They all stared at each other a moment. As one, they set out at a run for Catherine Mathley's boudoir.

"You two check her dressing room," Melinda ordered her sisters, "we'll search the bedroom."

"Right," said Annabelle.

"Come on!" said Margaret.

"And quickly!" Melinda urged.

"Is not one of us compromising the other?" Lord Carlton inquired, warily eyeing the confection of down and satin and lace that was Mrs. Mathley's bed.

"Only if we get caught. Don't just stand there gaping, Peter, start looking!"

"Never," said Lord Carlton on hands and knees, "did I think to find myself peering under a married woman's bed."

"Nonsense!" Melinda said heartily. "I dare swear you've hidden under numerous matronly beds in your time." She, too, was on her hands and knees, looking under the bedside table.

"Someday I am going to have to tell you the entire story of my life, if only to disabuse you of these ludicrous fantasies of yours."

"Oh, don't tell me that you haven't hidden under at least one bed?"

"Of course I haven't!" Lord Carlton snapped. "It's the first place any self-respecting husband would look."

A giggle escaped Melinda as she crawled to the foot of the bed. "Where does a gentleman hide when surprised by the lord of the manor?" she inquired, lifting up the pink bedskirt and peering underneath.

"The outside window ledge," Lord Carlton replied, also crawling toward the foot of the bed. "My childhood adventures have stood me in good stead over the years. The window ledge is drafty and a trifle dangerous, but far less so than being caught by a jealous husband."

"My horizons expand each hour in your company, Peter."

"From what I can tell they were bloody well broad enough when we met!"

Still searching for the two snakes, they were watching the floor, rather than their paths, and promptly bonked into each other.

"Ow!" said Melinda, rubbing her head.

"Hell and damnation," said Lord Carlton, similarly employed.

They sat side by side on the floor rubbing their respective bumps.

"Ah, the glamorous life of the polite world," Lord Carlton rhapsodized, which set Melinda to giggling.

"I do seem to lead you into the oddest scrapes," she said.

The earl shook his head. "You enjoy walking on the precipice of disaster, don't you?"

She laughed openly at him now. "Not at all. You're just such fun to tease!"

"Oh, you only like me because I'm an easy target," Lord Carlton said with an answering smile. "Come along, lass, we've snakes to find."

Twenty minutes of careful searching elicited a tiny shriek from Melinda. She threw herself back from a curtained window seat and pointed a finger that trembled slightly. "There."

Lord Carlton, far more fond of reptiles than she, strode past Melinda, bent down, and lifted the slumbering Archie and Fanny from behind the velvet curtains. "Wastrels," he chastised them. They flicked their tongues at him. "Annabelle! Margaret! Come fetch your snakes."

With a squeal of delight the twins bolted out of their mother's overburdened dressing room.

"Oh, Lord Carlton, how clever you are!" said Annabelle, clasping Archie fondly to her breast.

"I knew we'd find them with *you* helping in the search," Margaret said, relieving him of Fanny's company.

Melinda looked sourly upon her sisters and struggled to her feet. "I want Archie and Fanny and the rest of their crew, and any other creature in your room, placed in the barn with at least two locks on their cage before I see you again today," she informed them.

The twins, of course, vehemently protested this cruel banishment, but were overruled and bribed by a promise that they might attend her ball that evening "*If* I find those . . . those *serpents* safely locked in the barn this evening," Melinda said, before sweeping majestically from the room.

"Pudding heart," Lord Carlton called after her.

"Snake charmer," she retorted, closing the door behind her.

Lord Carlton helped the twins transplant the snakes to the barn, assuring them they would be far happier in an environment so rich with the edibles snakes most enjoyed, and then hurried, for he was late, back to the hall for his daily chess battle with Mr. Mathley.

"I apologize for my delay, sir," he said, striding into the study. "I was helping Melinda look for something."

"Look for something?" snapped Mr. Mathley as he glanced up from a book. "Melinda never loses anything.

197

Annabelle and Margaret, however . . ." Mr. Mathley stopped and peered knowingly up at Lord Carlton. "What ungodly creatures have they misplaced now?"

"The . . . ahem . . . creatures have been located and removed permanently to the barn, sir. You need have no fears of anyone, including Mrs. Mathley, suffering spasms on their account."

"Thank God," said Mr. Mathley feelingly as he set aside his book. "Sit down, Carlton, I've a new strategy I want to try on you."

Lord Carlton obligingly took his chair opposite his host.

"I hate to admit it," Mr. Mathley said as he made his opening move, "but you're not such a bad fellow as I first thought you, Carlton."

"Sir!" Lord Carlton said, looking up in surprise. "You honor me."

"Now, don't put yourself into transports. You may not be the scoundrel I first thought you, but I still neither like nor approve of you and I still don't want you to marry Melinda."

Lord Carlton was very still for a moment. "Of course not, Mr. Mathley."

"But you're not a monster," said his host, relaxing a little on his chaise. "In fact, you've been a most welcome tonic."

"How so?" Lord Carlton uneasily inquired as he advanced a pawn.

"Well, as long as Melinda has known you, she hasn't been involved in any scandal, and I can only credit your influence, for nothing else in her life has changed that would account for her no longer making a public spectacle of herself."

Lord Carlton thought it wisest not to correct this erroneous impression. "Melinda has a talent for trouble, I agree, sir. But it springs only from the best motives, and she has, you must own, a remarkable knack for bringing everything about right in the end."

"Yes, but it's the difficulty in getting there that's turned my hair gray," said Mr. Mathley, capturing the earl's pawn. "I just wanted you to know that I don't think you're a bad sort, as long as you don't marry into my family. I'll be sorry to see you go at the end of the summer. You are very good at losing at chess."

The two men shared a smile of understanding and continued their game.

Later that afternoon, Melinda was just starting back downstairs after enjoying a few minutes of peace in her room when voices caught her attention. She would have hurried down to extend a Mathley greeting, but she heard Lord Carlton behind her and waited until he was at her side before continuing downstairs.

"Good God, what new invasion is this?" he demanded.

"I fear it may be the Vandeveres," Melinda replied.

He caught her arm and pulled her to a stop. "You invited the Vandeveres?"

"Peter, we are supposed to be engaged! It would have been a *terrible* snub had I failed to invite your relatives to my birthday ball. I never thought they'd actually come."

"Well, it might have been a pleasant evening," Lord Carlton said with a sigh.

"But Peter, you don't understand! I've no rooms prepared for them! Somehow I've got to find three suitable chambers, have them cleaned, fresh linens brought out, flowers arranged—"

"Or Reeves and Mrs. Grant could do all of that while you enjoy a hideous tête à tête with my relatives."

Melinda stopped and pursed her lips. "I have always longed to converse with the Vandeveres," she said at last, "if I might be permitted to have just a word with Reeves first?"

"That's my girl," Lord Carlton said approvingly. "I knew you had it in you. You may bend Reeves's ear for as long as you choose," he said as, pulling her arm through his, they continued downstairs.

The scene below quickly came into view. An elegantly

dressed quartet, dusty and peevish, was surveying the grandeur of Putnam's entry hall as Mrs. Vandevere brittlely informed Reeves that yes, certainly they were expected and they wished to be shown to their rooms *now*.

"None of your northern attic rooms, mind," an elderly gentleman said with a stamp of his cane upon the floor. "I require a bedroom and sitting room on the first landing, south facing, with a good fireplace that doesn't smoke."

Reeves drew himself to his full height. "*None* of Putnam's fireplaces smoke, sir," he replied.

Once again Lord Carlton pulled Melinda to a stop, this time in shock rather than in outrage.

"Good God, that's Uncle Gilford!"

"It can't be," Melinda said. "I sent him an invitation, but out of courtesy only. He's dying, isn't he?"

"Not by the looks of it," Lord Carlton said grimly as he pulled Melinda down the stairs. "Aunt Vandevere, Cousin Fitzwilliam, Cousin Andrew, how good to see you," he said smoothly as they reached the entry hall. "And Uncle Gilford, this is a wonderful surprise. You look hale and hearty, sir."

"Far from it, young whelp," Lord Gilford said with a stamp of his cane.

"Well certainly, sir, you look far better from when I last saw you."

"Rumgumption!" said Lord Gilford. "I'm a dying man, as I've told you often enough. Can't you remember a simple thing like that?"

"Your pardon, Uncle Gilford. You seem full of vinegar just now. What do the doctors say?"

"*Doctors!*" barked Lord Gilford. "You could give a farthing for the lot of them and you'd be overpaying. Doctors! Why, I've had dozens of them these last few years, and do you think they can discover what's wrong with me? No!"

"It is the fire in your eyes and the strength of your spirit that has deceived them, sir," Melinda said, hurriedly stepping into the breach. "I am Melinda Mathley, Lord Gilford, and I am so pleased that you could come to my birthday ball."

"You may thank my niece, Alice," Lord Gilford snapped, looking with disfavor upon Mrs. Vandevere. "She insisted I come. Practically carried me out of my own house."

"Well, it is an honor to have you here, Lord Gilford, although I had no thought you would actually come, for I understood you to be on your deathbed."

"Humbug! I'll not let even the gravest illness keep me from the birthday ball of my future niece-in-law," said Lord Gilford, taking Melinda's hand and looking her up and down. "Well, you're not much to look at, but you've got manners and character as anyone can see. And a good head of hair. You'll do."

"Thank you, sir," Melinda said faintly in the face of such awesome condescension. "Peter, if you will take your family into the yellow drawing room, I will have refreshments brought to you immediately while I insure that their rooms are properly prepared."

"Coward," Lord Carlton murmured in her ear.

"Not at all, sir. I am merely performing my duties as any good hostess should. Run along now."

Lord Carlton cast her a glowering glance, and then escorted his family into the yellow drawing room.

"We must act quickly, Reeves," Melinda said in an urgent undertone.

"Yes, indeed, miss."

"Fortunately, Elizabeth Jonson occupies rooms in the south wing that may be converted into Lord Gilford's use. She will understand the need to move, I'm sure. I will speak to her myself. Have Mrs. Grant sent for immediately. Tell her that I want the three rooms currently vacant in the west wing made ready for the Vandeveres. And note this, Reeves: She is to place the portrait of Queen Elizabeth that we have in storage in the largest of the three chambers, and she is to refer to the room continually in front of Mrs. Vandevere as the Queen's room. Is that clear?"

Reeves, with some difficulty, withheld a grin. "Perfectly clear, miss."

"Good. I'll go speak to Elizabeth. On your toes, Reeves. We are about to avert a crisis."

"Very good, miss."

Miss Jonson was amenable to moving part and parcel from her rooms in the name of familial harmony to claim instead a smaller room in the east wing on the second landing.

Ten minutes later, having given concise instructions to Mrs. Grant, the housekeeper, Melinda ran downstairs and, taking a deep, calming breath, entered the yellow drawing room.

"Ah, thank you for your patience," she said. "We've had a few household crises that have distracted me. Your rooms will be ready in just a moment. Is the tea still hot? Lord Gilford, shall I refill your cup?"

Thirty interminable minutes later, Reeves and Mrs. Grant appeared and, with barely perceptible nods at Melinda, indicated that all was ready.

Melinda's relief was vast. It had been the most trying half hour of her life. Hildegarde Wells might be a plague, but Mrs. Vandevere was a fiend who delighted in directing her poison-tipped arrows at Lord Carlton. On several occasions Melinda had been on the point of entering the lists on his lordship's behalf. Only the barely perceptible shake of his head and the twinkle in his blue eyes kept her silent. *He* might be amused by such waspishness, but she was not! Only the civility drummed into her over the years held her to obeying the earl's silent command.

She rose gratefully from her chair when the servants entered. "Mrs. Grant will escort you, Mrs. Vandevere, and your sons to your rooms. Reeves, if you will be so good as to escort Lord Gilford to the . . . King Charles's suite," Melinda said to Reeves, who stood at Lord Gilford's elbow. "I hope you will find it to your liking, Lord Gilford. I'm sure you must wish to rest after your long and arduous journey."

"Aye," said Lord Gilford, stamping his cane as he began to walk toward the door. "Why are we forever paying tolls if the roads are never repaired? I'm black and blue from the jouncing I've suffered these last few hours."

"I'll have a cup of tea and some cool compresses sent to you immediately, sir," Melinda replied, as Reeves escorted him from the room and Mrs. Grant escorted the Vandeveres off.

Melinda sagged with relief as she closed the drawing room door behind them.

"A fine kettle of fish," Lord Carlton pronounced behind her.

She turned, regarding him with apparent surprise. "What? Are you still living?"

A reluctant grin tugged the earl's lips. "Just what do you mean, my girl, by leaving me in my family's coils for a quarter of an hour?"

"I *am* sorry, Peter," Melinda said in all sincerity as she advanced on him. "I did my very best not to meddle, but I had to ask Elizabeth personally to give her rooms to Lord Gilford, for it would have been most unfriendly to have Mrs. Grant do the fatal deed."

"I'm proud of you, my dear," Lord Carlton said sincerely. "I know what it must have cost you to let others do their jobs."

"Reprobate," Melinda said with a grin. "It *was* hard, and I am very proud of myself for succeeding in my first great challenge. I would be feeling on top of the world except, what on earth is Lord Gilford doing here? You told me he was dying!"

"Aye, that's what he told *me*," Lord Carlton said grimly, releasing her hands. "According to my beloved uncle, he should have crossed the river Styx at least twenty times in the last two years. It seems my only remaining uncle is a secret hypochondriac."

"And I thought him incapable of coming. Have I put you in the soup once again?"

"Nay, lass," Lord Carlton said, his expression grim. "*This* is entirely my own doing."

Several hours later, houseguests and relations began to troop upstairs to change for dinner. Melinda was one of the last to go upstairs for she had attended her father in his study in a partially successful attempt to cajole him into a good enough humor to withstand the coming festivities.

Basil Hollis, too, had been detained by a letter that had arrived a few minutes before. He read it in glowering fury, stamping up and down the conservatory. His man of business was once again taking it upon himself to try to curb Mr. Hollis's personal expenditures, if he had any desire to avoid bankruptcy. Mr. Hollis allowed no one to dictate to him, particularly a servant. Even his formidable uncle could not get him to bow to any decree he chose to refuse.

Thus, Mr. Hollis was in no charitable mood when he stomped toward the stairs.

"You'd better hurry, Basil," Melinda unfortunately commented as she left her father's study and began walking across the entry hall. "I understand it takes a good hour to properly pad your shoulders into some semblance of virility."

Mr. Hollis turned on his cousin, the letter in his pocket, the injuries he had suffered at Lord Carlton's hand that morning still fresh in his mind.

"A broad shoulder is nothing to rely on, Cousin Mel," he said with a glittering smile. "It will quite fail you where Carlton is concerned. He has no intention of marrying you, you know."

"Whyever not?" said Melinda politely.

Mr. Hollis's smile grew. "I've been speaking with the Vandeveres. They had quite a tale to tell. They're feeling ill-used, you see. A fortune that was to go to them may instead go to Carlton. Lord Gilford has demanded that he . . . ahem . . . *behave* for a full month. If he succeeds, Gilford

204

leaves him every shilling. If he fails . . . Well, that's where you come in, Cousin Mel. Engaged to the daughter of one of England's best families? Most impressive to a crotchety old man. Once Carlton is assured of the Gilford fortune, he'll have no need of your dowry or your protection, such as it is, in society. I do assure you, Cousin, that he'll drop you as soon as Gilford renders up his brass."

"A charming picture," Melinda agreed. "And why would not an avaricious gentleman like Lord Carlton want both his uncle's fortune and mine? With both he could blaze a trail of debauchery around the world."

"Yes, but he's a man who likes to live single. I do not say *alone*, merely single. Best be on your guard, Cousin."

Lord Carlton, having observed from the first landing this *tête à tête*, strode downstairs toward Melinda as Mr. Hollis gleefully made his way upstairs. Seeing the earl approach and in no condition to greet him calmly, Melinda hurriedly turned away and would have fled into a parlor, a drawing room, the back stairs, but Lord Carlton's concern was too great and his legs too long and he quickly caught her up.

"Melinda."

She had to stop and turn and regard him with what poise she could muster. "Hello, Peter. Dressed already? You look splendid."

"Melinda, what has Hollis been saying to you?" the earl demanded.

"Why, the usual chitchat."

"Melinda, don't lie to me. You're no good at it."

"Aren't I?" she said faintly.

"He has said something to distress you deeply. I pray you, tell me what it is."

"It is nothing to call him out about, Peter."

Arms akimbo, Lord Carlton glared at Melinda. "I do not make it a habit of calling out vermin," he retorted. "Although blacking an eye or two may be called for on this occasion. What has he said to you?"

Melinda's throat was so tight she had to force each word

out. "He merely explained to me why you won't marry me."

"Has he?" said Lord Carlton, his hands falling to his sides.

"As I never expected you to marry me, his word of caution was quite unnecessary."

"What did he say?"

Melinda held up a hand, as if to fend him off. "Peter, please. We both selfishly entered into this false engagement to rid ourselves of certain troubles. That has not changed."

"I will not be put off, Melinda. What did Hollis say?"

Melinda studied a button on her sleeve. "He merely told me about the month-long privation your uncle Gilford insisted upon as the condition for you inheriting his fortune. Really, Peter, there's nothing—"

Lord Carlton swore bitterly. "Melinda, I meant to tell you long before this."

"Peter, there was no need—"

"There was *every* need!" Lord Carlton declaimed to such effect that Melinda took a step back. "You have been honest with me from the beginning, and I have told you but half truths that are as good as lies. I *have* disliked being an outcast of society, Melinda. And I do need that inheritance."

"Well, of course you do," said Melinda. "You can't be an earl without money."

"I can't renovate my estates without money, Melinda."

She stared up at him a moment. "What *were* you doing up in Yorkshire for three years?"

An admiring smile touched his lips. "Oh, you are quick. I was improving my farms to the best of my abilities on my very limited income."

"Good God!" said Melinda, pale with shock. "The rake has become a farmer."

"Well, not entirely," Lord Carlton temporized. "I have discovered that I don't enjoy being a rake and a scoundrel all the time, neither do I enjoy being a farmer all the time."

206

"You could try walking between the two paths. Then you might find things aren't so dull."

"Oh, I haven't felt dull for some weeks now, Melinda."

A soft blush crept into her cheeks as Lord Carlton continued to stare down at her. She couldn't help herself; she looked away. "Well, now that everything is open and aboveboard, there's no more to be said."

"Melinda," said Lord Carlton, his hand reaching out, his fingers caressing her cheek, turning her head so she had to look up at him, "I never meant to hurt you."

"Oh, honestly, Peter," said Melinda, shivering inwardly at this touch, "how you do go on."

"I wanted to tell you the truth a hundred times these last few weeks, but I was . . . afraid. Don't look so astonished! Even scoundrels know fear now and then. From the first, Melinda, you have taken me on faith, treated me with friendship, ignored my past ignominy. I was afraid if you knew that my decision to enter our engagement was based on mercenary considerations alone, I would lose your respect, your sweet friendship, the . . . ease we have together."

"Silly man," Melinda said softly, her fingers brushing his taut cheek. "To seek a fortune that is rightfully yours so that you may attend to your estates as your honor demands is wholly admirable. How could I think less of you?"

Lord Carlton's expression was harsh. "Because I have used you and lied to you! Those are wrongs not easily redressed. But Melinda, I will never hurt you again. This I swear."

"You're very kind, Peter. Now, if you'll excuse me, I must go change. It would be improper to be late to my own birthday dinner."

Melinda hurried upstairs to her room where she locked the door and, rather than changing for dinner, sank onto her bed and cried for the next half hour, sobbing into her pillow so that no one would hear her. When she was quite cried out, for now, she lethargically began her toilette.

Fortunately, for all her mad starts, Melinda was a practical young woman and knew which eyewashes and compresses to use to remove any trace of red from her eyes, to remove all swelling, to in effect hide any trace of her storm.

When she went down to dinner, dressed in a low-cut gown of green silk, Lord Carlton's ruby and gold necklace gleaming against her throat, no one save the earl noticed that she looked in the least pale. Neither had much of an appetite.

* Chapter 13

To the great shock of Mrs. Grant, the housekeeper, Melinda had left all the details and their execution for her birthday dinner and ball solely in her hands. Seeking to prove herself worthy of this unexpected trust, Mrs. Grant surpassed herself. The house was festooned with garlands of flowers. Every surface gleamed. There were two courses at dinner of fourteen dishes each, everything from stuffed quail to the Putnam salad their chef had invented some years ago to raspberry trifle. Reeves had personally selected the wines to go with each dish. It was, on the whole, a cheerful table save for Lord Carlton, Melinda (who feigned pleasure), and Mr. Mathley who had been seated beside Lord Gilford.

"The migraines began back in ninety-six," Lord Gilford rattled on as he sliced into a partridge, "and had me bedridden sometimes half a year! But that was nothing to the nervous complaints that developed soon after. James's Powder had no effect. Prostrate I was—yes prostrate!—day after day, week after week. I couldn't abide any company. I could scarcely tolerate my housekeeper. One doctor after another came to me, examined me, and declared he could find nothing wrong. Bah! *Doctors*," said Lord Gilford with disgust. "A pack of know-nothing thieves intent on skinning us alive if we let them have their way."

"Mm," said Mr. Mathley morosely as he took a sip of wine. He had heard this same accusation, and variations thereof, repeatedly in the last hour. Mr. Gilford poured forth an unabridged history of the rest of his many ailments, with Lord Carlton looking on occasionally and thinking sourly that this was a most suitable punishment for the man who had caused so many others so many unhappy moments.

The difficulty of Mr. Mathley refusing to receive Louisa, Clarence, and General Hyde-Moore into Putnam that evening was easily resolved by pleading his broken leg. He was not in the receiving line when the dinner party broke up and advanced to the ballroom, but was installed instead on a chaise at a whist table in the red saloon, a suite that took up a good quarter of the first landing.

Thus was Melinda able to greet the Hyde-Moores with all of the effusiveness she desired. She made it plain to all about her that her father might disown the Hyde-Moores, but she never would.

"Well, Mr. Hyde-Moore," Lord Carlton said, shaking the young man's hand, "marriage seems to agree with you."

Mr. Hyde-Moore grinned. "Oh, it does that. You don't know what it's like, Carlton, to realize what you've always considered an impossible dream."

"No, I don't believe I do."

"Where's the holy terror? I mean, Mr. Mathley."

"Your esteemed father-in-law is holding court at a whist table."

"Thank God," Mr. Hyde-Moore said feelingly. "We shan't have him glowering at us while we dance. That's a relief."

"For one and all. It is entirely Melinda's doing. She handled him superbly."

"I owe her more than I can say."

"As do I," Lord Carlton murmured as Mr. Hyde-Moore passed down the line. "General Hyde-Moore!" he greeted the next guest. "An honor, sir."

"Lord Carlton," the general wheezed.

He was a stout man in his late fifties, almost completely bald. Retired life apparently agreed with him. The buttons on his coat and waistcoat threatened to burst off at any moment.

"I felicitate you, sir, on acquiring so estimable a daughter-in-law," said the earl, now well accustomed to attending to the conversational niceties.

"She's a pretty little thing," the general said, smiling genially upon Lord Carlton. But then, he smiled genially upon everyone. He passed down the line.

As it had been agreed earlier that afternoon that Mr. Mathley would hold court in the red saloon and need not even appear in the ballroom, it became Harry's duty to lead his sister out for the first dance at her birthday ball. This Harry was loathe to do, but his father had rung a peal over his head for a good half hour, and so he had formally and most unwillingly tendered his request to Melinda that she honor him with the first dance at the ball. Melinda then gratified his brotherly feelings by thanking him for the honor, but informing him that Lord Carlton had already claimed her for the first dance.

She then went off to inform Lord Carlton that he had claimed her for the first dance.

Thus, the earl escorted her out onto the gleaming ballroom floor for the first dance, a cotillion. She was quickly followed by her sister and brother-in-law and the rest of her family, save for Mr. Mathley and the twins who had been informed by their eldest sister that they might certainly attend her ball, but only if they remained inconspicuously concealed in the gallery. She promised to supply them with as many cakes and glasses of lemonade as they could consume.

Everyone had been attended to, but how, Melinda wondered rather desperately as the music began, was she to survive the next several minutes in close proximity with a man whom she loved but who did not love her? Would he ever love her? Could he ever love her? Melinda forced back the lump in her throat and banished the unshed tears from her eyes. She was a Mathley, after all, and she had her pride. Never would she let Peter Carlton know what she felt.

"You have surpassed yourself, Melinda," Lord Carlton commented as they danced past a bank of flowers.

"It is nice, isn't it?" she said simply. "I had nothing to do with it, of course. It is all Mrs. Grant and her staff. It is very lowering to be shown up so soon after embarking upon the path of right. And I have a new problem to fidget me: How am I to keep myself occupied if I do not meddle in the household affairs?"

"There is always needlework. I shall procure you a workbasket."

"I'll have your head if you do any such thing! Why are you looking so pleased in the midst of the most boring romp of this summer?"

The earl smiled down at her. "Ah, that is because I have some hopes of getting through the evening unscathed. The only time I have been safe in your company was at our first meeting and that, too, was at a ball."

"Oh, you *are* a scoundrel!" Melinda stated and then hurriedly looked away. She loved that he teased her. She loved him. "Don't Clare and Louisa look well together?"

Lord Carlton glanced at the newlyweds, who were glowing.

"Bursting with happiness," he drawled.

"Well, they've every right to be!" Melinda protested. "Never did I think that Louisa could become more beautiful than she was born. But la, Peter, is she not exquisite tonight?"

"Indeed," Lord Carlton said, gazing down at her. "Are you not the least bit jealous of *La Belle du Ton*?"

"Jealous?" said Melinda, staring up at him in honest surprise. "Of Louisa? Are you mad?"

"Most elder sisters denied the many blessings of nature that Louisa can claim, let alone the pack of eligible men dancing to the tiniest crook of her little finger, could not but feel some resentment," Lord Carlton opined.

212

"What a ragbag bunch of females you must have known in your life! I was never one to lament what I did not and could not have." Melinda cringed inwardly at this and hurried on. "Nor am I so mean-spirited as to begrudge Louisa the many gifts, as you say, nature has bestowed upon her. *I*, after all, have a good head of hair. Your uncle said so. And don't forget, *she* gave up a marquess for a mere nonentity, while I continue to remain engaged to an earl. I stand quite high in Father's favor just now, thanks to you."

"But *such* an earl!" Lord Carlton protested.

"Not that he would want you for a son-in-law, of course," Melinda calmly agreed. Her beloved had a most annoying knack for recollecting and uttering her pet phrases. "Still if you could prove yourself a decent hunter and recount to him one or two of your meetings with Mr. Jackson at his pugilistic emporium, he might begin to think kindly of you."

"But what of your determination to use me to browbeat your father into recanting his threat to marry you off to the next man who offers for you?"

"Oh, Louisa has taken care of that very well, thank you."

"Louisa?"

"Why certainly! *Her* offense is so much greater than mine that Father has quite forgotten, I daresay, that he ever made that odious threat about marrying me off. You will undoubtedly be free of Putnam Park and the mad Mathleys within the next few days."

This pronouncement wholly failed to bring cheer to either party.

"And who is on your dance card for the second dance?" Lord Carlton at last inquired.

"Clare, of course."

"You do believe in making public statements, don't you?"

Melinda shrugged. "My sympathies are wholly with Louisa and Clare. I don't see why the world should not know it."

213

"Have you ever done a selfish thing in your life?"

"Oh, this is too bad of you!" Melinda said. "You are making me blush at my own ball! However shall I come about? How shall I put you in your place?"

"You need only observe that Lord Gilford is the furthest thing from dying," Lord Carlton said, nodding at the elderly gentleman who stood against the wall, tapping his cane in time to the music and bending the ear of Sir Cedric Creighton, the local magistrate.

"He *is* the furthest thing from dying, Peter," Melinda quietly replied. "What will you do?"

"Finish out my month in society, and then run, not walk, back to the healthful climes of Yorkshire."

"Yes, but Peter, how will you get on? How will you manage without your uncle's fortune?"

A sardonic smile touched the earl's lips. "Oh, I've learned a good deal these last three years. I shall contrive, Melinda, never you fear."

"I've no doubt of your ingenuity and determination, Peter. But you need that money, and you need it now. Lord Gilford will die someday, yes, but he's the sort who will hang on forever just to spite you. I know!" Melinda said with sudden inspiration. "Couldn't we arrange some sort of accident? An overturned carriage? A hunting accident? Or perhaps a footpad! Josiah Barney would undoubtedly be most willing to cooperate in exchange for our dropping our charges against him."

A low chuckle escaped the earl. "How do you do it?" he demanded.

"Do what?"

"How do you contrive to make me laugh in the face of so bleak a future?"

"I was only trying to be practical about the situation."

They continued in pleasant conversation the rest of the cotillion, and then Melinda, with a secret sigh of relief, left Lord Carlton's arms and accosted her brother-in-law. It was doubly painful to love the earl and to know that she was, in his view, merely an expediency. Charming, he might be. Helpful, undoubtedly. In love . . . she might whistle at the moon. She had not realized until that evening as Basil Hollis had spewed forth his poison, how much she had begun to hope that she was capable of capturing Peter Carlton's heart. The pain she felt now told her just how much she *had* hoped.

"You should not be sad on your birthday," Mr. Hyde-Moore said gently.

Melinda forced a brilliant smile to her lips. "I am not at all sad."

"Pensive then. Have you quarreled with Lord Carlton?"

"Not at all! We get along famously."

"I am glad," Mr. Hyde-Moore said simply. "You are well matched and I like him. I will be proud to call him brother on your wedding day."

Melinda sank rapidly into gloom.

She was occupied for the next two hours dancing without pause with a good many of her masculine guests, even pulling General Hyde-Moore out onto the dance floor, despite all of his protests that his youth and dancing days were over. Even with his bulk, however, he acquitted himself admirably in the country dance and left the floor, panting and perspiring and exclaiming himself demmed if he wouldn't lead her out into another dance before the night was through.

She had just completed a dance with Mr. Fitzwilliam Vandevere, a tedious exercise for all he could discuss were the newest fashions issuing from Paris, and was leaving the floor on his arm when Lord Carlton stepped before them and intervened.

"Your pardon, Cousin, but I have promised Melinda to rescue her from the rigors of her own ball and lead her out to some quieter employment. If you will excuse us."

Not waiting for a reply, he looped Melinda's arm through his and led her to the outer balustrade, where steps on either side led down to the gardens below.

"Thank you, Peter," Melinda said. "I confess to being a trifle weary. I love to dance, but conversing with some of our young blades can be quite trying."

"Say no more," Lord Carlton said, removing two glasses of champagne from a passing footman's tray and handing one to Melinda. "I haven't been able to get near you since our first and only dance. You are most popular tonight."

"Duty only. It is my birthday ball, after all, and the gentlemen feel themselves obliged to dance with me."

"What a rapper! You're the best dancer in the room, and every man knows it. Dancing with you is pure selfishness on their parts, I assure you."

"Peter, darling, is that you?"

Melinda turned to find one of the most beautiful women she had ever seen advancing on them. She was a little tall with a fine figure, glossy black hair styled into an abandonment of tiny curls, and green eyes wide with surprise and pleasure.

"But it is you! How charming to see you after all these years," this vision said with a strong Polish accent. "What has it been? Five years?"

"Six," said Lord Carlton tersely.

"Oh, darling, you remember! You *do* care!"

Melinda began to loathe the Polish beauty.

"And is this the child who is to be your bride?" the beauty burbled. "Oh, you needn't look so surprised, Peter. I do read the papers. My dear, you're a sweet little thing and just the sort to make my Peter the happiest of all mortal men, I am sure! Oh, but where are my manners? I, my dear, am the Countess Rulenska."

"Melinda Mathley," Melinda said with a semblance of a smile. "You are . . . an old friend of Peter's?"

"An old acquaintance, merely," the countess said, wafting her Chinese fan through the air. "We met in Venice at one of those wonderful masquerades they give. I was quite enthralled with Peter, of course, as what woman would not

216

be? But he would not give me a tumble. He was undoubtedly holding out for you, my dear."

"That is quite enough, Rosalind," Lord Carlton said sternly.

The countess's green eyes widened. "Why, whatever can you mean?"

"Melinda, this ... this *creature* before you is no more the Countess Rulenska than I am!" Lord Carlton declared. Melinda began to have horrific visions of a past affair but was fortunately soon put to rights. "The last time I met her was indeed six years ago in Venice, but she called herself Rosalind Chalmers then and was as English as any of us."

"Now hush, Peter," the *countess* said in a whispered, unaccented English. "I have a role to maintain."

"What the devil are you doing here, Ros?" the earl demanded, arms akimbo.

"I am the guest of Lord and Lady Buntersham, of course. We met in Paris this last spring. They asked me to visit them this summer, and I have done so."

"I don't quite ... understand," said Melinda in some confusion. "If you are Rosalind Chalmers, English born, why are you pretending to be the Polish Countess Rulenska?"

"It is a delicate matter, my dear."

Melinda blushed.

"She is a *thief*," Lord Carlton stated.

Melinda stared up at him, for the first time in her life thoroughly nonplussed.

"Oh, Peter, I wish you would not be so ... so blunt!" said Miss Chalmers. "I simply acquire property that others are too careless to properly protect."

"A thief?" Melinda said, and then hurriedly lowered her voice. "A thief? But how wonderful!"

It was now Miss Chalmers and Lord Carlton who stared at *her*.

"I've never met a thief before," Melinda happily continued. "Josiah Barney was a mere footpad, after all. But do you steal from everyone?"

"Only the rich my dear," said Miss Chalmers, making a smooth recovery. "They're the only ones who have anything worth stealing."

Melinda turned glowing brown eyes up to Lord Carlton. "What an *amiable* creature you are, to be sure, to have so broad an acquaintance!"

Miss Chalmers uttered a most attractive gurgle of laughter. "Peter, she's a darling! No wonder you fell for her!"

"Oh, we're just indulging in our own little masquerade," Melinda said.

"Melinda!" said the earl.

"Well, we know her secret, why shouldn't she know ours?"

Melinda quickly and succinctly explained the faux engagement.

"But this is delightful!" cried Miss Chalmers. "You are a rogue, Miss Mathley. Yes, I say it, a rogue, and I am so glad that I have met you! To know that there are two of us in Europe . . . It does my heart good."

Melinda laughed. "*You* are not at all what I thought a thief would be."

"And you are not at all what I thought a young lady of the ton *should* be."

"Ah. Well, as to that," said Melinda, "I'm not. As my relations are forever telling me. But I manage to get by."

"I hear a waltz," Lord Carlton tersely interrupted. "Ros, will you oblige me?"

"But, of course," Miss Chalmers said, resuming her Polish accent. "I delight in the waltz."

Lord Carlton led her away to interrogate her within an inch of her life, to discover what she was doing in England, let alone in Putnam Hall. But Miss Chalmers had dealt with more determined men than he, and she was able to turn aside every question with a quip or a flirt or a laugh.

Melinda, watching this performance from the balustrade

218

doors, was forced to acknowledge in her heart of hearts that Peter and Rosalind looked well together, fit well together. Like was drawn to like. He was an adventurer. She was an adventurer. He was beautiful. She was beautiful. They were perfect together. Many a head turned to survey the couple as they swirled around the dance floor, Rosalind laughing up at the earl.

For the first time in her life, Melinda knew what it was to feel jealous, and what it was to feel despair. How could she ever hope to win Peter Carlton's heart when Rosalind Chalmers romped through the world?

The dance ended. He procured the "countess" a glass of wine and abandoned her to Lord and Lady Buntersham before returning to Melinda on the balustrade.

"She's up to something," he said without preamble. "But the devil take her, I can't discover what it is."

"Perhaps she just came to dance, Peter," Melinda said, *with you,* she silently appended.

"My brief acquaintance with Rosalind Chalmers in Venice leads me to believe that she never *just* does anything. There is purpose in every word, in every act."

"However did you meet?" Melinda said, a trifle faintly.

A reluctant chuckle escaped the earl. "She tried to steal my purse."

Melinda stared up at him. Then she, too, began to laugh. "Even I should not attempt that form of introduction."

"No, you've got a good deal more sense and eschew any form of obliqueness. You simply march up and introduce yourself."

"Ah. Well, I wanted to meet you, you see."

"Yes. I'm not entirely certain that *Rosalind* wanted to meet me, but she was forced to do so anyway."

"And you didn't have her arrested?"

"Look at her, Melinda. Could any man have that sprite arrested?"

"No," Melinda said softly as she gazed at Rosalind Chalmers dancing with Sir Cedric Creighton. "I quite take your point."

"Come," Lord Carlton said, turning to her, "we have dallied here long enough. Let us go survey your ball, Melinda. Guests must be attended, curried, and petted."

"You make them sound like horses or dogs."

"It is trying being at the center of the polite world."

"But you seem to be surviving it very well."

"Only with you to sustain me, my sweet. Come," said Lord Carlton, taking her arm, "let us stroll with regal bearing among your many subjects."

Their progress was necessarily slow through the crowded ballroom, but once they had escaped that, they could stroll without fear of being jabbed with an elbow or having toes crunched by a passing dowager. They entered the red saloon to find twenty tables set up. Nearly eighty people were at play, all intent upon their cards and keeping their wineglasses filled to the brim.

"Hello, Father," Melinda said, dropping a kiss on the top of Mr. Mathley's head. "Are you winning?"

"Of course I'm winning!" Mr. Mathley stated. "I know a hand of cards from a handbasket, my girl."

"Yes, of course you do, Father." Melinda smiled at Lady Jersey, Sir Cedric Creighton, and Princess Esterhazy. "I trust my father is not leaving your pockets totally to let?"

"We shall come about, Miss Mathley," Lady Jersey proclaimed. "The night is young."

"Then we'll leave you to it," said Lord Carlton, taking Melinda's hand in his and pulling her away. "Does everyone lose to George Mathley?"

"Everyone with their wits about them."

"I begin to feel a part of society after all."

They entered the supper room where a large buffet had been set up to succor the guests through the night.

"Oh, bother, there's Basil," Melinda moaned.

"Never fear, Lydia and Jerry will rescue us," Lord Carlton stated.

And so they did. The Fenwychs had entered the room just a moment earlier and, seeing their friends, hurried up, took them in hand, and insisted that they must share a table together.

It was quickly noted by everyone else in the room that their table was filled with the greatest amount of hilarity and *bon ami*. Some envied them, some tried to emulate them, some smiled indulgently. Only one glowered, and this, of course, was Basil Hollis.

He was a little drunk, but then he was always a little drunk at these functions. He was also feeling ill-used. Lord Carlton had felt it incumbent upon him to pull Mr. Hollis aside prior to the ball and inform him in no uncertain terms that if he ever said a word to Melinda again that made her unhappy or in any way uncomfortable, he would reduce him to rubble and gladly. As Lord Carlton surpassed him by a good six inches and many more muscles, Mr. Hollis could not but take this threat to heart.

But Mr. Hollis was not used to being threatened. The majority of the ton was afraid of his scathing tongue and his propensity for telling the most malicious truths whenever his ire was raised. He was therefore treated . . . delicately by the ton. Yet here was Lord Carlton with his ham-handed tactics and his rag manners informing him . . . *him* . . . that he would call him out on the field of honor at the next hint of provocation.

Well, the Earl of Carlton, the *notorious* Earl of Carlton, would soon find that Basil Hollis was a man who did not threaten easily. When the Fenwychs, Carlton, and Melinda adjourned for an after-supper stroll through the gardens, Mr. Hollis followed in their train.

"Ah, the bride and groom," he proclaimed as he caught up with them and surveyed the Fenwychs through his quizzing glass. "But where's the by-blow? Tucked into his little bed?"

Lord Fenwych, his face flushed with anger, curled his

hands into fists at his sides. "You're drunk, sir, if you dare to impugn the honor of any lady!"

"Lady? You call a wife who gifts you with some footman's brat a lady? Ha! You're much more generous than I."

Lord Carlton started forward, but Lord Fenwych held him back.

"You forget, Peter, whose wife she is." Lord Fenwych turned and planted Mr. Hollis a very neat facer that succeeded in blacking his eye and rattling him, but he was still on his feet.

Lord Carlton, therefore, followed this up with his own blow, which laid Mr. Hollis out cold on the ground.

It had all happened so quickly, that few if any in the garden realized what *had* happened as Lord Carlton summoned two footmen to carry Mr. Hollis to his room, loudly lamenting that any man should hold his wine so poorly as to pass out before midnight.

Lydia fluttered around her husband, ascertaining that his dear hand was not in the least injured, saying over and over again how brave he was and noble, and how she should never have married him if she had known it would bring him to such a pass. Lord Fenwych was occupied in assuring her that she was the greatest gift he had ever received and he'd be damned if he gave it back.

No wife could withstand such a declaration, and Lydia happily allowed herself to be enfolded in her lord's arms.

Melinda, meanwhile, took Lord Carlton's right hand in both of hers and gazed up at him. "Thank you," she said. "It's been a long time in coming."

He smiled down at her. "You're welcome. But 'twas a tad indecorous, don't you think?"

"If Lord Gilford is a man, he cannot help but applaud your defense of your best friend and his wife," Melinda said stoutly. "I shall bear you witness, as shall Lydia and Jerry. Come, let us stop the tattlemongers before they start and tell your uncle ourselves."

They bid adieu to the Fenwychs, who were wholly occupied in reassuring each other, and left the garden arm in arm. They entered the ballroom and immediately began to search for Lord Gilford when a thought struck Lord Carlton with considerable force.

"Good God, where's Rosalind?" he exclaimed.

Melinda's hand spasmed on his arm. "I don't . . . see her," she said.

"Nor do I," Lord Carlton said grimly. "I must leave you to face Lord Gilford alone, Melinda. I must find Rosalind and find her now."

"Peter—" Melinda began, but Lord Carlton had already disappeared into the crowd.

With a sad little sigh, Melinda made her way to Lord Gilford as Lord Carlton searched fruitlessly through the ballroom, the card room, and the supper room. Feeling downright grim, he returned to search among the guests taking the cool evening air on the outer balustrade. He saw that several people were still strolling through the Mathley gardens and started down the stairs to continue his search there. He soon ran Rosalind to ground as she stood sniffing the soft orange petals of a rose.

"Are they not lovely?" she said in her Polish accent.

"Stunning," he said. "Hand them over, Ros."

She turned to him, clearly startled. "Hand what over, my dear friend? The roses belong to the Mathleys, do they not?"

"As do the Mathley sapphires."

"The what?"

"Don't play games, Ros," Lord Carlton said grimly. "I was at a stand to know why you would deign to come to a country ball. Your standards are so much higher than this. And then it occurred to me that there was booty even in this house to attract your interest. The Mathley sapphires. You must have them. Hand them over."

"I'll do no such thing!" Miss Chalmers roundly retorted.

"Then I will take them from you before this host of polite society."

"You wouldn't dare," Miss Chalmers stated, taking a step back.

"Oh, wouldn't I?" said Lord Carlton, taking a step forward. "I am appalled at your manners, Rosalind. To steal a family heirloom from your hosts is very shabby."

"The Mathleys are the most delightful creatures, of course," Miss Chalmers agreed, "but the sapphires deserve a better home, a more understanding and appreciative owner."

"They deserve to be locked back in their safe, and I will do so the moment you hand them over."

"Now, Peter, do be reasonable."

"I think that I am being very reasonable, Rosalind. I ought to have you arrested here and now, but I won't, if you give me the sapphires, make your excuses to our hosts, and decamp, never to enter a Mathley home again."

"I find you are not at all as agreeable as I remembered you from Venice," Miss Chalmers said, whipping out her fan to cool her heated cheeks.

Lord Carlton smiled at this performance. "I am an uncivil boor, I know. Hand them over, Ros, or I'll search you here and now."

"Oh, very well," she said with a disgruntled sigh. She bent down and lifted the hem of her dress, removing the sapphires from a hidden pocket in her skirt.

Lord Carlton barely glanced at the sapphires as he stuffed them into his coat pocket.

"However shall you return them?" Miss Chalmers inquired. "*You* don't know the combination to the safe."

"Neither did you, but you succeeded."

"Ha! My dear Peter, I have had years of practice."

"Yes, but *I* have the eldest daughter of the house."

Miss Chalmers observed Melinda on the outer balustrade speaking with the Hyde-Moores.

"She is a fetching little thing," she commented. "Are you really going to marry her?"

"No," Lord Carlton tersely replied.

"Whyever not?"

"Her father objects."

"You could always elope."

"No. I've seen the toll elopement has taken on Melinda's sister. Even if I could earn Melinda's regard, I could never ask her to choose between her father and me, as Louisa was forced to do. Besides, if Melinda has any fondness for me, it's more for my reputation as a rake and a scoundrel than anything else. And really, it's too wearying maintaining that reputation. I'd like to assume a more prosaic mode of life. I don't think that would do for Melinda at all."

"I think you underestimate both her and yourself. You will never be prosaic, Peter, however stuffy you may behave with me. And she, I think, could be happy in any mode of life as long as you continued to smile at her. She would suit you, if you'd let her. She's the most darling girl I've ever met."

"Aye," Lord Carlton said, gazing at Melinda, whose twinkling brown eyes peeped mischievously over her fan as she gazed at the sumptuous throng in the ballroom, "she would drive any man mad with longing."

"You are very different from the man I knew six years ago," Miss Chalmers said quietly. "You should marry her, Peter. I think she's the only thing in this world that can make you happy."

He glanced at the thief. "I'll choose my own course, thank you, Rosalind."

Miss Chalmers sighed. "Shall you report me to the Bow Street Runners or to the militia or to whoever they use out here?"

"Nay, I'll keep your secret if you'll keep your word."

"Have no fear. I shan't rifle the Mathleys again. I hope we meet under more pleasant circumstances next time."

"As do I," said Lord Carlton, raising her hand briefly to his lips. "Now get out before I have you thrown out."

She laughed and turned and sauntered through the gardens and back up the stairs. She paused to say something to Melinda, and then continued into the ballroom. Melinda, in turn, hurried down the stairs and ran across the gardens to Lord Carlton.

"The Countess Rulenska," she said, imitating Miss Chalmers's heavy accent, "said that you wished to see me?"

"I do," said Lord Carlton, leading Melinda farther into the gardens.

With their backs turned to the rest of the guests, a hedge hiding them from view, he pulled the sapphires from his coat pocket.

"I need your help in returning these," he said.

"Peter!"

"Now, you can't think that I—"

"No, no, no, you goose! Certainly Miss Chalmers stole them. But however did you get them from her?"

He stared at her a moment. "You are not stunned? You are not appalled? You are not horrified that Rosalind Chalmers nearly made off with the Mathley sapphires?"

"Good heavens, why should I be? I'm merely impressed by her skill. However did she discover where the safe was, let alone how to open it?"

Lord Carlton took a breath. "That we must leave to the realm of conjecture. The more weighty question before us is, how are they to be returned? Do you know the combination to the safe?"

"Well, of course I do! I knew it when I was ten, not that Father knows, of course."

"Of course," said Lord Carlton with a smile. "But how are we to break away from your guests and disappear without rousing suspicion?"

"Ah. You are forgetting the many benefits of our betrothal. What could be suspicious in your stealing me away for a few private moments on my birthday?"

"You have an admirable mind, Melinda."

"Thank you, sir," Melinda said, dropping a quick curtsy. She looped her arm through Lord Carlton's. "Come, let me

226

tell Louisa what we are up to so she will not worry and can fend off any impertinent questions. Then we can wander off for our *tête à tête*."

"You were born to plot and scheme. It is useless trying to curb you."

"Have you been trying to curb me?" Melinda asked with interest.

"No, I've merely been trying to keep up with you!"

After speaking a moment with Louisa, who had some difficulty in comprehending what was told her, Melinda led Lord Carlton on a leisurely path around the perimeter of the house and through a side entrance that led to the back stairs. Avoiding every servant and every guest, they at last made their way into a little-used parlor on the second landing in the north wing. Melinda quickly lit a lamp and held it up to brighten the room.

"I see no safe," said Lord Carlton.

"Look behind the Van Dyck," Melinda instructed.

"Old George is craftier than I thought."

"On the contrary," Melinda said as Lord Carlton removed the Van Dyck to expose a small wall safe, "this was installed by Great-Great-Grandfather when he was given the sapphires by Queen Anne as recompense for services unspecified. I've spent many a happy hour trying to puzzle out what exactly Great-Great-Grandfather might have done for the poor Queen. Brought her secret whisperings of the Marlboroughs' doings at Blenheim after they had been banished from court, no doubt. The Mathleys were never noted for any grand gesture on behalf of the crown."

"Blasphemy!" Lord Carlton declared. He stopped and considered her with a most forbidding frown. "How is it that a once sane lord of the realm finds himself with purloined sapphires in his pocket, a single female alone in his company, and a safe waiting to be opened?"

"It must be the company you keep," Melinda retorted.

"You know," said Lord Carlton, removing the sapphires from his pocket and considering them in the lamplight, "if

227

we sold these, we would have enough money to enter upon any adventure that comes our way. It would be interesting to see what mischief you could conjure up in another country. Egypt comes to mind."

"I have always longed to travel," Melinda conceded. "I've seen most of England and Scotland and even a bit of Ireland and Wales, for the Mathleys know everyone, of course, and we have a family tradition of making others cover our expenses by paying a lot of lengthy visits. But I have never seen the rest of Europe, let alone the Americas, or Africa, or Turkey. What fun it would be!"

"You would make an excellent traveler for you regard every new prospect or person with delight. I would greatly enjoy showing you Alexandria or the Greek isles. Shall we?" Lord Carlton inquired with a sardonic smile, dangling the sapphires before her.

Melinda nibbled on her lip. "Only as a last resort. If Father breaks his other leg, I will personally sell the sapphires to the first buyer you can find for me. But for now, replace them as you should."

"Oh, very well. The combination, if you please."

Alas, Melinda was unable to tender this important information for Louisa burst into the parlor.

"Melinda! Melinda!" she cried. "Oh, there you are! You must come quickly!"

"What on earth is amiss, Louisa?" Melinda demanded, hurrying up to her sister.

"Aunt Wells claims that brigands have assaulted Cousin Basil, and she is demanding that the house be searched and the villains arrested."

"Oh, good God," Lord Carlton said in disgust. "Hollis *would* tell such a fairy story!"

"And Aunt Wells would react in just this manner," Melinda said with equal disgust. "Come along, Peter. The combination will have to wait. Disaster is looming."

With a sigh Lord Carlton replaced the Van Dyck, and the three of them quickly made their way downstairs and entered the red saloon. There they found an unpleasant scene. Mrs. Wells was stentoriously demanding that Mr. Mathley avenge his nephew. Mr. Mathley, in turn, brutally informed Mrs. Wells that he'd never heard such bird-witted twitterings in all his born days.

"Why would any brigand assault my nephew?" he demanded.

"Robbery, of course!" Mrs. Wells cried.

"Robbery?" Mr. Mathley snorted. "When there are so many better pickings in this damned crowd? You're off the mark, Hildegarde. The fellow probably got drunk, fell down, and is trying to cover his embarrassment with this absurd story."

"Not entirely," Lord Carlton said smoothly. "I can assure you, Mrs. Wells, that there are no brigands on the property. Lord Fenwych and I are wholly responsible for your nephew-in-law's present condition."

This brought the room to a stunned silence.

"Oh, Peter!" Melinda moaned.

"Your niece and a few others were witness to the altercation," Lord Carlton continued before Mrs. Wells could express her outrage or Mr. Mathley could commend him. "Mr. Basil Hollis, I regret to inform you, madam, was a trifle the worse for the wine he had consumed, as Mr. Mathley suspected. Rather than falling down, however, Mr. Hollis insulted Lady Fenwych in a manner that no gentleman could tolerate. Lord Fenwych and I reacted appropriately to the provocation."

"Mr. Hollis, sir," Mrs. Wells said, her voice shaking with fury, "is a gentleman."

"Not when he's foxed!" Melinda roundly retorted. "He said the most vile things to poor Lydia Fenwych, and we have witnesses, Aunt Wells! So before you go accusing Lord Carlton or Lord Fenwych of any mischief, look to Basil first!"

"I told you it was all a hum, Hildegarde," Mr. Mathley said with great satisfaction. He had never been fond of his sister-in-law or his nephew. "Tell my nevvy to stop making up such faradiddles when there are witnesses to dispute him."

Mrs. Wells was about to retreat in high dudgeon, when suddenly her eye was caught by something glinting from Lord Carlton's coat pocket. "What is that?" she demanded sharply.

Everyone looked around.

"What is what?" Mr. Mathley said peevishly, for he wanted to get back to his winning hand of cards.

"That!" said Mrs. Wells, pointing a finger at Lord Carlton. "Is that not a sapphire?"

Melinda and Lord Carlton glanced down at his pocket as one, and groaned as one. In his haste, the earl had carelessly let the tip of one of the Mathley sapphire earrings poke out of his coat pocket.

"It is nothing," Melinda said hurriedly.

"A present I meant to bestow on Melinda at the end of the evening," Lord Carlton said easily. "But you have ruined my surprise, Mrs. Wells."

"There's one brigand in this household, sir," Mrs. Wells cried, "whatever George may say, and *you* are he!"

"Aunt Wells, calm yourself," Melinda began.

"Show me your present to my niece," Mrs. Wells snapped.

"Hildegarde, you're making a damned fool of yourself," Mr. Mathley stated.

"Show me!" Mrs. Wells thundered.

Melinda gazed helplessly up at Lord Carlton. With a crooked grin at her, he put his hand in his coat pocket and removed the Mathley sapphires.

A horrified silence filled the room.

"Thief! Blackguard! Demon!" Mr. Mathley bellowed as he struggled onto his crutches.

"Father, no! You quite misunderstand. This isn't at all what it seems," Melinda cried, to no avail.

"So this is why you insisted on becoming engaged to my

daughter, eh?" Mr. Mathley growled as he stomped up to Lord Carlton. "You only wanted access to the Mathley sapphires. How dare you, sir? How *dare* you?"

He slapped Lord Carlton hard. There was a shocked gasp from the spectators. Miss Wells fainted into Mr. Wentworth's arms.

"Father, no!" Melinda moaned.

Lord Carlton stiffened, his blue eyes glittering. But he made no attempt to answer the insult. "You are mistaken, sir," he said calmly. "I was returning the sapphires, not stealing them."

"A likely story," Mr. Mathley scoffed.

Any retort Lord Carlton meant to make was forestalled by Mrs. Mathley—gorgeously arrayed in a gown of gold satin—as she burst into the room. "George! George! Have you seen Melinda? No one has seen her this last hour, and I'm so afraid she may have eloped with . . . Oh! There you are my dear! And Lord Carlton, too! How . . . How nice."

Mr. Mathley, if it was possible, turned a darker shade of vermilion. "Not only do you steal from your hosts, you seek to compromise my daughter as well?"

"*No*, Father!" Melinda said, catching his arm before Mr. Mathley could once again strike Lord Carlton. "I have not been compromised in any way, I do assure you!"

"You are the last person I would care to believe in this matter, Melinda."

"I think if anyone would know if I had been compromised, it would be me," Melinda retorted. "Peter told you the truth. He was not stealing the sapphires, he was returning them with my help."

"Have you become so besotted with this blackguard that you would lie to defend him?" her outraged father demanded.

"Can you know me so little, Father, that you think I would lie about a matter of such importance?" Melinda said quietly. "Peter obtained the sapphires from the real thief, whom you know as—"

231

"Melinda, no!"

Melinda stared up at Lord Carlton.

"I gave my word," he said gently.

"I've heard enough. Sir Cedric!" Mr. Mathley bellowed. "Sir Cedric! I want this fellow arrested this instant and jailed and brought before your bench on the morrow! You there!" he roared at two footmen, who trembled at the fury directed upon them. "Take this man in hand until the authorities arrive. If he escapes, it will be your heads!"

Lord Carlton stared at the terrified footmen and suddenly burst out laughing. This adventure was wholly of his own making, and it was a greater disaster than ever Melinda had contrived. He shuddered to think what she would do to top it.

✱
Chapter 14

MELINDA HAD NEVER known a more wretched night. Of sleep, there had been none; of worry, aplenty. She had no doubt that her father would charge Lord Carlton with theft and, with his influence, see him in jail for the rest of his life. Blast Peter for being a man of honor! All he had to do was identify Rosalind Chalmers as the thief, have her captured, her confession duly recorded, and all would be well. It was not that she wanted Miss Chalmers to suffer such a fate—despite her jealousy, Melinda rather liked the pretty thief. But she wanted Lord Carlton to suffer such a fate even less.

But directing justice toward Miss Chalmers was out of the question. Lord Carlton had given his word, and it was not in Melinda to break it. She damned herself as every kind of selfish fool for entangling Lord Carlton with her family. He would not be in this predicament if it weren't for her using every scheme at her command to keep him near. She was wholly responsible for the night he was spending in jail, and it was up to her, somehow, to get him out of this mess and free from any future entanglement with her family.

How this was to be accomplished had Melinda pacing her bedroom floor for the rest of the night. Only now when she could not call on his aid did Melinda realize how much she had come to depend on Lord Carlton's advice and help, just as Miss Jonson had recommended so many weeks ago in London. Well, she was on her own once again. The man she loved was in jail, and it was up to her to get him out and keep him out.

The wild and impractical schemes that came to her mind were soon discarded. They would, she thought glumly, only place the earl in deeper hot water. No, the time for schemes was over. Something new must be tried, something even more treacherous and dangerous than any scheme she had ever contrived.

The problem was, did she have the courage to carry it off? Serious doubts arose in her mind as she considered the consequences of such an act. She would lose much, including Peter Carlton forever. This seemed impossible to contemplate. For an hour she wrung her hands and wept and paced and would not let herself make that final leap. But at last she told herself that she had never had Lord Carlton, so how could she lose him? More importantly, how could she not do everything in her power to keep him from prison?

She was responsible for his current plight; only she could rescue him from it.

Melinda appeared at breakfast the following morning wan but resolute. The shadows under her eyes went unquestioned by any of the others who had come down to breakfast. Indeed, she was greatly pitied. To be used in such a fashion—to be the dupe used to acquire the Mathley sapphires!—was reason enough for her condition, and they let her be. Except, of course, for Mrs. Wells.

She swept into the breakfast room in all her glory. Every horrific prophecy she had made upon reading of her niece's engagement to a rake and a scoundrel had come to pass, and she was very pleased with herself for being so prescient.

"So, you are up, are you?" she said to Melinda as she took her place at the table. "I'm glad to see some proper spirit in you, Melinda. You have the honor of your family to uphold this morning. You acted the fool in becoming engaged to the fellow, of course, and in remaining engaged to the fellow despite all of my warnings, despite my pleading

234

with you and your parents to act in a sensible manner. This is the result, and I hope it has taught you to heed my words in the future. Now, all that we can do is disassociate ourselves from Carlton with every means at our command. You, of course, must speak against him at the trial this morning. I have written out a speech that you must memorize and—"

"Speak against him?" Melinda cried, rising from her chair and trembling with fury. "Speak against a better man than anyone in this house? I'll do no such thing!"

An uncomfortable silence settled upon the two dozen people seated at the table.

"You will correct your wild and impetuous nature this instant!" Mrs. Wells commanded. "You have a duty to your family to publicly denounce Lord Carlton, and you are going to do so!"

"I have a duty, yes, to tell the truth and not the lies you have undoubtedly written in your little speech! Lord Carlton has been grievously injured and unjustly imprisoned, and that I *will* denounce!"

"Headstrong and unnatural girl!" Mrs. Wells cried in severely high dudgeon. She, like Mr. Mathley, was not used to having her decrees ignored. "If you have no thought to the public spectacle you will make of yourself, think then on your poor mother who suffered hysteric attacks all night long! Think on your father whose hospitality and generosity have been so badly abused. Think of your sisters who must have been corrupted by that vile man's company this last fortnight. Think of your *family* and the honor and duty you owe them, not some devil-may-care rogue who undoubtedly used pretty words to turn your weak head!"

A terrible calm settled over Melinda. "You are a guest in this house, Aunt Wells, and have the right to be treated with civility by everyone in my family. But if you say one more word against Lord Carlton, I will have your bags packed and two stout footmen escort you to your carriage within the hour!"

With that Melinda stalked from the room and thence from the house to walk through the woods for a good two hours to get her temper and her nerves under better control. Passion would not serve her in court today.

As this was neither a quarter nor a petty session, Lord Carlton was brought before Sir Cedric Creighton, the local magistrate, at Sir Cedric's house, a large, commodious affair of Tudor lineage situated in a pretty park overlooking the river Wye. On those occasions when Sir Cedric held court in his home, he generally used his library, a most imposing room guaranteed to instill in the prisoner charged before his bench a respect for the law that had brought him to his current plight.

But as this matter was so very grave, and as it seemed that half the county had come to observe these unique proceedings, Sir Cedric ordered his ballroom to be made ready for the hearing. As it was but half the size of the Mathleys' ballroom—and that was being generous—only a hundred could be squeezed between the paneled walls. The Mathleys and their relations, of course, occupied the first row of seats. Behind them sat their houseguests. Behind these were the major landholders in the area, including the clergy; behind these sat the townspeople and some of the militia who had come for a morning's entertainment. The rabble—as Sir Cedric termed them—took up the last five rows of seats.

The noise was deafening. Everyone was talking to everyone else, most of them wondering if an earl really could be charged with theft and hung for the offense, the majority declaring that no nobleman in the land had ever suffered such an indignity, while the rest loudly proclaimed this to be fustian. Theft was theft and the earl was bound to swing for it.

Lord Carlton was at last escorted into the makeshift courtroom by two lieutenants in perfectly pressed red coats, which had half the young women in the room nearly swooning from rampant admiration. The earl had contrived to appear in proper morning clothes, his neckcloth respectably tied, his black hair swept back from his beautiful face, his Hessians gleaming, the other half of the young women in the room nearly swooning from the effect. As the spectators either cheered or called out to him, Lord Carlton made his audience a most elegant bow, and then took his seat to a smattering of applause.

Sir Cedric Creighton, bewigged and robed, at last appeared, the assembly rising for him as he took his seat in his favorite leather chair that had been moved to the front of the ballroom for this occasion. He rested one hand on the table before him and called the proceedings to order.

Order, alas, did not last long. Sir Cedric had no sooner told the prisoner to rise and had begun to read the charge for which he was brought into court when a gray-haired man in the audience claimed that that was no more the Earl of Carlton than he was.

"What's that?" Sir Cedric demanded in a sharp voice. "How dare you interrupt, sir?"

"But I tell you, you've got the wrong man!"

Everyone turned to regard the uniformed man who stood up to better make his case.

"And who are you?" Sir Cedric querulously demanded.

"I'm Captain Benjamin Reynolds," the captain stated, "and that man is Mr. Millard Vance. He captured Josiah Barney, a notorious footpad, less than a fortnight ago. I took his statement myself."

Sir Cedric peered intently at Lord Carlton. "It comes to me that I know you by another name as well! You are Adney Brewster, are you not?"

Melinda heard Lord Carlton groan. Her gaze flew to him to discover, not despair, but an incipient tendency to burst out laughing.

"He's the Earl of Carlton!" roared Mr. Mathley. "Have you all lost your senses? I tell you, he's the Earl of Carlton and a lying, thieving, scoundrel!"

"I'm not at all surprised that he has assumed a number of different names," Mrs. Wells declaimed. "Undoubtedly to lure innocent young girls into illicit rendezvous!"

"He's fought at least ten duels," Mr. Fitzwilliam Vandevere offered.

"It has even been said," Mrs. Vandevere stated with a shudder, "that he is a frequent participant in *prizefights*."

"Hey, didn't I see that bloke in a mill at the last county fair?" someone from one of the back rows called out. "Won ten shillings on that fight, I did."

"No, you've got it all wrong," said a man in the row before him. "That was Beau Bixby at the last fair."

Everyone in the room began to argue whether Lord Carlton *was* Lord Carlton or Adney Brewster or Millard Vance or Beau Bixby. Mr. Mathley was roaring for the earl's head on a platter; Mrs. Mathley, in between reviving sniffs of her smelling salts, was tearfully proclaiming that whoever he was he had to marry Melinda after compromising her so badly the night before; Basil Hollis made mention that several pieces of jewelry had turned up missing at the last house party Lord Carlton had attended; and Lord Gilford was demanding with every other breath to know what the devil was going on.

Sir Cedric Creighton, who had consumed too much champagne the night before at the Mathley ball, had a roaring hangover that could kill a horse. He could follow none of this.

At last, Melinda could take no more. She climbed upon her chair and yelled at the top of her voice: "Silence!"

A shocked quiet followed this command. Mrs. Mathley fainted into her husband's arms at so outrageous a display, prohibiting him from bringing his eldest and most lunatic daughter to order. Sir Cedric Creighton regarded Melinda with the utmost gratitude.

"Sir Cedric," said Melinda, climbing down from her chair, "if you will be so good as to keep this rabble quiet, I can explain everything."

238

"I should be forever in your debt," Sir Cedric replied. "Come forward, Miss Mathley. And the rest of you," he said, directing a stern gaze at the audience, "keep quiet or I'll have you all arrested!"

Melinda began to approach the magistrate, but Lord Carlton reached out and caught her hand, stopping her.

"Melinda, don't," he said quietly.

She smiled sadly at him. "It's all right, Peter. I promise. It's my fault you're in so much trouble, and I've got to make it right."

"There's no need."

"There is every need."

She pulled free and walked up to Sir Cedric, grateful to be facing one man, trying to pretend that a hundred people weren't staring at her back. Trying to pretend she didn't feel Peter's gaze on her.

"Everything is entirely my own fault, Sir Cedric," she began in a firm voice. "So far from Lord Carlton compromising me, it is I who have compromised *him*. I fell in love with Peter, and all I could think to do was to stay with him as much as possible so perhaps he would fall in love with me. I was not thinking clearly—I was in love, after all—or I would have realized that there wasn't a chance of Lord Carlton's falling in love with a lunatic like me."

Melinda was wholly unaware that Lord Carlton had risen from his chair.

"You cannot love that . . . that rake and scoundrel!" her father bellowed. "I forbid it, Melinda. Sit down at once and stop making a spectacle of yourself!"

"He is *not* a rake and a scoundrel!" Melinda cried, furiously stamping her foot as she turned on Mr. Mathley. "*Nor* is he a thief! He is kind and generous and honorable and he loves to laugh and he has the most wonderful laugh, and no sensible woman could help but love him and I am always sensible!"

Melinda was wholly unaware of Lord Carlton's precipitous return to his chair.

"Any woman who loved him," she continued, turning back to the now wholly conscious Sir Cedric, "would want to do everything in her power to help him. Unfortunately, in trying to protect *his* reputation so that he could inherit the fortune he deserves, I wove a series of lies and false identities that have led him to this outrageous finale."

"Melinda!" barked Mrs. Wells. "Do not bring further shame to your family by continuing on this outrageous path! Do not slander what remains of your reputation by taking on the blame for this monster's horrific actions!"

"Oh, hush, Aunt Wells," Melinda said crossly.

"*Melinda!*" gasped Mrs. Wells. "How dare you speak to me in such a manner?"

"I agree with Miss Mathley, madam," Sir Cedric said. "You will be silent, or I will have you removed from my courtroom! Pray continue, Miss Mathley," he urged over her aunt's outraged gasp.

"Well," Melinda said, knotting and unknotting her fingers before her, "it all began when Lord Gilford said he would leave his fortune to Lord Carlton if he could behave like a gentleman for one month. Lord Carlton has extensive estates in Yorkshire that he hopes to renovate, but his family has done such an excellent job of running through the Carlton fortune that he has very little money to do the work his honor demands of him. As a landowner yourself, Sir Cedric, you must understand the onus that lay upon Lord Carlton to do everything in his power to improve his holdings. Lord Gilford offered the challenge; Lord Carlton could not but take it up."

"Perfectly reasonable," Sir Cedric agreed.

"At the same time," Melinda continued, somewhat reassured by the magistrate's kindly smile, "my father challenged me with marrying the next man who offered for me. This was an intolerable threat, for there was a very good chance that the next man who offered for me would be a complete nincompoop. So I suggested to Lord Carlton that we might be of use to each other. If we pretended to be engaged—"

"Melinda!" Mrs. Mathley quavered.

"Lord Carlton would have the entrée to society that he needed," Melinda resolutely pressed on, though her hands trembled somewhat, "and I would be able to offer my father so horrific a match that he would have to retract his odious threat."

"An excellent scheme, Miss Mathley," said Sir Cedric. "I commend you. Pray continue."

Melinda drew a shaky breath. "Lord Gilford was never far from my mind. As you know, I have the most annoying tendency to land in the most absurd scrapes, none of which would give Lord Carlton the character his uncle demanded for this month. Just after we decided on our false engagement, I met Lydia Brooke who had been cast off by her family and Lord Carlton very kindly agreed to help her."

"So the by-blow is yours, is it, Carlton?" Mr. Basil Hollis taunted. "I thought as much."

"Tristan is *my* son!" Gerald, twelfth Viscount of Fenwych, declared, rising so that everyone in the courtroom could hear and see him. "I abused this good lady's friendship, and she has been so good as to forgive and marry me. Any fool can see that Tristan is mine. He has the Fenwych ears!"

There was a buzz in the room as the spectators debated the varying qualities of the Fenwych ears.

"There will be silence in this courtroom!" Sir Cedric stated, rapping his gavel. "Silence, I say!" He at last was obeyed and once more urged Melinda to continue.

"Well," she said, running a hand through her already tousled auburn curls, "then Harry was so foolish as to call out Jasper Wilmingham, and you *know* how deadly Wilmingham is with a gun, and I couldn't just stand by and watch him be killed, so I turned once again to Lord Carlton."

"Ah, ha!" Harry shouted. "I knew you were behind it all the time. I knew it!"

"You called out Jasper Wilmingham?" Mr. Mathley demanded as he turned on his son, looking quite vermilion. "You had the imbecilic gall to call out the most notorious duelist in all of England?"

"Father, you don't understand—" Harry began.

"You will resolve this domestic quarrel at a later time if you please, gentlemen," Sir Cedric intervened. "Tell me, Miss Mathley, what exactly did Lord Carlton do to stop this duel? It was stopped, wasn't it?"

"Oh, yes, dead in its tracks," Melinda assured him. "Peter ... I mean, Lord Carlton ... was quite brilliant and even contrived to have Wilmingham flee the country, convincing him that a charge of murder had been lodged against him. Well, as you can see, Lord Carlton acted from the best of motives and with the purest of intentions, but still these adventures were not the thing to get back to Lord Gilford's ears and we tried to keep everything secret. When we fell into the river Wye and you happened by, I was afraid to tell you that he was Lord Carlton because you would undoubtedly have thought it a very good joke, which it was, and told all of your cronies, who would have told their cronies, and word would eventually have gotten back to Lord Gilford."

"It was not to be thought of," Sir Cedric agreed.

"My point exactly! When Louisa and Clare decided to elope, I quite naturally wanted to help, and I wanted to keep Lord Carlton with me as much as possible, as I explained before, so I browbeat him into helping them to elope."

"He was wonderful," Louisa stoutly declared to one and all. "He fully entered into our feelings and assured us that it was far better to marry for love, when there was some income to depend on, than to marry for title and be miserable the rest of my life."

"But Louisa," Mrs. Mathley remonstrated, a bottle of smelling salts gripped tightly in her hand, "you would someday have been a duchess!"

242

"I never cared for that. I only wanted to be Clare's wife!"

The crowd murmured their approval of this devotion.

"I don't care who takes issue with me," Mr. Hyde-Moore loudly stated, "Lord Carlton is the best man in England, and I'll fight any man who says differently!"

"I trust that will not be necessary, sir," Sir Cedric intervened. "Now, please do try to hold your tongues everyone, I think we're getting to the juicy bit. You were saying, Miss Mathley?"

"Well," Melinda said, nibbling on her lip as she tried to remember where she had left off. How wonderful of Louisa and Clare to publicly stand up for Peter! "Well, when we were returning to Putnam Park after helping Louisa and Clare to elope, we had the great misfortune to be held up by Josiah Barney, apparently a *most* notorious footpad. Lord Carlton acted perfectly splendidly in capturing him, but then there we were with a criminal on our hands and no desire to take him home. So we took him to Captain Reynolds. We couldn't explain how we came to be on the road so late at night, because word would have gotten back to Lord Gilford that Peter had assisted an elopement, so I gave Lord Carlton the name of Millard Vance and said that I was his sister. *That* is why so many people think he is not Lord Carlton. And, of course, he *is* Lord Carlton."

"That is quite clear," Sir Cedric murmured, his gray eyes beginning to twinkle. "Thank you for clearing up that little confusion, Miss Mathley. But about the Mathley sapphires—"

"I was coming to that," Melinda said. Never had she thought her face could be so hot. "Rather than acting the thief last night, Lord Carlton acted the hero. He knew the thief, you see, having nearly lost his purse to this . . . person in Venice some years back. So when he saw the thief among our guests, he was very naturally suspicious. Being clever, he deduced that the Mathley sapphires were the lure, accosted the thief, and retrieved the sapphires before they could be carried off. He asked me to help place them back in their safe, for I know the combination, you see. We were just about to open the safe when Louisa interrupted, asking us to intervene before Aunt Wells had the house searched for footpads who existed only in my cousin's imagination. We went downstairs, the sapphires were discovered in Lord Carlton's pocket, and you know the rest."

"Indeed I do," said Sir Cedric, rubbing his throbbing temples. "But why didn't he say all this last night and save us all this trouble this morning?"

"He tried! But no one would listen. And he could not reveal the true thief because he gave his word he would not if the jewels were returned to him, and they were. He is a man of honor, Sir Cedric. He could not go back on his word, even to defend himself. He was trying to protect my family, he *did* protect my family, and now is being punished for it. He may once have been a rake and a scoundrel, but he is not one *now*. He is the best man I have ever met. What other man could have put up with my mad starts? He would not be here now if I had not cajoled him into entering into my lunatic scheme of a false engagement.

"You see," Melinda pleaded, "all of this is *entirely* my fault, and I do most humbly beg your pardon—as I beg Lord Carlton's pardon—for causing so much confusion and trouble. It was never my intention . . . but then, it never is," she concluded sadly.

"You have surpassed yourself this time, Miss Mathley," Sir Cedric said gravely, but his gray eyes were kind and Melinda began to hope. "You have explained everything to this court's complete satisfaction."

"*What?*" erupted Mr. Mathley.

"Hush up, George," Sir Cedric snapped. "Anyone can see the girl is telling the truth. And it is my opinion," he said, directing a severe glare at Lord Carlton, "that any man in England would be proud to claim so honest and courageous a young woman as his wife. This case is dismissed. Lord Carlton is free to go."

The ballroom was engulfed in a roar of noise as one hundred people rose as one to cheer or to argue or to try to untangle the skein of adventures that had entrapped the earl.

Melinda, believing she had humiliated both herself and Lord Carlton before the whole county, and ruined any chances he might have had of inheriting his uncle's fortune, ran weeping from the room through a side door. It led out to a gravel path that led through a topiary. She saw neither green giraffes nor artfully shaped peacocks. She saw nothing at all for her tears and so tripped and stumbled a good deal as she tried to get as far away from the makeshift courtroom as possible.

She was entirely unsuccessful. She had not gone more than a dozen yards when someone gripped her shoulders and pulled her to a stop.

"Melinda," Lord Carlton began.

"Let me go!" she cried, struggling to free herself. Instead, by what course she was unaware, she found herself turned toward the earl and bundled close against his broad chest. "I won't blame you for hating me. I'm awful, I know!" she sobbed. "I'm so ashamed."

"Nay, lass," the earl said gently, "I'll not let you browbeat yourself like this. You're the most wonderful woman I've ever known, and you can stop struggling right now for I'll not release you until you agree to marry me."

This stopped Melinda cold. "Don't be an idiot, Peter," she said gruffly, taking a step back and hastily wiping away her tears. "You don't have to marry me. Our engagement was never real."

Lord Carlton's fingertips brushed the remaining teardrops from her face. "Yes, that's what I've told myself these last three weeks. But I've discovered my heart has always held a different opinion. We got into this adventure together, and we will end it together. Marry me, Melinda."

Melinda was finding it increasingly difficult not to fling herself at the earl and sob all over his morning coat. "Peter, just because Sir Cedric practically ordered you to marry me doesn't mean you have to sacrifice yourself to protect my honor."

"The devil take Sir Cedric! What about *my* honor?" Lord Carlton demanded. "You stated before half the county that you had compromised me. I must and shall have satisfaction."

"Don't be gallant, Peter. You promised—"

Lord Carlton gave up trying to reason with her. He pulled Melinda roughly back into his arms and kissed her with a violence that Melinda insensibly returned, trembling at his soft moan.

"Sweet loon, don't you know I adore you?" he murmured, cradling her in his arms. "I set out to snare a fortune and found myself captured by love instead."

"But you can't!" Melinda could not help but protest. "I have nothing to recommend me."

"Nothing but your honesty, courage, good humor, and a heart large enough to see the man behind the reputation. You will have to reconcile yourself to my love, Melinda."

"But you had a horrible three weeks with me!" she said, her cheek resting comfortably against his broad chest. "You've been bloodied, thrust into a duel, suffered untold abuse at my father's hand, and nearly drowned. You've been held up, jailed, and accused before all of Hereford of being a thief!"

"Yes, I know," said Lord Carlton, smiling tenderly down at her. "It was the best three weeks of my life. I plan to spend the rest of my days falling into one scrape after another. Heaven knows what mischief matrimony will inspire in you! It will be the grandest adventure of all."

"My point exactly! I'd make you a wretched wife."

"You will make me the happiest man in England," Lord Carlton said sternly. "You will agree to marry me, Melinda, or I'll carry you off to Gretna here and now."

"No, sir!" Mr. Mathley thundered as he stumped up behind them on his crutches. "I'll have no more elopements in this family! You will be married in a church with the entire family present or, by God, I'll have you whipped through the streets!"

Lord Carlton and Melinda turned to stare at Mr. Mathley in the utmost astonishment.

"Father?" Melinda said hesitantly.

"Did I or did I not order you to marry the first man who asked for your hand?"

"Well, yes, but—"

"And is Lord Carlton, or is he not, that man?"

"Yes, but—"

"And am I, or am I not, a man of my word?"

"*Always*, Father," Melinda murmured, her eyes shining.

"Then you will marry this fellow before Michaelmas. I will brook no opposition in this matter!" Mr. Mathley stated.

"Opposition was the furthest thing from my mind, sir," Lord Carlton said with a broad smile. "And thank you. I shall be forever in your debt."

"We will discuss Melinda's portion later, sir," Mr. Mathley retorted.

"I didn't mean—" Lord Carlton began, but Melinda jabbed him in the side with her elbow.

"He is tweaking you, Peter," she informed him. "My father has been known, on occasion, to crack a joke."

"This is a day of marvels," Lord Carlton murmured. "Come, Melinda," he said, pulling her back into his arms, "you have confessed before the whole county that you love me, and I confess before the whole *country* that I love you. We have your father's approbation. All that remains is for you to say 'Yes, Peter, I will marry you.'"

Melinda Mathley considered herself practical in all her adventures. She looked up at Lord Carlton, heart in her eyes, and said "Yes, Peter, I will marry you."

There, before the entire county, Lord Carlton kissed his

247

fiancée, and she, unmindful of their audience, kissed him
back with a thoroughness that left no doubt in his mind that
she fully returned his regard.